BALEFIRE

OTHER BOOKS FROM JORDAN L. HAWK:

<u>Hexworld:</u>
Hexbreaker
Hexmaker
Hexslayer

<u>Spirits:</u>
Restless Spirits
Dangerous Spirits
Guardian Spirits

BALEFIRE

(Whyborne & Griffin No. 10)

JORDAN L. HAWK

Balefire © 2018 Jordan L. Hawk
ISBN: 978-1720604747

All rights reserved.

Cover art © 2018 Lou Harper

This book is a work of fiction. Names, characters, places, and incidents are products of the author's imagination or are used fictitiously. Any resemblance to actual events or locales or persons, living or dead, is entirely coincidental.

Edited by Annetta Ribken

CHAPTER 1

Griffin

There were monsters in the woods.

I stood in the heart of the Draakenwood, before the twisted tree, in what had once been the seat of Theron Blackbyrne's power. The place where Nyarlathotep, the Man in the Woods, had taught magic to generations of ambitious sorcerers in exchange for absolute loyalty.

The Draakenwood belonged to him no more. Widdershins had taken it, and the monsters now floating through the boughs and burrowing beneath the soil answered to no creature of the Outside.

The umbrae had placed the entrance to their burrow in the collapsed basement that once underlay Blackbyrne's manor. Newly churned soil, heaps of stones, and other detritus showed evidence of their digging. The murmur of their conversation thrummed in my skull, like voices half-heard from another room. A worker slithered past, and I stretched out a hand to touch its gelid form.

"How are you settling in?" I asked.

If anyone had told me even as recently as two years ago, that I would stand unafraid among the creatures that haunted my worst nightmares, I would have called them mad. If they'd told me I would willingly invite the umbrae into the forest immediately outside of a populous town, my reaction would have been one of unmitigated horror.

Now, the Queen of Shadows regarded me through a single burning eye with a tripartite pupil. She coiled in the main entrance of the new nest, her segmented body just small enough to fit inside a freight car. Someday she would be as vast as her mother in Alaska, as long as the train that had brought her here.

Her voice replied in my mind. *"This is a good place, Brother. We burrow into the tunnels already here, expand them. Some are blocked; we will excavate them and learn where they might lead. The first gardens are already planted. The first nursery will be ready soon."*

"That's good," I said. "I'm glad to hear it."

"Your brother-by-blood did not come with you today?"

"No." Jack had accompanied the new queen, her attendant soldiers, and her workers on the long trip from the Alaskan wilderness. The bribes to get the cargo crates they hid in from Hoarfrost to a Whyborne Railroad train in San Francisco had been enormous, but Niles bankrolled the project and put Jack in his pay during the transfer. "Jack is working with me now. I've hired him on to assist with my detective agency."

Money and detectives meant nothing to the umbrae. But they understood family very well indeed, so I let her feel my joy at seeing Jack again, along with my hopes for working with him in the future.

Pressure spiked in my head, and the taste of blood began to seep into my mouth. Human minds weren't meant to communicate with the umbrae. *"He will remain here with us,"* she said. *"This is good."*

"Widdershins knows its own," I said ruefully. "And the Draakenwood belongs to Widdershins now. Somehow." I wasn't entirely clear on what the maelstrom had done to expand its influence after defeating Stanford and breaking the hold of the Man in the Woods.

A worker—perhaps the one I'd touched before—ventured toward me. This time its gelatinous body glided over my feet, picking away leaf detritus from my shoes, in much the same way as it would have cleaned any debris from the Queen of Shadows.

"All the children recognize you as one of ours." The Queen of Shadows touched me with one of her feelers, slick and cool against my face.

I should have been horrified by the thought. Or wondered what was wrong with me, that my adoptive human mother had rejected me, but the Mother of Shadows and all her spawn claimed me as one of their own.

This was the second of her daughters I'd met. The first little queen had hatched prematurely, thanks to the Endicotts, and would never have a warren of her own. The queen before me was her younger sister, laid and hatched later. We'd never set eyes on one another before last week, but that meant nothing to a species which communed directly from mind-to-mind.

The tang of blood grew stronger in the back of my throat. Though I had been changed by my encounters with the umbrae, I could still only remain in telepathic contact for a short time. "I'm glad you're settling in. I'll come back soon."

"You can always use the Occultum Lapidem," she reminded me. *"It will be easier to speak to me through it, than with our mother so far away."*

"I know. Thank you." I stood up and dusted myself off. "I'll call upon you if I have any need, trust me."

"You will have need." She paused. *"When the masters return, we will all have need of one another."*

It was why we had brought her here, to the Draakenwood. And yet, her words threatened to peel back the thin veneer covering my fear. The masters were coming, unless we discovered some method of stopping their arrival. Even if we fought them and triumphed, the thought of what we might lose in the process filled me with dread. The people I loved most in the world would be the first to fight, and I couldn't allow myself to consider the prospect all of us might not survive.

"You're right," I agreed as I turned away. "We most assuredly will."

CHAPTER 2

Whyborne

"Done?" I asked my husband as he emerged from the pit where the entrance to the umbrae's tunnels lay.

Summer had come to Widdershins, which meant my wait had been at least superficially pleasant. The roots of the gargantuan tree overlooking the ruins of Blackbyrne's house offered a relatively comfortable seat, and a nearby sapling a convenient place to hang my coat and hat. Fireflies danced amidst the dense green foliage, like a thousand fairies tempting incautious mortals to join their revels. Night birds called to one another: whip-poor-wills whistled madly, occasionally falling silent at the hoot of an owl.

The scene would have been perfect, if it hadn't also been where I'd murdered my brother.

Murdered was perhaps too strong a word. Persephone and I shoved him through a rip in the veil and into the Outside, where he had presumably perished. Though Stanford had a better chance at survival than most, having grafted something of the Outside onto his own body, Nyarlathotep showed no mercy toward those who had failed him.

Griffin approached my perch, dusting off the knees of his trousers as he did so. "Yes. I think the umbrae will flourish here." The light of my lantern revealed his smile. "I'd never have thought I'd sleep sounder knowing there are monsters in the woods, but there you have it."

I summoned a chuckle, though I didn't really feel like laughing. "Agreed."

Griffin cocked his head. "Is something wrong, my dear?"

"Oh, nothing." Or everything. I'd settled dangerous creatures beneath the woods adjoining a busy town. There was a very long list of people who wanted me dead. The end of the world was coming, and I didn't know how to stop it. "I'm fine. It's a beautiful evening, isn't it?"

I glanced reflexively at the gigantic trunk of the tree as I spoke. The very spot where we'd tossed Stanford out of our world.

Griffin, of course, noticed immediately. "I'm sorry. I didn't think. Naturally you have bad memories of this place." He put a hand to my shoulder. His wedding ring flashed in the lantern light, the white pearl glowing like the fireflies. "I should never have asked you to come with me."

"I imagine you have bad memories as well," I protested. "After all, Stanford kidnapped you, locked you in a cage, and threatened to kill you."

"True, though the umbrae have at least done such extensive remodeling of their new home, I couldn't even tell you where the cages were."

I had no such troubles recalling where Stanford had strangled me, demanding Father choose between us. Or where I'd stabbed him with Griffin's old sword cane.

Or had my last glimpse of his face, distorted in pain and terror as he vanished from our world forever.

Stanford had tried to kill me first, of course. He meant to seize the fragments of the maelstrom within my flesh and that of my twin sister, and use its power to serve the masters. He would have hurt my town, hurt all the people the maelstrom had collected, and reduced Widdershins to nothing more than a tool to welcome the masters back into the world so they could enslave everyone.

We hadn't exactly been close.

"It isn't that I feel guilty about killing Stanford," I said.

"Nor should you." Griffin sat beside me, slipping his arm from my shoulder to around my waist. I leaned into him gratefully. "For heaven's sake, Ival, not even Niles blames you. Stanford murdered your older sister, he meant to kill Persephone, and intended to sacrifice the rest of us to Nyarlathotep. Not to mention the fact he murdered the heads of the old families, and worked with Bradley Osborne to take over your body, and—"

"I know; I know." I held up a hand. "Stanford was a terrible person. We loathed one another since childhood. He left Persephone and me no choice but to put an end to him. Believe me, I'm well aware of all of this."

"And yet you still wish things had been different," Griffin suggested.

"Of course I do." I stared down at my hands. My wedding ring bore a black pearl in contrast to Griffin's white, its surface rich with hidden colors. "Why couldn't he have just stayed in the blasted asylum? Why couldn't he have left us alone?"

I'd thought the same thing many times throughout childhood. Bullying me had been Stanford's favorite sport. If he had just let me be, how different things would have been for us all.

"It's his fault, not yours." Griffin's hand stroked my arm soothingly. "You bear no blame in this."

"I know. I'm not blaming myself. I'm not—not remorseful, or guilty, or..." I let out a long sigh. "I don't know what I feel."

"Family is difficult, sometimes."

Heaven knew, Griffin understood that. He had a better relationship with the Mother of Shadows than with the human woman who had raised him.

He pressed a kiss into my cheek. "Sitting here won't help things. Let me take you home."

I nodded. We rose to our feet, and I put my coat and hat back on. Two soldier umbrae detached themselves from the upper boughs of the great tree, one gliding ahead of us down the path, the other behind. An escort, courtesy of the Queen of Shadows, as Griffin called her to distinguish her from the

Mother of Shadows in Alaska. The umbrae served as guides as well; I was no woodsman, and the dense forest remained as confusing to me now as it had the first time I'd set foot in it.

Still, with the help of the umbrae, we navigated the Draakenwood quickly enough. The easiest path out was through the graveyard, and I tried not to look too closely at the mausoleums as we passed. Miss Lester had restored the damage Stanford did to the cemetery when he raised the dead of the old families against us, but I'd never forget the sight of Guinevere's corpse lurching toward me, trailing her winding sheet behind.

We'd parked the motor car at the gates. The police, under Chief Tilton, were familiar with our vehicle and knew to let us be. I supposed there were some benefits to my new status.

When we arrived home, it was to find a note wedged into the crack of our front door. Griffin and I exchanged a glance, and he pulled it loose. For a moment, I indulged in the optimistic thought that a potential client had come seeking his abilities as a detective. His business had taken a sharp uptick since February, especially among the old families. The decision to hire Jack to take on some of the simpler investigations had come from necessity rather than simple familial loyalty.

"It's addressed to you," he said.

Drat it. I took it from him and unfolded the paper. The stationery bore the imprint of the Widdershins Arms Hotel. Written in an elegant hand, it read:

Dr. Whyborne,

Please join me for a late dinner at the Widdershins Arms at your earliest convenience.
It's time.

Sincerely,

Rupert Endicott

CHAPTER 3

Griffin

"It's just like an Endicott to show up with no warning and expect us to drop everything," Christine complained. "Some of us have other things to do. Like sleep."

Though I didn't believe the Endicotts meant to spring an ambush on us, going to the meeting without Christine and Iskander had been out of the question. Whatever Rupert meant to say likely concerned us all, one way or another. So the four of us had wedged ourselves into my motor car, with Christine perched in Iskander's lap and Whyborne sandwiched between Iskander and myself. She'd recently taken to wearing skirts much looser than current fashion dictated, and Whyborne kept flipping the excess fabric out of his lap, only to have it blow back onto him.

"Perhaps you should have stayed home, dearest," Iskander said as I parked along the curb outside the hotel.

Christine gave him a withering look. "Don't be absurd."

"It is inconvenient," Whyborne agreed. "Which I suppose we should have expected. No word from the Endicotts for almost four months, during which I might have been translating the Wisborg Codex, if they would have only given me the key to begin with. And now they wish us to set aside everything else and attend to their problems."

Though Whyborne had agreed to help them in exchange for the Codex's cipher, I remained unsure about the decision. The masters wouldn't remain in the Outside forever, and Whyborne was needed to help defend the town, not play errand boy to the Endicotts.

Even so, I agreed we should at least hear Rupert out. "I doubt the delay was purposeful." I climbed from the car and went around to open the door for Christine. She had already exited by the time I arrived, so I exchanged a fond look with Iskander, who seemed more harried than usual. "Things may have occurred of which we have no knowledge."

Whyborne muttered something I couldn't quite hear, but judging by his mulish expression, he was less inclined to give his English cousins the benefit of the doubt.

"By the way, Whyborne," Christine said as he extracted himself from the car, "whatever cologne you've taken to wearing, you should continue doing so. It suits you quite well."

Whyborne stared at her blankly. "I haven't put anything on since this morning." He sniffed cautiously at his sleeve. "I don't smell anything." He glanced anxiously at me. "Griffin?"

I shrugged. We'd been pressed together in the motor car, and I'd noticed nothing beyond his usual scent of salt and ambergris. "You smell quite pleasant, my dear, but no different than ordinary."

"Honestly, Whyborne, there's no need to make a fuss," Christine said with a roll of her eyes. "I was simply offering a compliment. Come along and let's locate Rupert."

As we entered the hotel lobby, the manager spotted us and hastened up. "Dr. Whyborne! Always a pleasure to see you, sir."

"Uh, yes." Whyborne's ears turned pink. He and Christine had attempted to come here incognito last year, wearing possibly the worst disguises I'd ever laid eyes on in my years of detective work. "Always, er, a pleasure to be here. I received a note from my cousin, Mr. Endicott, inviting me to dinner?"

"Mr. Endicott, yes. I was unsure of his claim of relationship, but..." The manager trailed off. Rupert was a man of color with a refined English accent; no doubt he had resorted to some show of sorcery to convince the manager of his story. "At any rate, he's awaiting you in a private room. I asked the cook to remain so we'd be able to supply you with dinner. On the house."

"Very kind of you," Whyborne said, looking like a man going to his execution rather than the table.

The manager led us to a small room off the lobby. The electric lights of the chandelier flashed off Rupert's spectacles as he looked up from the book he'd been pouring over. "There you are," he said, as though we were the ones to have inconvenienced him. "Where have you been?"

"Talking to umbrae," Whyborne said. "We abominations like to keep in touch."

Interest sparked in Rupert's gaze. "I imagine so."

"Just don't think to send another of your more expendable family members to procure an egg," I warned him as I took a seat. "Did you realize Turner would have betrayed you as well, if we hadn't stopped him?"

To my surprise, a shadow fell across Rupert's face. "Betrayal from within is something we've become all too familiar with as of late, I'm afraid."

The waiters appeared with a light dinner, which they spread out before us before retreating. The manager offered a bottle of wine for Whyborne's approval, poured, then withdrew as well.

Christine sniffed her glass and made a face. "I think it's gone off."

Rupert took a sip. "Pedestrian, but sufficient."

"It seems fine to me," Iskander said. "Shall I pour you some lemonade, Christine?"

Her face brightened. "That would be perfect, Kander, thank you." She set to her meal with enthusiasm. "So, Mr. Endicott, I believe you were saying something truly shocking, along the lines of a family of traitorous snakes eating their own."

"Christine, please," Whyborne said with an exasperated look. "Cousin, I assume from your message that the Endicotts are ready to take back the family estate? When we last saw you in February, you said it had fallen to the Fideles."

"It has, and remains under their control." Rupert's full lips pressed into a thin line. He'd selected the sea bass au gratin, but only stared at it on his plate. "I'd hoped to return much sooner.

But we've had a bit of a problem."

"Which I take it is about to become our problem as well?" I inquired.

"Alas, Mr. Flaherty, you are correct." He lifted his glass in my direction. "Perhaps I should start from the beginning."

I watched him carefully, but his face remained schooled. "That's usually for the best."

He turned to Whyborne. "Did Theo and Fiona ever speak of Balefire Manor?"

An expression of discomfort spread over Whyborne's face. Theo and Fiona Endicott had embraced him as one of their own, a lost cousin found again. Until they'd learned of his ketoi blood, upon which they'd decided to raise a tidal wave to destroy Widdershins. Whyborne and Persephone had fought them; it hadn't ended well for either Endicott.

As with Stanford, Whyborne hadn't been left with a choice. But Rupert had surely known Theo and Fiona—had no doubt mourned their deaths, along with the rest of the family.

"No." Whyborne set to cutting up his fish into smaller and smaller pieces. "I take it that's the name of the family seat?"

"Given to us by the crown in 1498, after the Cornish Rebellion." Rupert folded his hands before him on the table. "For services rendered, one could say. Balefire was the name we gave to the manor house we built on the estate. It stands on Carn Moreth, a tidal island intermittently connected with the headland of Penmoreth."

He paused to remove his spectacles and draw out a handkerchief to clean them with. "Last December, on the longest night of the year, we lost all contact with Balefire Manor and Carn Moreth. No one has left the island since. Anyone who tries to reach the island by crossing the causeway during low tide gets about halfway—then suddenly finds themselves walking back toward the headland with no memory of having turned around. We tried going by ship, of course, but the local ketoi somehow learned of our troubles and decided to take advantage of our temporary weakness. The waters between Seven Stones Reef and Carn Moreth are impassable now thanks to them."

"Do you think they're helping the Fideles?" I asked. The cult wished to complete the Restoration and return the masters to our world, presumably in exchange for personal power. Though at least one of them, Mrs. Creigh, believed cooperation now was the only means to ensure the survival of any part of humanity later.

Whyborne frowned at me. "The ketoi wouldn't do that."

"Persephone contended with traitors among her people," I reminded him. "There's no reason to believe the Cornish ketoi wouldn't have such problems as well."

"God knows, I would prefer to blame this all on the ketoi," Rupert said. "But our feud with them is long, and there seems to be no connection. The unfortunate truth is, it would take one of our own blood to lower the enchantments that kept Balefire safe. A member of the family must have been the one to hand control of Balefire over to the Fideles."

"This traitor you mentioned." Having scraped her own plate clean Christine leaned across the table and speared a piece of asparagus from Whyborne's. "You weren't going to eat this, were you?"

Whyborne made a face and edged his plate in her direction. "Help yourself."

Rupert put his spectacles back on and carefully straightened them. "Balefire has stood for over five-hundred years and never fallen to an enemy."

"Of which you've made quite a few," I observed. "Are you certain the Fideles are the ones who have taken Balefire from you? You've hardly made yourself popular with other sorcerers."

"Abominations and traitors who consorted with the Outside," Rupert snapped. Then he caught himself and took a deep breath. "I will not apologize for what the Endicotts stand for. We are the shield set between the human race and the forces of darkness. But I regret calling you an abomination, Cousin."

Whyborne made an impatient gesture. "Yes, yes. I've been called worse many times. A...*colleague*...from another museum who disagreed with a translation once referred to me as a 'rich dilettante, who can barely distinguish Akkadian from Aramaic.'"

A smile curved Rupert's mouth for the first time. "How vicious. As for why we believe it is the Fideles who took Balefire, I can only tell you those who seek the Restoration have good reason to be interested in Carn Moreth."

More secrets. I pushed my plate away. Christine snatched the remains of my roll from it. "What sort of defenses are we talking about?"

"Again, I must beg your indulgence, but the Seeker would nail my hide to the gates as a warning to future generations if I answered that," Rupert said. "But I assure you, whoever has done this had to have been inside them at the time."

"So we're to go blind into this?" I asked, at the same moment Iskander said, "The Seeker?"

Rupert seemed to struggle a moment; no doubt this was one of the things Endicotts didn't care to speak of to anyone outside the family. "We Endicotts have two heads of household, one might say. The Keeper of Secrets and the Seeker of Truth. Though in this case they are brother and sister—twins—the position isn't hereditary. Rather, they are chosen from the strongest in magic, but also by disposition. It would do the family no good to have a powerful sorcerer with access to every secret and weapon, if he were also mad for power and cared nothing for the rest of us."

"And what exactly do these titles mean?" Whyborne asked with a frown.

"The Keeper of Secrets remains at the estate at all times. Once elected to the position, he or she never leaves Balefire Manor again. The Seeker is often at the estate, but her duty includes travel if necessary to uncover...whatever it is she seeks to uncover. The locations of monsters to be eradicated, the houses of bloodlines similar to our own, some arcane artifact which must be brought under our protection."

Whyborne snorted. "Your protection. What a quaint way to refer to hoarding magical weapons."

"It keeps such instruments out of the hands of those who would use them against the human race," Rupert snapped.

"And now this arcane armory is in the hands of the Fideles," I said. "I suppose you can't tell us what precisely was in it, either?"

"I don't know everything myself. And even if I did..."

"You wouldn't be allowed to say." I was liking this less and less. "So you don't know what happened? No one has come in or out of the estate for almost six months?"

"We have a constant watch set on Penmoreth. There's been nothing. And telescopes and the like aren't...useful...for observing the estate more closely."

"Part of the defenses, I assume." Whyborne sat back in his chair, his expression shuttered. "What precisely do you want from me, Mr. Endicott? I assume you're at least allowed to say that."

Rupert didn't rise to the bait. "The Seeker wishes to take Balefire back from the Fideles. Rescue the Keeper."

"Assuming he's even alive," Christine said. "If no one has come in or out, what are they doing for provisions? Food and water?"

"Do you really think we never planned for a siege?" Rupert asked.

"Oh, yes, doesn't everyone?" Whyborne muttered. "I can't imagine why Father never put a well into the basement of Whyborne House. I suppose the wine cellar would have to do."

"If the heart of the maelstrom was within some sort of fortification, you wouldn't have had to battle the Fideles in the streets last summer," Rupert pointed out.

Whyborne scowled. "Or they might have taken and held it, as they have Balefire."

"There's no point in arguing," Iskander said. "Mr. Endicott, how does your Seeker intend to take back the estate?"

Rupert looked pained. "I can't—"

"Say," I finished for him. "Why didn't the Seeker come herself? If securing Whyborne's cooperation is so important to the Endicotts, surely she could do us the courtesy of speaking with him directly."

To my surprise, Rupert only chuckled. "She's not a young woman, Mr. Flaherty, and is used to having things her way. You'll understand better when you meet her."

"And where and when will this be?" Whyborne asked suspiciously.

"We have a three-masted schooner docked in Widdershins now. It will take us from here to the Isles of Scilly, off the coast of Cornwall. What remains of the family is gathering there."

Christine finally put down her fork. "You're asking a great

deal of us. The last time we saw you, Miss Endicott was threatening to slit Whyborne's throat. Why should we leave with you, when you won't tell us anything? Surely it would make more sense for Whyborne to remain here, in case the masters return."

"If you want any hope of fighting them, the Wisborg Codex is the key," Rupert replied. "As for Hattie's actions...I will not lie to you, Dr. Whyborne. There are other members of the family who do not trust you. Who believe we would be better off fighting this battle ourselves. They have argued very strongly against bringing a being such as yourself onto the estate and into proximity of the magical artifacts gathered there."

I tightened my grip on my wine glass. "Whyborne is a person, not a 'being.'"

"I meant no offense." Rupert inclined his head to Whyborne. "But let us not pretend you're human. I was there when you fought your brother in the Draakenwood. My advice to the family has been to respect you, and give you no reason to turn your wrath against us." Rupert lifted one shoulder in a half shrug. "Needless to say, not everyone agrees with my assessment. The Seeker believes the risk is one that must be taken."

"How flattering." Whyborne folded his arms over his chest and hunched his shoulders. "I can't wait to meet the rest of the family."

"We're going, then?" Christine asked with a frown. "How certain are you we actually need the Codex?"

"The invitation was only extended to Dr. Whyborne," Rupert said.

"If you lot think the rest of us aren't going with him, you're delusional," Christine replied bluntly.

"I'm not convinced any of us should go." I glanced at Whyborne. "With all due respect, Mr. Endicott, you have avoided giving us any particulars—under orders from the Seeker, but that doesn't change the fact you're asking us to leave Widdershins with no real idea of what we can expect to face."

"I know." Rupert sighed heavily. "If you'd like to discuss things further, I'm staying aboard ship—the *Melusine*. And I have one more thing to ask of you. Or rather, of your sister, Dr.

Whyborne."

Whyborne frowned. "Persephone? What do you want from her?"

"We need her to dispatch her most trusted diplomat with us." He paused. "After four-hundred years of war, the Endicotts wish to broker a treaty with the ketoi of Cornwall."

CHAPTER 4

Whyborne

"If the Endicotts think Persephone will help them convince the ketoi to end the war, they're mad," I said to Griffin, when we returned home.

"Mad, no. Desperate, yes." He locked the door, while our cat Saul twined first around his ankles, then mine, leaving behind a film of orange fur on our trousers.

"They've killed countless ketoi over the centuries. And hybrids." I scowled. "And ruined Mother's health for decades, and nearly murdered Persephone and me."

Before I knew of my heritage, Theo and Fiona Endicott had related how a number of our family members had died in a ritual gone wrong. The Endicotts tried dark sorcery on a ketoi prisoner, hoping to kill anyone who shared its bloodline. I didn't know the identity of their victim, but they had been a relative, however distant. The spell had nearly cost Mother her life and caused her to deliver Persephone and me into the world early.

Mother's health had been ruined as a result, and I'd been a sickly child, seeming to succumb to every cough or ague. The Endicotts would have been pleased if they'd known; they had no pity for ketoi, and even less for those of us they considered hybrid abominations.

And that was even before they'd tried to overwhelm Widdershins with a tidal wave.

I made my way upstairs and slumped into a seat by the cold hearth. "Why does everyone in my family want to kill people? Don't I have any non-murderous relatives?"

"Your mother?" Griffin suggested. He poured us each a tumbler of brandy, then came and sat beside me on the couch. "Persephone?"

"Persephone sawed off Dives Deep's head in front of the rest of the museum staff and most of our donors," I said sourly. "I know Persephone had to kill her to secure the chieftainship, but did she have to be so...so *excessive?*"

"At any rate, I'm not at all certain we should go with Rupert." Griffin leaned against me. "Not without knowing more about what we'll face. We won't exactly be leaving Widdershins unguarded, but..."

He trailed off. Persephone would still be here, but the two of us were far more powerful together. If the masters came through the veil while I was gone...

The Wisborg Codex could surely tell us when they would make their appearance. With luck, it held within its pages the secret to defeating them. But the code it was written in had proved uncrackable to every method I'd applied.

"The masters are unlike anything we've ever faced," I said at last. "They created the ketoi and the umbrae. The rust. The maelstrom itself, when Nyarlathotep shaped the arcane lines at their command."

"You do realize the Endicotts may have no plans to hold up their end of the bargain," Griffin said. "They're likely to turn on us the moment we're of no use to them."

"They'll wait until after the masters are defeated to do that." I swirled the brandy in my glass, then drained it in a gulp. "Dr. Hart won't be happy if I ask for leave yet again."

"If you believe this is the only course we can take, I think the director will understand." Griffin finished his own drink and put it aside. "Tell him you're studying Cornish."

I frowned. "It's a bit outside of my normal purview. The

language itself is extinct, or nearly so, though there are murmurings of an attempt at revival in the linguistic journals." But a serious attempt would mean finding anyone who still spoke even a few words, and I doubted the director would believe I'd voluntarily track down strangers to talk to them. "The museum *does* have a copy of Pryce's *Archaeologia Cornu-Britannica—*"

Griffin pressed his lips to mine, silencing me. "We've talked enough for one night, my dear. I have a better use for that clever tongue of yours," he murmured when the kiss was done.

I smiled, and my heart lightened unexpectedly. No matter what other worries plagued me, there was always this. Us.

Joy.

"Do you now?" I shifted off the couch and onto my knees. "Does it involve me at your feet?"

His breathing thickened. "It does indeed."

I shed my coat and vest, then slid my hands teasingly up his thighs, feeling the curve of muscle beneath cloth warmed by his skin. A breeze blew through the open window, chasing away the summer heat that tended to collect on the second story. His erection already began to tent his trousers, and my own body responded to the sight.

I took my time, slowly undoing each button. Watching him watch me, his green eyes dark with desire. I teased him a bit, rubbing his cock through the soft cotton of his drawers. The tip of his tongue touched his lip, and he whispered my name.

When I'd made him wait long enough, I tugged down his drawers and pulled his prick free. The familiar feel of the silky skin against my lips thrilled me, and I swallowed him down slowly. His hand gripped my hair, and his breathing grew heavier still.

After all our years together, I knew him well enough to play his desire like an instrument. Faster, then slower; a pause here, a quick lick there. I drew myself out and stroked an accompaniment, sometimes lazily, sometimes faster, until the taste of him sharpened in my mouth. Then I set myself to the task, his moans and pleas driving my own lust higher, until his hips arched off the couch and his hand clenched in my hair.

I let him slip from my mouth, pressed my face into his

trembling thigh, and let ecstasy crest through me as well. "Yes, my dear, let me see you," he said, and I tipped my head back, raw and vulnerable, shuddering as I came.

He traced a thumb over my lower lip, then kissed me. "My Ival."

"Always."

He drew me onto the couch beside him, and we twined into a sated tangle of limbs. The curtain billowed in the breeze, and fireflies danced in the backyard beyond. "I love you," Griffin said, trailing his fingers through my hair. It needed cut, but I'd been too busy to attend to it as of late, so the locks stuck out in all directions. "I trust your judgment. Just...be cautious of the Endicotts. Please. Even if Rupert is honest, I fear those he answers to may have no intention of honoring any bargain with you."

"Agreed," I said ruefully. "But as you said, enough for tonight. All of our problems will still be waiting in the morning."

"Unfortunately," he agreed, and led the way to our bedroom.

CHAPTER 5

Whyborne

It was strange how routine waiting for the world to end could become.

The next morning after breakfast, I went to my employment at the Ladysmith Museum, just as I had nearly every day for the last nine years. The guards nodded to me, as did some of my colleagues, while the hadrosaur skeleton in the grand foyer loomed silently over us all. I passed through the exhibit halls and through a staff door, to my office.

My original office had been in the basement; though my status had changed, the work remained largely the same. Scraps of cuneiform tablets waited to be pieced together, a half-written paper begged me to complete it, and piles of correspondence from my philological colleagues around the globe silently accused me of neglect.

As I hung up my hat and coat, Miss Parkhurst stuck her head in through the open door. "Good morning, Dr. Whyborne."

"Good morning, er, Miss Parkhurst." I was never quite certain whether or not to suggest a different level of formality, given the romantic attachment between my secretary and my sister. I didn't wish anyone at the Ladysmith to imagine our relationship in anyway untoward, so I had avoided use of her familiar name thus far. "Anything of interest in the newspapers today?"

Miss Parkhurst had spent the past few months combing a wide variety of international newspapers in search of anything which might signal Fideles activities. Unfortunately, it was sometimes difficult to discover whether or not an article truly indicated unnatural happenings, or merely that the writer had an unusually fevered imagination. Had the passengers aboard a steamer—suspiciously unnamed in the article—actually seen a sea monster of some kind, or had a bored reporter invented the story from whole cloth? What about the report of a flying creature snatching away an intoxicated man in Virginia?

"Nothing, Dr. Whyborne. Or at least, nothing that seems connected to the Restoration."

I dropped into my chair. My unanswered correspondence had taken on mountainous proportions, and I shoved away a flare of guilt. "I have a favor to ask of you."

She straightened, and her golden earrings flashed in the light streaming through my window. Yet another gift from my sister, no doubt. Why on earth Persephone was waiting to propose, I couldn't imagine. "Of course, Dr. Whyborne."

"If you would be so kind as to leave early—with a full day's pay, naturally—I need to speak with Persephone." Of course I was perfectly capable of summoning the ketoi myself, but Miss Parkhurst might appreciate the excuse of spending a few hours together in an isolated cove.

Her face brightened in response. "Oh, yes! That is, I'd love to. Love to help, I mean." A blush spread across her cheeks, and I felt my own ears turn hot. "What do you need to speak to her about?"

"The Endicotts have returned."

"I see." Her expression turned sour. She'd had fewer interactions with my cousins than the rest of us, but she'd been there when Hattie threatened to cut my throat and Persephone's.

"Indeed." I rubbed at my eyes. "And of course nothing is ever simple with them. They have a favor to ask of the ketoi."

"Oh dear. Persephone won't be pleased to hear that."

"I can't say I'm particularly pleased, either. But they have something we need." Perhaps. Maybe. Assuming they wouldn't decide Persephone and I posed too great a threat.

Rupert had overruled Hattie in the Draakenwood...but that didn't mean he didn't have other family members who would happily spill our blood the moment we had served our purpose. Even if that meant facing the masters and fighting with only their own arcane power. None of the Endicotts I'd met had lacked for confidence in their sorcerous abilities, that was for certain.

"I'll leave around two o'clock, then," Miss Parkhurst decided. "In the meantime, would you like your morning coffee?"

I attempted to whittle down my pile of mail, but my mind refused to settle to the task. As I'd mentioned to Griffin the night before, the museum library included at least one tome on Cornish language. If Rupert wouldn't tell us anything about Balefire Manor, perhaps I could learn something useful from books. I couldn't recall anything specific to Cornwall in my previous arcane researches, but I dimly remembered the landscape was dotted with prehistoric stone circles and menhirs. Which could mean nothing, but my past experiences suggested sites of greater than normal arcane power were often marked by some sort of stones or structures. The obelisk and fane in Egypt, the clusters of standing stones around Widdershins, and the stele near the city of the umbrae in Alaska had all indicated places touched by the Outside in some fashion. Perhaps the same held true of the henges.

If nothing else, someone might have written about the manor house itself. Surely a Tudor-era mansion, built on a tidal island, would have caught the attention of some architect or antiquarian. Even if I could find only a journal article, I might learn something useful about my cousins. And about what awaited us, if we should decide to help retake the manor.

I quit my office in favor of the library. Mr. Quinn immediately marshaled the junior librarians to comb the stacks. I'd never set out to have a cult of librarians who answered only to me and my sister, but it did come in handy whenever I needed to do research.

Unfortunately, most references to Cornwall concerned either tin mines or Arthurian legends. I was already familiar with those legends—my mother had read them to me a thousand times, starting when I was a babe in arms.

None of it seemed of particular interest. As for Balefire Manor, it existed only in references. A single line here, a footnote there. Other manor houses of the era such as Cotehele or Trerice had their long histories laid out in detail, accompanied by illustrations of Tudor ceilings or stone dovecotes.

The Endicotts, it seemed, had been very effective at keeping their secrets over the centuries.

Out of linguistic curiosity, I asked Mr. Quinn for Pryce's book. Knowing my own propensity to become sidetracked in matters of academic interest, I forced myself to turn to the vocabulary section. Carn Moreth was the name of the island Rupert had given.

Carn translated to "a high rock" or "rocky place." *Moreth* as "grief." Hill of grief? Rocky outcropping of grief?

Why did that sound familiar?

I stared at nothing for a long moment, wracking my memory. Was it connected to some legend? I envisioned my mother's room in Whyborne House, the sound of her voice as she read to me in French and German.

King Arthur. Merlin. Tristan and Iseult.

Lyonesse.

I started to my feet. "Mr. Quinn!"

Mr. Quinn must have been lurking just out of sight, because he appeared almost instantly. "Yes, Widdershins?"

I wished he would stop calling me that. "I need one of the books kept under lock and key."

A smile crawled over his thin lips, and he laced his hands together. "One of the forbidden tomes? Excellent."

CHAPTER 6

Whyborne

Christine wasn't in her office, but one of the secretaries directed me to the storeroom where Iskander was carefully photographing some of the more obscure artifacts from one of her digs. He'd rigged up a series of lights and neutral backdrops, and was in the process of adjusting the position of a small amulet shaped like a bird. At the sound of my steps, however, he looked up.

"Good morning, Whyborne," he said. "It is still morning, isn't it?"

"Barely, but yes. Do you happen to know where Christine is?"

"Sorting through one of the crates from the Nephren-ka dig, I believe. She's writing a paper on ushabti." He paused. "Is there anything I can help you with?"

I started to deny it, but caught myself. Given Christine's temper, Iskander might be better suited to accompany me after all. "Yes, actually. I need to speak with Rupert Endicott. I've come across some information about the estate. If I'm correct, we're all in a great deal of danger."

He turned off the hot lights. "Say no more. I'll accompany you at once. I won't claim to have much influence over the Endicotts, but thanks to my mother they're more inclined to look favorably on me than the rest of you."

"And you're less likely to start a fight with them than Christine," I agreed. "We'd better hurry before she returns and catches us slipping out."

The docks bustled with activity. Stevedores shouted, nets filled with heavy cargo groaned, and a pair of captains engaged in a shouting match over which of them was the proper husband to a certain lady, and thus had the right to see her first on the unfortunate occasion of having docked at the same time.

The *Melusine* was a sleek vessel, but it was clear even from a distance that she didn't sacrifice elegance for function. Her brass fittings gleamed, as did her teak deck. A canopy amidships formed a comfortable workspace; Rupert stood beneath it at a teak table, grinding something into powder in a mortar.

He looked up at our hail. "Ah, Dr. Whyborne, Mr. Putnam-Barnett. I've been expecting you. Do come aboard."

Iskander and I exchanged a wary glance. I'd certainly had no plans to come here. Perhaps Rupert merely meant to keep us off balance. "Mr. Endicott," I said coolly. "We would like to speak with you. In private."

"Of course." He took off the apron he wore over his impeccable clothing and folded it neatly on the table. "This way, gentlemen."

He led the way below decks to a dining room equipped with a table, comfortable couch, library, and grand piano. I perched on the edge of the couch, gripping my knees. Iskander sat beside me.

"Would you care for some tea?" Rupert asked. "I imagine poor Mr. Putnam-Barnett hasn't had a decent cup since relocating to this benighted colony."

A look of longing passed over Iskander's face, but he only said, "Another time, perhaps."

"We're not here for pleasantries." I folded my arms over my chest and fixed Rupert with what I hoped was an intimidating stare. "It seems you've left out some very important facts about the Endicott estate. Or was Von Junzt referring to a different hill of grief, when he spoke of the place the Eyes of Nodens conducted their rites to call upon the dweller in the deep?"

To my surprise, a satisfied smile curved Rupert's lips. "I was expressly forbidden to speak about such things with you. Alas, my small slip allowed you to discover it for yourself. I suppose there's nothing for it but to reveal all."

Blast the man—he'd deliberately used me as a way around the orders he'd been given. He hadn't lied at all when he'd said he'd been expecting us.

"Such a shame," Iskander agreed dryly.

Rupert crossed his legs and rested his hands on his knee. "What else did Von Junzt have to say about Carn Moreth?"

"I'm sure you've read the *Unaussprechlichen Kulten* yourself," I replied stiffly. "Most of what he had to say about the Eyes of Nodens was vague, merely veiled hints of their relationship with the ketoi and the gods. He mentioned the focus of worship was something called 'Morgen's Needle,' and suggested it had something to do with the drowned land of Lyonesse." I paused. "Morgen was an early name for Morgan Le Fay. It means 'sea-born.'"

Iskander frowned. "Do you think it referred to a ketoi hybrid?"

"It could, at least in this case." Rupert said. "Of course, Morgen's Needle has nothing to do with King Arthur, any more than Merlin's Cave or any of the other stones and places associated with the legend. Morgen's Needle is a single, tall standing stone, much, much older than any human myths. It stands at the highest point on Carn Moreth, at the center of an arcane whirlpool. Of course, our vortex is quite small compared to the maelstrom of Widdershins, and is unlikely to have developed any sort of sentience, let alone housed pieces of itself in flesh."

Curse Stanford and his plotting. He'd exposed our nature to the Endicotts, which no doubt meant they would eventually attempt to use it against Persephone and me somehow.

"That was where the spell against the ketoi was performed," I guessed. "The one Theo spoke of." The one that had wrecked Mother's health and forced my sister and me to be born before our proper time.

"Yes. And the backlash killed some of our most talented sorcerers, so you can consider your aquatic kin avenged." He paused, as though deciding what to reveal. "The arcane energy was too strong—it flooded into them with such power it scorched them from the inside and stopped their hearts."

Iskander winced. I'd sent a shock of arcane power through him once, to destroy the rust that had taken over his mind and body. Even that short burst had been enough to knock him unconscious.

"So the Fideles have access to Morgen's Needle," I said.

"Yes." A troubled look passed over Rupert's face. "As I said, the vortex is quite small compared to Widdershins. But Morgen's Needle...it has similar markings as the Eltdown Shards and the stele in Alaska. The stone it was carved from resembles nothing found in Cornwall...but it is similar to that which the Occultum Lapidem are made from. I fear no human hands raised it, but that it is a tool of the masters, abandoned when they left our world."

Wonderful. "That's why you believe the Fideles were the ones to take the estate, rather than another of your many enemies. This isn't just an attempt to destroy the Endicotts, but to continue the Restoration."

"Indeed. Crippling our family's ability to fight them is likely no more than a bonus for achieving their true goal. As to what they mean to do with it..." Rupert removed his spectacles and rubbed tiredly at his eyes. "You mentioned Lethowsow—Lyonesse, as it is more commonly called. I assume you're both familiar with the legend?"

"Of course," Iskander said. "It's a mythical drowned country, which lay between Cornwall and the Isles of Scilly. Supposedly created when Merlin raised the waves to destroy the forces of Mordred."

"It is all only legend, but a legend that we believe contains a kernel of truth." Rupert put his spectacles back on and turned his dark gaze on us. "Seven Stones Reef, said to be the remains of the capital city of Lyonesse, marks the ketoi city. We think that, at some point in the past, an ancient counterpart of the Eyes of Nodens used the Needle to inundate a vast swath of land. Why, I couldn't say—perhaps as some favor to the ketoi, or in tribute to their god. The devastation must have been unimaginable. The height of Carn Moreth became a tidal island, renamed to commemorate those killed by the sudden flood, along with the new headland, now called Penmoreth. If we are right, if those who know how to properly use it can command such destructive forces...well. I'm certain you can imagine what they might do with it."

It was what I'd feared from the moment I'd recalled Von Junzt's words. Some ancient thing of the masters, left behind so their minions could wreak destruction and terror now. "We need to take it back from them. Why the devil did you wait so long?"

"It wasn't by choice, I assure you." Rupert's lips thinned unhappily. "We needed a way to get through the defenses surrounding Balefire, and for that the Seeker required a particular artifact. A pendant with very specific properties. Others among the family searched for it while Hattie and I came here. Unfortunately, they only recently retrieved it from a stronghold in the Balkans."

He bowed his head. "You see why we are so desperate for your assistance, cousin. Why even the Seeker, who isn't known for her tolerance of ketoi hybrids, is willing to join forces with you. To make peace with the ketoi themselves. To give you the key to the Wisborg Codex, which may help us stop the masters—but may also contain arcane secrets that a being such as yourself might use to take their place in subjugating the world." He tilted his head back up and met my gaze steadily. "Morgen's Needle drowned Lyonesse a thousand years ago. Should the Fideles use it, Widdershins—along with a good part of this state—may follow it to the bottom of the sea."

CHAPTER 7

Griffin

I SPENT THE afternoon preparing Jack for the prospect of taking over my detective duties, should Whyborne choose to throw in our lot with the Endicotts.

"I don't know, Griffin," he said as we sat together in the parlor room that served as my office. "I'm only just learning the trade. I don't have your contacts, or your skill, or—"

"I'm not expecting you to replace me," I assured him. "But you can take some of the simpler jobs, ones that don't require anything beyond a facility at asking questions, combined with a bit of charm."

Jack grinned and cocked a brow. "I might be able to manage that part, anyway."

I snorted. My brother had been adopted separately from the orphan train, and ended up running away from the cruel family who had wanted a laborer rather than a son. After a brief stint with a traveling circus, he'd roamed the country, living off his quick wit and easy smile. He'd learned to lie with a grin, and do it so effectively he'd even deceived me for a time.

"Nothing unsavory," I reminded him. "Keep to my usual rates, don't add anything unnecessary to expenses, and absolutely no taking reward money."

"You're no fun," he groused. "Don't worry about that, Griffin. I didn't decide to stay in Widdershins just so I could let you down."

"I know." I met the gaze of eyes as green as my own. "I remember."

I'd glimpsed his thoughts briefly in Alaska, when my mind had been possessed by the little queen. His pain and his love. Jack wasn't perfect, far from it, but he wouldn't do anything to hurt my business or my reputation.

The ring of the phone interrupted our conversation. When I answered it, Niles Whyborne said, "Griffin, I've just heard from Percival. We're to meet Persephone at the usual place this evening."

"Before sunset?" I asked. Normally the ketoi came ashore only after dark, when they were less likely to be spotted by curious humans.

"Apparently there is some urgency involved. I'll come fetch you in the touring car. Percival suggested bringing your brother as well."

When I hung up, Jack said, "Who was that?"

"Niles Whyborne." I sank slowly back into my chair. "How would you like to meet your sister-in-law?"

Jack barely spoke on the ride to the beach. He seemed overawed by Niles, who rode in the back of the touring car with us while Fenton drove. As usual, Niles wore a suit straight from the most expensive tailor in New York, his Tiffany tie pin, emerald-studded pocket watch, and diamond ring casual reminders of the wealth controlled by the Whyborne empire.

"How has the sword cane served, Griffin?" he asked as Fenton guided the car out of the city and onto the lonely coast road.

"Very well, thank you." The cane had been a gift after Whyborne destroyed my original one. Unfortunately, he'd been stabbing his brother with it at the time.

Niles had still loved Stanford, despite everything the man had done. And yet he'd put a bullet in him in an attempt to save Whyborne. I suspected that day—that moment—haunted Niles.

He'd aged in the past few months, the lines on his face more deeply graven, his shoulders not quite so straight.

Fenton pulled the car to the side of the road, and we made our way down to the hidden beach. The sun sparkled off the water, the retreating tide leaving behind strands of kelp. The others had arrived before us. Maggie Parkhurst perched on a rock, while Whyborne chased Persephone through the surf, yelling at her to give back his hat.

Jack gaped at Persephone's sleek orca skin, the tendrils of her hair, and her batrachian feet. He'd met the umbrae, of course, but they were vastly inhuman in appearance. The ketoi were similar enough to our species to be disturbing in a different way.

"That's Whyborne's twin, Persephone," I said with a nod.

Whyborne stepped into a tidal pool and cursed loudly. Persephone put his hat onto her tentacles and laughed at him.

"And they're supposed to be key to saving the world?" Jack said incredulously. "You're having me on, brother."

I winced. "No. No, I'm afraid not."

Niles sighed heavily, then called, "Persephone! Give your brother back his hat. Percival, it is beneath your dignity to run about shouting like some sort of delinquent."

"But she took my hat!" Whyborne objected. "Oh, very well." He trudged up the beach to join us. Persephone sprinted past him, tossing his hat onto his head as she passed.

"Hello, Father." She grabbed Maggie about the waist, grinning cheerfully. "Do you remember my cuttlefish?"

Maggie's face went scarlet. At the sight of his sister hugging his secretary, Whyborne also blushed furiously. Niles sighed again.

Perhaps in a fit of chivalry, Jack approached them. "A pleasure to meet you, Miss Parkhurst, Miss Whyborne," he said, as though there was nothing at all strange about the situation. "I'm Griffin's brother. Jack Ho—Flaherty," he corrected, having only recently changed his name back to the original.

"Brother's husband's brother," Persephone said. Jack glanced worriedly at Niles, even though I had assured him Niles was well aware of my relationship with his son.

"Mr. Flaherty," Maggie said faintly. Her nerve failed her

altogether with Niles. "S-Sir."

"Hello, Maggie," I said. We'd formed something of a friendship over the last few months. While Whyborne and Persephone practiced sorcery, or manipulated the maelstrom, there was little for us to do besides watch and talk. As a result, I likely knew more about her than Whyborne did.

"Griffin. It's, um, good to see you." She took the opportunity to slip out of Persephone's grasp, her face still blazing red.

Niles observed the two of us, as if silently asking himself why his youngest children had to be contrary enough to not only have an interest solely in their own sex, but—more importantly —to have contented themselves with riffraff such as ourselves. He finally settled on offering Maggie a regal nod and a polite, "Miss Parkhurst. It's good to see you under more pleasant circumstances."

"So." Jack tucked his hands into his pockets and rocked back on his heels. "I take it this isn't just a nice family outing on the beach?"

"No," Whyborne said quickly, as though happy for any topic of conversation that might relieve the awkward atmosphere. "Iskander and I saw Rupert Endicott today."

I stiffened. "And Christine?"

He cast me an exasperated look. "We weren't there to murder the fellow, Griffin. At any rate, Iskander agreed to relate our conversation to her tonight, which is why they aren't here as well."

"I like Christine," Persephone said. "She would have been a great chieftess among the ketoi."

"I'm certain she would agree," Whyborne muttered. The crash of the waves formed a backdrop to his words as he explained everything they'd learned from Rupert, as well as the request he'd made last night.

Persephone's expression grew more and more grim as he spoke. When he finished, she folded her arms over her chest. She was no longer Whyborne's light-hearted sister, but the warrior-chieftess of the ketoi. "They ask much."

"I know." He spread his hands. "But what choice have we?"

"The Endicotts tried to kill us. They would have slain all you land-dwellers. Mother nearly died because of them. And now you say I must send an envoy to my sister chieftess and ask her to ignore her own history with the Endicotts and make peace?" Her hair lashed around her shoulders. "I do not like this, brother."

"I'm hardly fond of it myself," he shot back. "But I'd be far less fond of the Fideles using the power of Morgen's Needle to drop half of New England into the sea."

Niles's frown grew deeper and deeper. "I dislike the idea of either of you leaving. We don't know when the masters will return, and we'll need both the land and the sea to have a chance at defeating them."

"The rest of us could go," I suggested. "I have my shadowsight, and Christine and Iskander know how to fight sorcerers. Christine's even been practicing with the bow and arrow, since those won't explode in her hands if a sorcerer decides to use fire magic against her."

"I'll come with you," Jack offered. "If you think I'd be more useful there than watching your business here at home."

But Whyborne was shaking his head. "The Endicotts want me. If I don't go, they won't give us the key to the Wisborg Codex."

"I don't see they're in much of a position to make demands," Niles replied. "Really, Percival, you never did know how to negotiate. You should have brought me to this meeting."

Whyborne's face took on the mulish expression he often wore around his father, and I mentally resigned myself to a stubborn outburst. After all these years, Niles should know any criticism on his part would inevitably cause Whyborne to react defiantly. It was a habit neither of them seemed able to break. "I'm not staying here and just hoping the Fideles don't kill us from afar. The Endicotts have plenty of experience fighting sorcerers, and as useful as Griffin's shadowsight is, he's only one man. They wouldn't have asked for me unless they believed my presence greatly improved their chances of taking back Balefire Manor."

"Damn it, Percival, listen to me!" Niles took a step forward. "I won't pretend I entirely understand this business with the maelstrom. But what happened in the Draakenwood made one thing clear. Whatever role the maelstrom means you and your sister to play, you are critical to the defense of this world when the masters return. You cannot risk yourself on some fool's errand to Cornwall." He gestured vaguely in my direction. "The rest of us may fall, but as long as the two of you are still standing, we have a chance."

Whyborne's eyes widened. "Don't be absurd! I'm not sacrificing anyone so I can sit back in safety, let alone my friends!"

I braced myself for his reaction, but it had to be said. "Niles is right."

His lips parted in shock. Then his brows dove down, eyes narrowing in anger. The wind picked up, flinging foam across the beach. "I can't believe you think so little of me."

"I don't," I protested. The fear and worry I routinely suppressed struggled to rise to the surface. Whyborne and Persephone were meant to face the masters; it was why the maelstrom had made them in the first place. They would be on the frontline, in the thick of whatever terrible forces the masters could wield, and the thought terrified me. But at least it meant he should stay here for now, rather than risk dying on behalf of the Endicotts on the other side of the Atlantic.

Niles glowered at Whyborne. "I thought you'd finally learned to accept your place in this town. The old families, the librarians, the police, all stand ready to fight at your command. And you want to abandon them and go haring off, with the Endicotts of all people?"

Whyborne's face smoothed into the expressionless mask that bespoke true fury, and I silently cursed Niles for making everything worse, for daring to imply Whyborne would abandon the responsibility he'd had such difficulty coming to terms with. The waves smashed into the strand with greater violence than before, and the wind turned to a snarl over the cliff. "I accepted that it is my duty to protect Widdershins," Whyborne said coldly. "You are my general, Father, and I'm leaving you with whatever army I can muster. But I will not sit here while the Fideles plot to use Morgen's Needle against us. I will not cower at home, while my husband and my friends attempt the task that is rightfully mine."

Niles's nostrils flared. "Persephone, tell your brother he's a fool."

Persephone had listened to their argument in silence, the look on her scarred face grave. "Among the ketoi, a chieftess leads from the front. Fire in His Blood may have the form of a land dweller, but his heart is surely of the sea." She met Whyborne's gaze. "I'll keep watch for us both. And I'll send an envoy with you."

"Thank you," he said. He swept a withering glare over the rest of us. "I'm going home. The rest of you can do as you please."

"Ival," I said, but he had already turned away and stalked toward the path leading away from the sea. His abruptness stung, but I knew Nile's words had hurt him.

"I agree Percival should stay here, Niles," I said, "but he's no coward, and you can't simply insult him until he agrees with you."

"Bah. You talk to him," Niles said, waving an annoyed hand. "Perhaps he'll see sense."

"Perhaps." But as I left the beach and hurried after my husband, I rather thought it was too late for that.

CHAPTER 8

Whyborne

I rode in the front of the touring car beside Fenton, my arms folded across my chest, with Griffin, Jack, and Father in the back. Miss Parkhurst had elected to remain behind with Persephone. No one spoke, but I could feel Father's disapproval beating on the back of my neck the entire trip home. As soon as the motor car stopped in front of our house, I hopped out and stalked toward the door without saying good night.

Jack and Griffin joined me on the porch, Jack looking rather unsure. "Should I come to Cornwall with you?" he asked, glancing back and forth, as though not certain which of us to direct the question to.

Griffin gave me the chance to answer. When I didn't, he rubbed at his eyes. "No. Stay here as we discussed earlier." He pulled his keys from his pocket and held them out. "Actually, why don't you keep the house while we're gone? It will be more comfortable than your boarding room, allow you to see clients, and watch over Saul. You can use the motor car as well, should you have need."

Jack nodded. "I'll come by in the morning with my things.

See you then, Griffin." He hesitated. "Goodnight, Whyborne."

"Goodnight," I said, a bit stiffly, but my anger wasn't directed at him.

As Griffin had relinquished his keys, I was forced to uncross my arms long enough to let us inside. Saul bounded to meet us, and I picked him up, cradling his warm little body to me. He purred and butted his head against my chin.

I carried him to the study, Griffin trailing behind. "Very well," he said. "I know you wish to argue, so out with it."

It was difficult to decide what part of the conversation had made me angriest. I sat in one of the chairs and settled Saul in my lap. "You think me faithless," I decided at last. "Or a coward."

Griffin let out a long sigh. "Ival, you're the bravest man I've ever met in my life. Do you recall when we first encountered the otherworldly, all those years ago? The Guardian in the warehouse?"

I frowned suspiciously at the apparent non sequitur. "Yes."

"Instead of running and screaming like a sensible person, you stood by me. We returned here, to this very room, and *that* was when you asked to be a part of my investigation. Not when it seemed to be an ordinary, if potentially risky, case. But when it became undeniable that anyone pursuing things further would be placing themselves in the sort of danger neither of us had even imagined could exist." His pointed to the other chair near the fire. "And I sat right there and fell completely, madly, in love with you. So please, don't insult me by suggesting I think, even for an instant, that you would act the part of a coward."

My heart softened, despite myself. I recalled the moment well, even though of course I'd had no idea Griffin desired anything of me past a brief joining of forces. "You told me you worked alone."

A smile curled near the corner of Griffin's mouth. "And you invited me to make use of you. Though, sadly, not in the manner I wished to."

I flushed at the recollection of my clumsy words. "Then why would you suggest I remain behind now?"

My husband bowed his head. "Because Niles is right. We must think strategically. Not act according to our hearts."

I hesitated. Father had fought in the War Between the States under General Grant, had commanded men on the field and off. Griffin's experience with the Pinkertons was far different, but he had at least planned ambushes when pursuing bank robbers.

"We need the Wisborg Codex," I said at last. "Otherwise we're fighting blind. Surely you must agree any knowledge of the masters will give us a strategic advantage. Do you truly believe the Endicotts will give us the key if I refuse to go?"

"We could try—"

"No." I looked down at Saul's ears. "No, Griffin. My mind is made up."

"I know." He came and knelt down by us. "I expressed my opinion, and now I must accept your decision. Don't be angry with me."

I cupped his cheek with my unscarred hand. "I hate to quarrel."

"So do I." He turned his head and kissed my palm. "I love you, Ival. More than I could have imagined, that long ago night."

I leaned over and kissed him, dislodging Saul from my lap as I did so. The familiar contours of his lips drew a gentle warmth into my chest. "Darling."

Our foreheads rested together briefly. Then Griffin pulled back. "Come to bed. Tomorrow will be a long day for us all."

CHAPTER 9

Griffin

THE NEXT NIGHT, we awaited the arrival of the ketoi at the *Melusine*'s berth.

The day had been one of frantic activity. Iskander and I devoted ourselves to packing and transporting our things to the *Melusine*, while Christine and Whyborne secured the director's permission to desert the museum for a few weeks. The man seemed to have become resigned to such sudden trips; though not a member of the old families, he rubbed elbows with them at clubs and galas, and knew enough to acquiesce without much grumbling.

All was in readiness by mid-afternoon. I said goodbye to Jack at home. Iskander and I met Christine and Whyborne at Marsh's for dinner, then made our way to the docks around sunset.

Rupert waited at the base of the gangplank. "The ketoi haven't yet sent their envoy," he said with a frown. "Though we are less beholden to the tide than most ships, I see no need to expend our energy on water magic without true need."

"Even in Widdershins, the ketoi can't parade up and down the docks in broad daylight," I replied. "They'll come."

Persephone wouldn't have changed her mind after siding with Whyborne last night.

We'd buried our brief quarrel; I'd always found it hard to stay annoyed once he wrapped his arms around me for the night, and he was the same. Still, I wished he'd agreed to at least try to bargain with Rupert. The entire situation sounded exceedingly dangerous, and we didn't know enough about Balefire Manor to anticipate what we might face. If something happened to him...

It would crush me, of course. I couldn't bring myself to even picture a life without my Ival. But more than my happiness depended on his safety now.

I wished we knew why, exactly, the maelstrom had decided to split off twin fragments of itself. To command the armies of land and sea against the masters seemed the most likely explanation, but surely there were easier ways.

The maelstrom was an inhuman sentience. But such a long, careful plan must have some understandable strategy behind it.

"There." Whyborne pointed at the water, interrupting my thoughts.

The waxing moon had broken the horizon a few hours back, and now hung high enough in the sky to reflect off the heaving waves. Fins breached the surface of the water just off the dock. First a few, then more, and still more. I shifted my weight uneasily and wondered just how many of her people Persephone had brought with her.

While most of the ketoi remained in the water, some swarmed up the pilings and onto the dock. Persephone came first. She ordinarily wore at least some ketoi jewelry—and not much else. Tonight, however, she dazzled the eye, with gold, coral, and pearls reflecting the light of the ship's lanterns as well as that of the moon. A tiara held back her ever-shifting hair, necklaces hung low across her chest, and layers of bracelets and anklets chimed with every step of the batrachian feet.

She cut a commanding figure. I wished Miss Parkhurst was here to see her.

An honor guard of ketoi carrying spears followed her and took up position to either side, their eyes hostile. "Hello, cousin," Persephone said to Rupert with a smile that revealed row after row of shark's teeth.

Rupert inclined his head slightly. "A pleasure to see you again. Is one of these your envoy?"

"No." Her hair seethed over her shoulders. "Before I send her with you, I want assurances, Endicott."

Annoyance flickered across Rupert's face. "I'm sure Dr. Whyborne informed you as to what is at stake should the Fideles use Morgen's Needle."

"Some of your lands will become ours," Persephone replied, cocking her head to the side.

"Including Widdershins!" Whyborne exclaimed. "Persephone, we talked about this last night. Must you always be so difficult?"

She didn't glance his way. "I asked the question of our cousin, not you."

The lights reflected in Rupert's spectacles, hiding his eyes. "Because once we have Balefire Manor back under our control, we can use its power to fight on your behalf. To stop the masters."

"You will swear an oath to do so?"

Rupert hesitated. "That would be the Seeker's responsibility. I can promise only for myself. But I will swear whatever oath you require of me."

"And your Seeker will approve?"

"Not at all." Rupert offered her a rueful smile. "But if it will help us defeat the masters, then I will do it. Nothing else matters."

Persephone regarded him for a long moment. Then she nodded. "Understand this, cousin. If any harm comes to our envoy under your watch, my brother will boil your blood in your veins."

Whyborne looked a bit taken aback at being assigned such a task. But there came the soft chime of gold on gold as the envoy climbed onto the dock, and I understood why Persephone had made such a threat.

Heliabel walked between the honor guard, her expression serene. Like Persephone, she dripped with gold and pearls. Fine gold mesh draped her body from shoulder to ankle, the closest thing I'd ever seen to a dress of ketoi make. Perhaps she'd had it crafted specially, or perhaps it was simply of ritual significance to her role as envoy from one ketoi city to another.

"Mother?" Whyborne exclaimed. His eyes widened. "You're coming with us?"

"I'm a matriarch," she said. "And I am related to both sides in this conflict. It makes sense for me to mediate between them."

Whyborne looked conflicted. But he'd always respected Heliabel's choices, so he only said, "Of course."

Rupert inclined his head. "Welcome aboard, Mrs. Whyborne."

"You may refer to me as Matriarch, or as Speaker of Stories," she replied coolly.

If Rupert was taken aback, he didn't show it. "As you wish, Matriarch. If we are quite done here, then, we should get aboard. The tide waits for no man." He smiled faintly. "Not even the Endicotts."

CHAPTER 10

Whyborne

"I CAN'T BELIEVE Persephone sent our mother," I said, as soon as the cabin door shut behind us.

Rather than reply, Griffin put his hands on his hips and surveyed the bed. "The accommodations aboard the *Melusine* are far superior to those we had while traveling to Egypt, don't you agree?"

Rupert had assigned us a stateroom in the port aft area of the lower deck, where the ship's crew had stored our things at some point earlier. I'd expected the polite fiction of separate beds, but the Endicotts had never been ones to feel themselves constrained by society. Our stateroom contained a single relatively large bed, desk, bookshelves—complete with brass railings to keep books from tumbling off during heavy seas—and dresser. Portholes showed the night sea beyond, and a skylight let in fresh air.

"We're still on the water," I muttered, wrapping my arms around myself. I despised boats, even when they weren't taking me away from Widdershins. "And you're changing the subject."

Griffin sat down on the edge of the bed and looked up at me.

"Heliabel is the logical choice, for the reasons she gave herself. And now that she is healthy, she's a fierce fighter. You should have seen her take on the byakhee."

"I was too busy trying to stop my brother. And that's beside the point." I leaned against the desk. "The Endicotts aren't trustworthy. If this Seeker of theirs tells Rupert to stab us all in our sleep, he'll do it."

Griffin's expression grew thoughtful. "I don't think so." When I snorted, he held up a hand. "Granted, I could be wrong. But Rupert isn't Hattie. Or Theo and Fiona. He cares about the family and wants what's best for them, but I don't think that means blind loyalty in his case. He thinks for himself." Griffin paused. "I wonder if that's why he was sent to contact you in the first place. Because the Seeker knew he would assess the situation fairly."

The sea grew rougher around us as we passed the breakwater. Outside the portholes, the moonlight glittered on the waves. I had to resist the urge to pull down the shade so as not to see it. I'd never be fond of water, no matter how many accursed ships I was forced onto.

Griffin must have noticed, because he patted the bed beside him. "Perhaps I can take your mind off of your worries."

At least we wouldn't be required to squeeze into a single tiny berth if we wished to be intimate. Or forced to share accommodations with several others, as we had on our voyage to Alaska. Before I could join him on the bed, however, there came a knock on our door.

Griffin gave me a rueful shrug. "Come in," he called.

Iskander poked his head in. "Do you chaps have a moment? There's something Christine and I would like to discuss with you."

"Now that we're out to sea and no one can start any nonsense about me staying behind in Widdershins," Christine added, pushing the door wide and inviting herself inside.

I frowned. "Why on earth would anyone suggest that? We need all the help we can get, and I doubt any of the Endicotts can shoot half as well as you."

"See, Kander?" Christine said, dropping into a chair. "Whyborne is sensible, at least." She considered. "Now there's a sentence I never thought I'd utter."

"You haven't told them yet," Iskander pointed out.

I gave Griffin a baffled glance, but his attention was focused on Christine. "Tell us what?" I asked.

Christine took a deep breath before speaking. "Good news, gentlemen. Our company will soon number five, rather than four."

Could she have been more cryptic? "Are you talking about Jack?" I asked blankly. "He's to work with Griffin, but I'm not certain he's as inclined to adventure as, well, you are."

"Of course I'm not talking about Jack," Christine said.

"I'm not putting Miss Parkhurst in any more danger than I must. I know she was of assistance last February, but—"

"I'm pregnant, you utter fool."

I gaped at this rather indelicate announcement. Christine, pregnant? Such a condition often accompanied marriage, and yet somehow I'd never imagined it would happen to her.

"Congratulations!" Griffin exclaimed, leaping to his feet. He shook Iskander's hand warmly. "This is wonderful news!"

I felt as though I'd had the wind knocked out of me. "You're going to have a baby?"

"That is the expected outcome, yes." Christine rolled her eyes at me. "You'll be the godfather, of course."

I blinked. "I will?" Then I recovered myself. "That is—of course—I'd be honored." A thought occurred to me. "But...dear heavens, it isn't safe for you to accompany us! Perhaps—"

"If you suggest I remain behind on the Isles of Scilly, I shall be very tempted to thrash you." Her dark eyes flashed. "As I told Kander, if we don't defeat the masters, there won't be a world left for the baby to grow up in. Besides, I won't be the first woman in this condition to take up arms. My own mother fought in the war beside a sergeant who rather unexpectedly gave birth to a baby boy."

"I suppose," I said doubtfully. "Are you feeling well, though?" I had the vague idea women in her state tended toward sickness.

Christine laughed at my concern. "Honestly, Whyborne, you know me. Never been sick in my life. I'm a bit peckish occasionally, and my sense of smell seems altered, but otherwise

I've suffered no effects."

Recalling the night we'd dined with Rupert, I was less certain about her description as being "a bit peckish," but kept the thought to myself.

"When is the, er, blessed event to occur?" I asked.

Christine stared at me as though I'd grown another head. "'Blessed event?' Really, man, what has gotten into you? The first half of November, based on my calculations."

I didn't know how one might calculate such a thing, which perhaps was for the best. "Oh," I said dumbly.

Christine rose to her feet. "At any rate, we'd best get back to our cabin, now that we've shared our news with you."

I hadn't said a word of congratulations. Ashamed of my lapse, I rose as well. "I am happy for you both. Truly." I held out my arms, and she stepped into the embrace. "Any child of yours will be amazing." I paused. "Are you sniffing my hair?"

"No," she lied. "Thank you, Whyborne, Griffin. We'll see you in the morning."

The door shut behind them. I sank down on the bed. "Is something wrong?" Griffin asked me.

"No," I said, because I didn't want to speak my fears aloud. But my entire life, I'd heard the story of how Mother had almost died when giving birth to Persephone and me. The two of us had nearly perished as well. I'd never thought of childbirth as anything other than fraught with peril.

Christine would be facing a danger that had claimed women throughout history, and there wasn't a cursed thing I could do to help her. All of my magic, and I had no way to protect my best friend.

Rising to my feet again, I said, "I'm going to talk to Mother."

CHAPTER 11

Whyborne

I FOUND MY mother in the cabin set aside for her. Smaller than ours, it contained two single beds, one mounted to the wall above the other. The top bunk offered a view out a porthole, and she lay there on her belly, peering out. Her gold mesh dress hung over the back of the chair, a small fortune tossed carelessly aside.

"Percival," she said. Shutting the porthole and securing it, she climbed down to my level. She gave me a smile, but there was a note of sadness to it that left me feeling uncertain. "A far cry from all the times you visited me at Whyborne House, isn't it?"

"It's good to see you like this." I gestured vaguely in her direction. The sea had transformed her in many ways, but it had healed her as well. Given her strength and freedom.

But a part of me missed our old visits. Missed knowing I could simply take the trolley to High Street, knock on the door of Whyborne House, and climb the stairs to her room. We still met once a month, on the deserted beach just outside of town, but it wasn't the same. Most of the time Persephone and I spent the hours practicing sorcery. Even when Mother and I did speak, it was no longer of the books we'd read, or the stories I'd translated.

Our world had changed, and us with it.

"Thank you." She perched on the edge of the bed, drawing up her long, frog-like feet and wrapping her arms around her knees. "It will take us a few days to arrive. I hope we'll find time to talk."

"I'm sure we will." I paused. "Actually, I wondered if you might speak with Christine."

She frowned and cocked her head. "Why?"

"She's...she's going to have a baby." I clasped my hands in front of me and stared down at them.

"I thought there was a new bulge beneath her skirt, loose as she's wearing it."

"Oh." I hadn't noticed. "I hoped...that is, I don't know if she has anyone to talk to about, er, such things. Her own mother is entirely estranged, and I doubt Miss Parkhurst would be as helpful as someone who has, ah, gone through the process." My face heated with embarrassment, but I persevered. "I know the two of you have only interacted a few times, and she might not ask for herself, but perhaps you could, I don't know, help in some fashion?"

"You love her very much, don't you?"

I looked up in surprise. "Of course I do. She's my best friend."

"I'll speak with her," Mother said. "If she wants my advice, I'm glad to give it."

"Thank you. I appreciate it." I hesitated, not wishing to pry, but the sadness hovering in her eyes decided me. "Is everything well?"

"Well enough," she said without conviction.

"Are you certain? You just seem a bit sad, that's all."

She sighed, and her shoulders slumped. "Is it wrong of me to mourn your brother?"

I opened my mouth, then closed it again. I'd wrestled with my own anger and guilt, and seen Father struggle to conceal his grief. But I hadn't spared much thought as to how Mother must feel, to have lost a second child.

How selfish I'd been.

"No," I said simply.

"Even after all that he did?" Her clawed fingers curled into fists. "He *murdered* Guinevere. He wanted to do the same to you and Persephone."

I pulled the chair out from the desk and sat down. "I know. But he was still your son."

She shook her head, but not as if to disagree with me. "He was such an active boy. I remember how loudly he screamed as an infant. His nurse feared Niles would be angered by all the noise, but your father only laughed and said Stanford had a good, healthy set of lungs. Whereas you were so quiet, I had to keep checking on you, to make sure you weren't lying dead in your crib." She stared down at her hands. "Stanford was four years old when the Endicott spell destroyed my health. I think, in some ways, that was when I began to lose him."

I'd never considered the time between Stanford's birth and my own. My image of my brother was always one of the cruel bully, older and stronger than me. But of course he hadn't come into the world that way. "I don't remember him visiting you, except when Father told him to."

"No. At first, I was too ill for a rambunctious child to visit. By the time I'd recovered somewhat…I suppose it was too late. I must have seemed like a pale stranger who'd taken the place of the mother he remembered." She tilted her head back, staring up at the bottom of the bunk above her. "The woman who'd danced and played silly games with him was gone, and I was left behind. Like a changeling in a fairy tale."

"I'm sorry," I said. "I didn't know. That is, I knew, of course I did. Only I never wondered what it must have been like for either of you."

"Understandable. You never knew me before I was sick." She looked at me again, her expression grim. "I can't stop thinking what might have been if the Endicotts hadn't cast their accursed spell. If I had never fallen ill. In the Draakenwood, before you came to our rescue, Stanford accused me of giving all my affection to you and none to him."

The devil? Anger fired my blood. "That's outrageous! How dare he say such things to you? Blame you for his ills, his choices?"

The ship rocked slightly, as though the sea had grown rougher. "Calm yourself, my knight," Mother said. "I'll be unharmed if the *Melusine* goes to the bottom, but I can't say the same for everyone else aboard."

I took a deep breath to steady my racing pulse. "Forgive my outburst. But he was wrong to say such things."

"He saw himself excluded from my sickroom, and you included."

"Because I almost *died!*" Curse Stanford for a willful fool. "It's a child's logic. Perhaps he felt that way when he was four, but he should have outgrown it by thirty-five."

"I know." She shook her head angrily. "That isn't even my point. If the Endicotts hadn't cast their spell, I might have been able to counteract some of Niles's worst indulgences of Stanford. Intervened when he picked on those smaller and weaker than himself. And perhaps it would have changed nothing—maybe I would have even made things worse, I don't know. But I can't overlook the possibility Guinevere, at least, would still be alive."

The pieces slipped into place. "Persephone didn't ask you to be her envoy. You volunteered."

Mother reached out and took my hand in her clawed one. "Let us say it was a mutual decision. I wanted to come because over thirty years ago, the Endicotts judged the ketoi, and those with ketoi blood, had no right to exist. Then they appointed themselves our executioners."

She paused and met my gaze. "And now they think I will simply forget and forgive. They think I will broker some fair treaty between themselves and the ketoi, which they will then break at their leisure. But they're wrong." Mother smiled, her mouth uncurling wider than a human's to reveal rows of shark's teeth. "One way or another, I mean to make the Endicotts pay for what they did."

CHAPTER 12

Griffin

Ival and I emerged onto the deck the next morning after a lazy breakfast. As we had no pressing duties, we'd slept late, emerging to find the dining saloon already deserted. Portions of a cold breakfast had been left for us, so we took our time eating and exploring the bookshelves. Unfortunately they seemed bare of the adventure fiction I preferred, but Whyborne had pulled down a grimoire for later study.

Iskander sat under the canopy amidships, reading a book while the wind tousled his thick hair. Christine stood near the bow, staring out over the sea.

"What on earth is she doing?" Whyborne exclaimed in horror. "She could be swept over the side at any moment!"

I glanced at the placid sea. "I don't think there's any chance—" I began, but he'd already scurried away. A few moments later, Christine's irritated, *"Good gad, man!"* echoed across the ship.

I suppressed a sigh and joined Iskander. "How are you doing?" I asked, with a nod in Christine's direction.

He set his book down. "Well enough. A bit nervous, of course, and I would have preferred Christine remain in

Widdershins. But I married her for her spirit, so I can hardly complain of it now."

"True." The same might have been said for Whyborne, I supposed. I'd wanted him to remain behind in Widdershins, but wasn't it his very courage that had drawn me from the start?

I settled back in the chair. The yacht was outfitted with every comfort; even the deck chairs were superior to those we'd had aboard the steamer to England. And of course the ships to and from Alaska had offered not even that much in the way of ease. "I hope you realize I'm at your disposal, should you ever need anyone to watch the little one."

A wistful tone must have crept into my words despite my attempt to suppress it, because Iskander gave me a thoughtful look. "You wanted to be a father, didn't you?"

I glanced automatically in the direction of the bow. Whyborne seemed to have given up on shepherding Christine farther back onto the deck, and now seemed to be trying to convince her to sit down on a nearby coil of rope.

He'd be lucky if she didn't throw him overboard before the end of our journey.

Ival and I were not made precisely the same; I preferred men, but women did not leave me unmoved. In some other life, I might have married a woman I loved and raised a family at her side.

But the maelstrom had collected me. Weighted the dice of fate, because it understood, in some way I didn't comprehend, that I belonged in Widdershins. With Ival.

"I would have welcomed the opportunity, had it presented itself," I said at last. "But I have no regrets as to the direction my life has taken."

Heliabel joined Christine and Whyborne. I couldn't hear what they spoke of, but Ival quickly left them alone.

"This ship is far too small," he declared when he rejoined us. "It would be much too easy to fall overboard."

I wasn't certain whether he spoke from his anxiety around water travel, or from misplaced concern for Christine. "The deck is far more cramped than the ocean liner, that's true. But there's room enough to take a stroll, so long as we watch our step."

I rose to my feet and set off. After a moment, he hurried to catch me. "What are Heliabel and Christine speaking of?" I asked him.

"Oh, you know." His cheeks reddened. "Womanly things."

"Ah." I glanced back at them. Christine had hiked up her skirt and seemed to be complaining about her ankles, while Heliabel nodded sympathetically. "Is that why you wished to speak to your mother last night?"

"Yes. Though we talked about other things." Whyborne hesitated. "I know she came as envoy, but she wants revenge against the Endicotts."

"Surely she won't do anything too extreme," I said.

Whyborne stared at me as though I'd lost my senses. "Dear lord, man, she literally stabbed herself in the chest to keep Fiona from using her as a hostage against Persephone and me."

"You make an excellent point." I absently ran my thumb over the head of the sword cane, tracing the Whyborne family crest hidden within the decorative engraving. "Do you think she'll refuse to act as go-between?"

"No. But she won't be as impartial as the Endicotts might wish." Whyborne sighed. "We'll need their help, Griffin, against the masters. Ordinarily I'd say let the Endicotts reap what they've sowed, but with the fate of the world in balance…"

He trailed off unhappily. I brushed my hand discreetly against his. "Don't fret so, my dear. Heliabel is no fool. She knows what's at stake just as we do."

"I suppose."

We fell silent as we reached the stern of the ship. A youth of perhaps sixteen years sat there in another deck chair, dressed in a fashionable suit and apparently at his leisure. Black hair blew in the wind, his olive skin glowing in the summer sun. His head bent over a book, and on the deck beside him a basket sat, containing what appeared to be knitted shawls, balls of yarn, and knitting needles.

All of which glowed with magic in my shadowsight.

He looked up as we approached—and a bright smile bloomed over his face. Leaping to his feet, he thrust his hand out to Whyborne. "You must be Dr. Whyborne! What a pleasure to meet you, sir!"

"Er," Whyborne said, obviously taken aback.

"And you are?" I asked.

The youth flushed. "Forgive me. My name is Basil Endicott."

He'd spoken Whyborne's name, but... "You do know who we are, don't you, Mr. Endicott?"

"Please, call me Basil." He finally let go of Whyborne and shook my hand in turn. "Otherwise, I won't know if you're referring to me or to Rupert. And yes, Mr. Flaherty, I've heard stories of you both."

Whyborne still looked nonplussed. "Forgive my surprise, but ordinarily Endicotts try to kill me. Or at least insult me."

"Ah, yes." Basil winced. "Some of them are still angry about Theo and Fiona. But the twins did try to kill you first—what were you supposed to do, refuse to defend yourself?"

"That is the response the rest of the Endicotts seem to have expected, yes," Whyborne said.

"Well, that's quite silly," Basil replied.

I watched him carefully, but he seemed to be exactly as he presented himself. His eyes told me he was a sorcerer—but I'd already guessed as much from the basket of knitting beside him. "And Whyborne's ketoi blood?"

"Why should that outweigh his Endicott blood? *Supra alia familia*, that's our motto, you know."

I glanced at Whyborne for a translation. "Before all other things comes family," he said.

"Precisely." Basil beamed at him. "You're one of ours. If Fiona and Theo had only realized that, so much unpleasantness might have been avoided. Imagine what we might have accomplished as allies."

A wistful expression crossed over Whyborne's face. Though I didn't think the Endicott twins had been a good influence on him—quite the opposite—he'd genuinely liked them both, up until they'd reacted with homicidal intent. "I can't disagree," he said at last. "Most of your family doesn't seem to share your assessment, however."

"The older generations are stuck in their ways." Basil waved a hand as if sweeping aside the past. "I hope in the future we will be more thoughtful and less quick to condemn."

"A good sentiment," I said neutrally. Even though I couldn't detect any falsity in his manner, I wasn't inclined to trust Basil.

Not yet, at any rate. "Might I inquire as to the contents of your basket?"

I expected him to demur, or lie outright, given how closely the Endicotts guarded their secrets. Instead, he declared, "I'm the ship's windweaver."

I glanced at Whyborne, but he seemed equally baffled. "The what?"

Now it was Basil's turn to seem puzzled. "Windweaver. You don't think we'd simply rely on nature to fill the sails, do you?"

Whyborne and I both turned to the sails. They seemed ordinary enough to me. "I can summon wind," Whyborne said. "But I'd be more likely to blow down the canvas than do anything useful. And it wouldn't last but for a few minutes."

"Ah, yes, Rupert said you lacked subtlety," Basil said guilelessly. "I suppose brute force suffices for you in most cases, but there are benefits to the more civilized magics."

Whyborne drew himself up, nostrils flaring in affront. "Brute force?" he sputtered. "Civilized? I'll have you know—"

"Do show us, Basil," I said over him. "I fear I'm but a layman in such matters, but I would love to know more."

"It's quite simple." Taking his seat, Basil pulled out what I had assumed to be a shawl of some sort. As he spread the square of cloth wide, the whole thing gleamed with arcane light in my shadowsight. "I learned this at my grandmother's knee. In the old days, this was considered women's magic, but I've always felt we of modern times should embrace all the arts, don't you?"

I wished Christine had joined us for this conversation. "How does it work?"

Basil took out a pair of glass knitting needles and a half-finished square. "Before our journey—or during, if the natural winds get too high—I bind the wind into the knitting. When the natural wind falls, I unravel the knitting a bit at a time, releasing the bound wind to propel us along. So long as I keep a close eye on the naturally occurring breezes, and adjust to them accordingly, we can travel quite swiftly."

"Fascinating," I said sincerely. "I should like to watch you work, if I may."

A flush touched Basil's olive cheeks. "Of course, Mr. Flaherty."

Whyborne's brows drew together in thought. "You've described magic before as a type of sewing, when I asked you to describe how casting a spell looked to your shadowsight."

I nodded. "Reality has a sort of, of warp and weft to it, normally unseen," I explained to Basil. "When a spell is cast, in a way it's like the sorcerer's will becomes a needle and thread, punched through the very fabric of the world."

"Then this could be a useful craft for you," Basil said, looking back and forth between us. "Or, if knitting doesn't suit, magic may be woven into other items as well. Rope work, particularly using knots to bind spells, is an ancient art."

My mind instantly leapt to the sorts of things we might do with rope magic. I glanced at Whyborne, who, oblivious, said, "Knots?"

"They're most often used to keep something from happening," Basil said. "To hold back an event, or a reaction. But other types of spells can be used with knots as well."

My cock swelled as my imagination ran wild. "The sun is a bit strong," I said to Ival. "Perhaps we could go below?"

"Beneath the canopy is pleasant," he replied. "And we endured far worse in Egypt."

"Perhaps later."

Clearly I'd puzzled him, but he nodded and we took our farewell of Basil. As we descended to the lower deck, I said, "Have you ever investigated such magic?"

"Knitting? No." He followed me to our cabin. "Mother knows how to knit, of course. The ketoi don't have cloth, but they use complicated knot work to make their nets and bags, so she might be able to utilize the same principles even beneath the sea. I wonder…"

As I hadn't intended to send him into deep contemplation, I shut the door behind us, then caught his wrists lightly. "I meant ropes."

For a moment he looked at me blankly. Then his cheeks reddened. "Oh." He pulled free of my grip and instead held my wrists captive. "We have used ordinary rope before. But it isn't just that, is it?" He leaned in and breathed in my ear. "Magic excites you."

I pressed my swelling cock against his thigh. "I do find

enjoyment watching you use your power. But it isn't the power or the magic. It's you. The way it affects you."

Desire darkened his eyes. He shoved me back on the bed, and I went without resistance. He swung a leg over to straddle my hips, catching my wrists again in his hands and pinning them over my head.

My breath caught. Most of the time, our love-making was a slow give-and-take. But a part of me thrilled on the occasions when he would take charge of me, ordering me to do his bidding, or holding me down as he did now. "Basil said the knots could be used to hold things back. You could use them to deny me release." I licked dry lips. "Torment me for hours."

His eyes widened at the thought. Then he kissed me hard. I sucked on his tongue and writhed beneath him. Passion thrummed through my veins like the fire that burned beneath his skin. When he was done, he sat back. "We will investigate that idea at our first opportunity. For now, undress me."

I did as he asked, my fingers trembling with desire. He was fire and heat, everything good in the world, and I tried to show him that every time I took him in my arms. I peeled away the layers of his clothing, unveiling pale skin marked by scars. The ugly knot of tissue where Nitocris had bitten him was quiescent to my shadowsight, but the lacework of scars marking his right arm seethed with hidden fire. I ran my fingers over them reverently, and he shivered at my touch.

"Take off your clothes," he whispered.

He watched as I did so, gaze searing my skin. When I was done, he dragged me down on the bed again, pinning me under him. I moaned into his mouth, then tilted back my head so he could bite me on the throat.

"Keep your hands above your head," he ordered. I did so, letting him do whatever he wished to me. He knew my body with a thoroughness no one else ever had, and I delighted in the certainty his familiarity brought. I expressed it in a laugh, and he raised his head, grinning back at me like a naughty schoolboy.

"Turn over."

I did. He kissed his way along my spine, bit the backs of my thighs. The sea air blew fresh and wild through the porthole above us, and the scent of clean sheets filled my nose as he pressed me into the bed. When he finally entered me, I had to concentrate on the motion of the boat to keep from spilling immediately.

We fucked with joyful abandon, lost in one another, while the rest of the world fell away. The ship rode the swells, lifting high then plunging down. I struggled to hold back, until I could take no more and muffled my cries in the sheets. A moment later, he bit the nape of my neck, body stiffening as he spent.

After a short while, he withdrew, collapsing beside me. We lay together, limbs intertwined and our breathing slowing as sweat dried on our skin. "I love you, Ival," I murmured when I could speak again.

He pressed a kiss into my shoulder. "I love you, too."

For once, we had nothing to do and nowhere to be. We lazed away the afternoon, talking, laughing, and wrestling playfully. Tomorrow was uncertain, but today was ours, and we took full advantage of it.

CHAPTER 13

Whyborne

WE PUT INTO the harbor at Old Grimsby a few days later.

Mother had left the ship miles out, slipping away over the side and vanishing beneath the waves. I didn't know how she meant to find the local ketoi, and didn't wish to inquire in front of the Endicotts, lest they somehow use the knowledge against them later.

I hadn't had the chance to question Mother any further on precisely what revenge she meant to exact from the Endicotts. She had spent time with Christine, who continued to insist on risking her life by venturing close to the side, where any errant wave might sweep her overboard. The sight of them laughing together warmed my heart. Christine was my sister in everything but blood, and I was gratified when she and Mother found common ground. They spent many an evening discussing scholarship beneath the canopy on deck, Christine's feet elevated on a second chair to alleviate their newfound tendency to swell.

Our journey aboard the *Melusine* had been surprisingly quiet. Only the ship hands and Basil had any particular work to do; even Rupert had abandoned his alchemical experiments, no doubt due to the motion of the ship making precise measurements difficult. Griffin and I watched Basil do his windweaving once or twice. To my eyes it seemed nothing more exotic than a young man knitting, or unraveling, his work. Griffin, however, was enthralled; clearly his shadowsight made the experience far more interesting.

The usual malaise I suffered while traveling set in as we left Widdershins farther and farther behind. I'd never cared to leave my home, but nowadays I felt drained and a bit achy unless I was close to an arcane line. The more power I used, the more my physical self seemed to depend on its presence for health. The thought disturbed me somewhat, but I consoled myself with the reminder that someday all this running about would surely come to an end, and I would never have to leave home again.

The summer days were long, and it was after nightfall when we put into the small harbor. We stood along the rail, watching the shoreline draw closer and closer. The harbor was far shallower than that of Widdershins, with two quays extending out from a wide, gently sloping beach. The town beyond clung to the curve of the cove, and looked to be composed of a handful of cottages and little else.

"Quaint," Christine judged. "Still, it will be good to stretch our legs. I'm used to traveling on much larger ships."

"Though with smaller quarters," Iskander added.

"Quite so." She glanced at Rupert, who had joined us at the rail. "Are we staying aboard, or at an inn? And will an adequate dinner be provided either way?"

Considering Christine had spent most of the voyage with a plate in front of her, I feared such a remote settlement might not be able to provide a dinner she judged "adequate." I didn't say as much, though, not wishing to have to swim the last distance to the shore.

"The Seeker awaits us at The Morvoron Inn." Rupert paused. "The name means mermaid in the old Cornish tongue, which may be a good omen or an ill one, depending on how our negotiations with the ketoi go. The place is too small for us to take rooms, but there will almost certainly be dinner."

"'Almost certainly?'" Christine repeated in alarm.

"I'll find something for you, never fear," Iskander said soothingly.

Griffin kept his gaze trained on Rupert. "And will the Seeker answer the questions you haven't?"

"I couldn't say." Rupert turned away from the rail. "Excuse me."

Basil took his place almost as soon as Rupert left. "Most of the other ships here belong to our family," he said, eyes shining as the quay drew closer. "Or, well, have been hired by them."

I looked around; there seemed far too many for my liking. "How many are there of you?"

"Of *us,*" Basil said. He continued to insist that I was a member of the family. Personally, I was of the opinion it was a trick on his part, and he would betray us at some critical juncture. I resolved to keep an eye on him at all times. "Not so many as you might think. The Seeker has called in every member of even the most subsidiary branch."

"Like Turner in Alaska?" Christine asked. "He seemed rather angry at the rest of you."

"I heard about that. Nasty business." Basil sighed. "But such things are what comes from ignoring the true meaning behind our family motto. Turner—and those who sent him after Dr. Whyborne—put their own prejudices above blood."

Christine rolled her eyes, but Basil was looking out over the harbor and didn't see.

There was a flurry of activity as the *Melusine* put in. Soon we were lashed to the dock and the gangplank firmly in place.

"Oh, do be careful!" I exclaimed as Christine marched boldly down the gangplank.

She paused just long enough to shoot me a glare, before continuing on her way.

A lonely path led out of the town—such as it was—and up a slight hill. Lights shone out from what must be the inn Rupert had mentioned. Basil led the way, but Rupert strolled at a more sedate pace, his expression dour.

"You don't look particularly pleased at the upcoming reunion," I remarked to him.

The wind stirred the grass and ruffled the hedgerows. Old Grimsby boasted little in the way of trees, either because of the constant ocean breezes or due to farming practices, I didn't know. A sign indicated we walked up Tommy's Hill, and I idly wondered who Tommy might have been, and what he'd done to have a hill—or perhaps it was the road?—named after him.

"There is little to be pleased about," Rupert replied. "We are here to plan a battle, from which some of us will surely not return. Beyond that, the Seeker will likely be less than happy I told you as much as I did. I still believe it was necessary to speak of Morgen's Needle, so you understood the magnitude of the threat. But the Seeker isn't exactly known for tolerating disobedience."

"You could tell her I had done research on the Endicotts before," I suggested. "Or even that Theo had spoken of it to me, before he knew about my hybrid nature. I doubt she has a very high opinion of my character to begin with, so it hardly matters if you blame me."

The moonlight flashed from Rupert's spectacles as he looked up at me. "A kind offer, Dr. Whyborne, but I will not hide behind you. I will face whatever punishment the Seeker deems fit."

The inn looked as quaint as the rest of the town: rough stone and timber walls, battered by wind and storm, pierced by mullioned windows whose bubbly glass gave only a distorted view of what lay within. Smoke streamed from its two chimneys, and the scent of cooked beef set my stomach to growling.

"Thank heavens there's something to eat," said Christine, currently finishing off a loaf of bread brought from the ship.

Griffin dropped back beside me. "Some sort of spell has been set on the doors and windows," he murmured. "Whether to ward off attack or to conceal what's inside from prying eyes, I couldn't say."

"I wonder if there's any way for you to learn to tell what a spell does by the way it looks?" Perhaps I should have suggested Griffin accompany me to the Ladysmith and peruse the tomes of lore we had within. Or even lent him the *Liber Arcanorum*. But would they tell him anything about the patterns formed by the warp and weft of magic? No other human, so far as I knew, had ever been able to perceive magic the way Griffin could.

"A bit too late to worry about it now," he said. "Just be aware."

The door swung open, and a familiar face looked out at us. "Oi, Basil, Rupert," Hattie called. "You brung the abomination, then?"

"A pleasure to see you again as well, Miss Endicott," I snapped. "I'd almost forgotten how very charming you are."

She let out a bark of laughter and slapped one trouser-clad knee. "I always said you're a funny one, for a monster. Iskander, good to see you. Maybe you'll decide to stay here in England with us, eh?"

He gave her a rather strained smile. "I doubt it."

"Enough pleasantries," Rupert said. "Where is the Seeker?"

Hattie stepped back from the door and gave us a mocking bow. "Right this way."

We entered into a long, low-ceilinged room that took up most of the first floor. Men and women ranging in age from youths to elders sat elbow-to-elbow within, their conversation falling silent as we entered. As they were dressed rather more finely than fishermen or farmers would be, I assumed they were yet more cousins. Had the family paid the inn keeper a generous sum to keep the locals out tonight, or used their sorcerous arts on him? Or both?

Tables dark with age and stains crowded so close to one another it would be difficult to navigate between them on a busy night. The far end of the long room, away from the bar, was much less cluttered. More of a parlor than a place to eat, it offered a scattering of chairs near a large, stone fireplace that looked as though it had stood for centuries. Likely it had.

A woman near Mother's age and dressed in black sat near the fire, knitting placidly. Strands of silver amidst her dark hair gleamed in the firelight, the lines in her pale skin a testament to a lifetime of toil. The glass needles flashed so quickly in her hands they looked like streaks of flame.

"Grandmother!" Basil exclaimed, bounding across the room to her. This, then, must be the woman who had taught him to windweave.

"You didn't send the ship to the bottom, I see," she said in a crisp voice. She reached the end of a row and set her knitting aside. "Well done, Basil. Rupert?"

Rupert slipped past us and went to her. "Allow me to

present to you Dr. Percival Endicott Whyborne, Mr. Griffin Flaherty, Dr. Christine Putnam-Barnett, and Mr. Iskander Putnam-Barnett." He turned back to us. "This is Minerva Endicott, the Seeker of Truth and current head of our family."

CHAPTER 14

Whyborne

"**Welcome to the** Isles of Scilly," the Seeker said. She didn't bother to rise to greet us.

"The ketoi envoy—Dr. Whyborne's mother—has departed to speak with their relatives beneath Seven Stones Reef," Rupert informed her. "Dr. Whyborne knows of Carn Moreth and Morgen's Needle."

Her eyes were sharp enough to cut. "Does he, now?"

Griffin folded his arms across his chest. "There is a great deal more we need to know. What sort of defenses surround Carn Moreth. How you mean to breach them. What sorts of magical weapons the Fideles might have taken from your armory to use against us."

Minerva looked at him silently for a long moment. He returned her gaze steadily, refusing to yield.

"You colonials have no manners." She stood slowly, her back straight as a queen's. "Demanding as spoiled children. There are few in the British Isles who would dare to speak so to me."

"Perhaps if your family hadn't tried to kill us more than once, I would be more deferent," Griffin replied. "We came at your request. But we will not go blindly into this. We're not here to die for you."

She glanced at me. "Do you allow your man to speak for you?"

Her tone implied Griffin was nothing more than a servant. "The four of us are united," I replied frostily. "And equals." Despite whatever Griffin thought about my role in defeating the masters.

"Ah, yes, you Yanks do love to talk about equality. I might respect it, if you followed it up with action, rather than keeping it an empty platitude those at the top of society can spout to make themselves feel better." Minerva turned to the door. "Walk with me, Dr. Whyborne. The rest of you will be given food and drink."

"Food?" Christine said hopefully. Then she shook her head. "No. We're not letting you make off with Whyborne, no matter how good that smells. Is it some sort of meat pastry?"

"Focus, dearest," Iskander cajoled.

I kept my gaze on Minerva. It seemed obvious she considered all of us beneath her, but equally that my magic gave me some rank above that of my friends. Turner had said as much in Alaska, that those without sorcery were considered lesser.

The Seeker was clearly a proud woman, used to obedience. I didn't intend to give it to her, but I had a better chance of learning more if I agreed to her suggestion now. "Mrs. Endicott wouldn't have gone to all this trouble if she meant to murder me," I said. "Go and eat. I'll be back soon."

Griffin didn't look at all happy, but refrained from arguing. Minerva put out a hand, and one of the other Endicotts sprang forward to place a blackthorn walking stick in it. Though it appeared nothing more than a cane, I suspected it was in fact her sorcerous wand. Certainly she didn't seem to lean upon it when she led the way back to the door and into the night air.

Hattie fell in behind us, a silent shadow. No doubt she meant to protect Minerva, should I suddenly take it into my head to attack.

We strolled away from the inn, toward a small ruin higher on the hill. What the square building had once been, I couldn't have said. Beyond, the ocean rolled and crashed against the shore. The occasional light across the water betrayed the presence of the other Isles of Scilly.

The Seeker stared out over the black waves for so long I began to wonder if she meant to speak, or merely wanted to put me in my place by forcing me to accompany her on a fruitless walk. Eventually, she said, "Can you imagine this land as it once was, Dr. Whyborne?"

The wind toyed with my hair and brought with it the scent of hearth fires, mingled with salt and fish. "What do you mean?"

She stretched out one gnarled hand, as though to pull aside a curtain and reveal a window onto the distant past. "Millennia ago, all of this was above the waves. What are now islands were hills. There were forests and fields, farmers and craftsmen, towns and cottages. All erased in a single night."

The ocean breeze seemed suddenly colder. "Lyonesse."

"I'm sure Rupert told you it was more than just a legend. In a time so long ago it was ancient when Arthur walked these lands, people thrived here. Humans. Now their bones rot beneath the waves, and ketoi swim amidst the ruins of their cities." She let her arm fall. "I want you to appreciate the power of Morgen's Needle. Of the incredible responsibility the Endicotts shouldered, when our ancestors agreed to take Carn Moreth."

"Mr. Endicott—Rupert, not Basil—said it was given to you by Henry VII, after the Cornish Rebellion," I said. "In return for some service he failed to specify."

Rather than answer directly, she said, "It's rumored you fought the Eyes of Nodens." She turned from the waves to look at me closely. "Did you?"

"They turned against the ketoi." Though I hadn't known of my heritage at the time. "The Eyes sought to compel the dweller in the deeps to walk the land and use its power against humanity."

"I see. The cult went by a different name then, but centuries ago, Carn Moreth was one of the sites where they performed their unholy rituals. Where the ketoi came up from the depths in answer to their summons." Her lip curled in disgust. "Where they took wives and husbands from the sea, and to which the abominable offspring of such unions returned."

She spoke as though she stated facts, as though her words couldn't possibly cause offense. I scowled. "Might I remind you I'm descended from a similar union?"

"As though I might forget. I'm simply explaining the situation to you." She turned away from me. "The Endicotts had already hunted monsters for centuries. Our ancestor, Richard Endicott, learned of the rites at Carn Moreth and of the dangers of Morgen's Needle. He went to the king in secret and told him what he knew of the cult and the ketoi."

"But not the Needle?" I asked.

"Of course not. Who would trust a king with such power? King Henry ordered him to put an end to the cult, or at least this branch of it. Sir Richard, along with the strongest of his family, went to Carn Moreth and waited until the celebrants were either drunk or exhausted from their unholy rites. Then the Endicotts struck. It's said the blood stained the headland for miles."

"And in exchange, the king gave them Carn Moreth," I said.

"Indeed." Minerva gripped her blackthorn cane more tightly. "Many Cornish lands were seized after the rebellion and given to loyal Englishmen, so it didn't seem an unusual gift. Sir Richard built his house around Morgen's Needle. He named it Balefire Manor, after the fires that had burned the night the Endicotts drove back the cult and the hybrids."

"I imagine the ketoi weren't pleased."

"No." A smile of grim satisfaction turned up the corners of her mouth. "But they've never been able to take it back from us, not in five-hundred years."

Silence fell between us. The wind sighed around the stones of the ruin, waves crashing against the shore. When she seemed disinclined to continue, I said, "Though interesting, I'm not certain why you felt it so important to give me a history lesson."

"So you understand what we are sacrificing by asking you here. By extending the hand of peace to the ketoi." She looked suddenly older, her shoulders slumping as if beneath the weight of years. "Your kind have killed so many of us. And now I must ask the murderer of my beloved niece and nephew..." Her breath caught sharply.

I wanted to argue that Theo and Fiona had tried to kill me

first. They'd meant to destroy my mother, my town, everyone I loved.

I didn't bother. As far as Minerva was concerned, I was like a stag who had turned on the hunters. In her eyes, they had the right to kill me. I had no such right to fight back.

After a long moment, she forced her shoulders straight once again. "We were never able to unlock the full potential of Morgen's Needle. We used its power as we could. Sir Richard was the most successful, using it to weave the barrier which prevents the ketoi from attacking from the sea."

"I encountered a similar barrier in the city of the umbrae in Alaska," I said. "It was a spell of the masters, meant to keep their rebellious slaves confined. So how did our ancestor learn of it?"

A line sprang up between her brows. "I...do not know. The Keepers of Secrets might have passed down such knowledge over the years, but if so they haven't shared it with the rest of us. Morgen's Needle was used to adjust the barrier more than once over the years, I do know that. First to keep out sorcerers, then anyone not of our blood, and finally to remain impermeable at all times unless the Keeper opened a gateway through it. The barrier didn't extend across the causeway, though that changed when Balefire fell. I had wondered how that might be possible, but if it is as you say a spell of the masters, the Fideles might have known it."

"So they likely are able to use the Needle."

"Indeed." She paused, as if debating with herself. "I will tell you one of the secrets of the Endicotts, Dr. Whyborne, and pray my brother the Keeper will forgive me for it. If he still lives. Obviously, you know of the arcane lines. Do you understand how they interconnect?"

"Not precisely." I didn't wish to reveal my ignorance to her, but a misunderstanding could be worse. "I know I've found them everywhere I've traveled. I know some of those in far flung places are connected to the maelstrom in Widdershins." Because it used them to collect people, but that I kept to myself. If the Endicotts realized the maelstrom had the power to influence others, even subtly, they wouldn't rest until Widdershins was destroyed. Starting with me.

"They are *all* interconnected." She gestured in what I

assumed to be the direction of Carn Moreth. "Just as all the veins and arteries in your body are connected. Some are larger, and some are smaller. Some are mere capillaries—tiny extensions of the arcane lines permeating reality, which allow us to cast spells even if we aren't directly on a line."

"Oh." It made sense, I suppose. "What does this have to do with Morgen's Needle?"

"It is our belief the Needle was created to function as a sort of master switch, to put it in modern terms. Someone who understood its workings and could control or influence any point along the arcane lines, could starve some places of magic, or flood others. Perhaps worse."

All the blood seemed to drain from my extremities. "Dear lord."

"That is why we're so afraid now." Minerva turned away from the ocean and back toward the inn. "That is why I'm willing to pardon you for the deaths you caused. The Fideles *cannot* have such power. They will use it to destroy their enemies and prepare for the coming of the masters. And I cannot allow that to happen."

I listened to the whisper of her footsteps receding toward the inn. But I didn't follow. Instead I stared out over the crashing waves in the direction she had earlier indicated.

Last February, I'd discovered Nyarlathotep, the Man in the Woods, the servant of the masters, was the architect of the enormous maelstrom beneath Widdershins. However the arcane lines had been formed, whether through some natural phenomenon or by the hand of the masters, he had been the one to twist them into a vortex. One large enough to tear a hole in reality of a size for beings as powerful as the masters to pass through.

Had he done that work here? Stood atop Carn Moreth when it was a hill and not an island, directed and redirected the flow of energy through Morgen's Needle and given birth to the maelstrom? To what would become sentient and, well, me?

If the Needle could do that, there was no telling what the Fideles had planned. If they tried to starve the maelstrom of arcane energy, it couldn't power the gateway to allow the masters in, so likely they wouldn't do that. But I didn't know enough about Morgen's Needle to begin to guess what other horrifying possibilities existed.

We had to take Carn Moreth back from them. That became more apparent with everything I learned about the Needle.

And if the Endicotts ever learned how to use it against me? Against Widdershins?

A chill that had nothing to do with the ocean breeze seized me. I crossed my arms for warmth, and turned back to the lights of the inn.

CHAPTER 15

Griffin

I sat with Iskander and Christine at one of the pub tables, keeping an eye on the door as we ate a hearty meal of crab soup, pasties stuffed with beef and onions, and whortleberry pie.

"I can't believe they didn't have lemons," Christine complained. "What sort of place doesn't have lemons?"

Iskander glanced in the direction of the waitress, who didn't seem to have overheard. "I expect on these islands they mainly eat what they produce themselves."

"Which apparently doesn't include lemons."

"Likely not, no."

She eyed him. "You think I'm being irrational."

"Not at all," he assured her hastily. "Really. Lemons should be, er, a staple of any establishment."

Most of the Endicotts present sat in small groups, speaking in low voices or not at all. Some stared into their drinks grimly; others sharpened knives or practiced lighting, then extinguishing, candle flames. No doubt many of them feared to learn the worst, that the Fideles had slaughtered everyone inside Balefire Manor.

Though the majority of faces around us were white, the

family included members with darker complexions: Rupert, of course, but also a sprinkling of those whose forefathers had hailed from India, Oceania, and the Arabian countries. Wherever the British Empire had set foot, no doubt the Endicotts had also gone, questing for magic and slaying monsters.

A bronze-skinned woman of about twenty sat at the next table, her shoulders hunched and her eyes red from tears. Seeing my attention on her, she leaned in my direction. "You came with the abomination, didn't you?"

Before I could reply, Christine said, "What the devil is wrong with you all? Whyborne is no more an abomination than anyone else. If you actually want our help, you ought to be more polite about it."

The other conversations fell silent, all eyes on us. "Padma," a man said, not exactly as a warning, but more as an urge toward restraint.

"I'm sorry. You're right." Padma swallowed hard. Tears gleamed on her lashes, threatening to spill down her cheeks. "If he can bring back my Sadik, I don't care *what* he is."

I took out my handkerchief and offered it to her. "Is Sadik your husband?" I asked.

"No. My little boy." She dabbed at her eyes. "He was in the crèche with the other children. I had just gone to London—an antiquarian there had received a book he thought I'd have interest in. Sadik was supposed to be safe on the estate, and now I haven't seen him in six months, and..."

"Chin up, Padma," said one of the other women. "We'll get them back."

I exchanged a horrified look with Iskander. Even Christine appeared stunned. "There were *children* trapped in Balefire?"

"Of course there were." Rupert emerged from a back room. "We Endicotts don't spring fully formed from the rock, you know."

The thought children might be at risk—or even killed by the Fideles—hadn't so much as crossed my mind. I felt like a fool for not having considered what now seemed obvious. "I'm sorry." I turned back to Padma. "We had no idea. Of course we'll do everything in our power to return him to you. All of them."

"How...how many?" Christine asked Rupert. She looked shaken in a way I'd never seen before.

"We think seven children were in the crèche when the Fideles struck." Rupert went to the bar and accepted a pint. "Ranging from two to eight years in age."

"God." I couldn't imagine how difficult the last six months must have been for the parents caught outside the estate. Not knowing if your child was afraid, or hungry, or even alive. "Why didn't you come to us sooner?"

"Hattie and I left for America two weeks after Balefire fell, when it became apparent there would be no quick solution." Rupert took a sip from his pint. "I hardly see how we could have moved any faster, especially as we didn't know if we could even trust Dr. Whyborne at the time."

"We still don't," someone muttered.

Rupert ignored him. "Unfortunately, as I told Dr. Whyborne back in Widdershins, we needed a certain arcane artifact—a pendant—that will allow the Seeker to breach the defenses. That was much less easily retrieved than you lot, and it was only recently located. I assure you, once we had it in hand, we moved as swiftly as possible." He half raised his pint again, but didn't put it to his lips. "The waiting hasn't been easy for any of us. It is a hard thing, not to know what fate has befallen those you care for."

"We'll get them back," Christine said firmly. "Whyborne is relatively competent when it comes to magic. I can shoot the wings off a fly at fifty paces, and if anything gets past me, Griffin and Iskander are quite able to take care of it."

"But what about the ketoi?" Padma asked. "Will they agree to let us through?"

Whyborne believed his mother meant to exact vengeance against the Endicotts. Judging by Padma's red eyes, the strained looks on other faces, they would pay whatever price she asked. Anything, if it put them one step closer to getting their children back.

"I'm certain Heliabel will be able to convince them to cooperate," I said. And hoped it was true.

CHAPTER 16

Whyborne

WE MET THE ketoi delegation at sunset the next day, on a stretch of beach near the ruins of King Charles's Castle. The sea wind whistled over the stones as the last, lonely gulls cried before settling for the night.

Tension radiated from the Endicotts around us. The ketoi had given very specific instructions, written in my mother's hand on paper and ink pilfered from some unguarded ship or cottage, and left pinned to the dock with a stone. Only a small delegation was to meet them in this place, and they were to come as unarmed as possible for a family of sorcerers.

Hattie had objected loudly, of course. But Minerva overruled her, and brought along only Rupert, Basil, and two more whose names I hadn't caught. I didn't trust the Endicotts not to pull some trick at the last moment, so I insisted on coming as well.

As the last light faded from the sky, the ketoi emerged from the waves. Though similar in dress to the colony outside of Widdershins, they wore the gold net of their clothing in a slightly different fashion, with subtle variations in the design of their jewelry. One of the Endicotts muttered an imprecation at the spears in their hands.

Their chieftess arrived last, accompanied by Mother. The Cornwall chieftess was a grizzled old ketoi, her arms scarred with what looked like enormous sucker marks, one fin missing altogether. The stinging tendrils of her hair had been amputated on the same side as the missing fin, as though something had sheared them away, along with her ear.

They walked past the honor guard and stopped a short distance from Minerva. The chieftess's remaining hair writhed and twisted in agitation. The look in her eyes when she beheld Minerva bordered on hatred.

Oh dear. That definitely didn't bode well.

Mother took up position slightly to one side and between them, so both were in her view at the same time. "I have come with Ship-bane, chieftess of the local ketoi, to speak with the Endicott known as Seeker of Truth."

Minerva's mouth tucked in at the corner. "Ah, Heliabel Whyborne, née Endicott. I confess I've been very curious to meet the Mother of Monsters."

I clenched my jaw but held my peace. Mother's teeth gleamed unnervingly in the light of the Endicott lanterns. "Indeed. Ship-bane, this is my son, Fire in His Blood."

I was uncertain of the etiquette of greeting unfamiliar chieftesses, so I settled on a slight bow. "A pleasure to meet you."

"Cousin," she said in a voice like waves over gravel.

"Enough of this." Minerva banged her cane on the stone. "I assume our need has been explained to you. Do you accept our offer of peace? We will not wage war on you for ten years from this time, unless you attack us first."

I glanced at Mother, but her gaze was fixed on Minerva. "Not enough," she said coolly.

Minerva's eyes widened slightly. How long had it been since anyone had told her no? "What do you mean?"

Ship-bane's eyes glittered with rage. "Thirty-one winters ago, your spell slew our elders, destroying the knowledge and guidance of the matriarchs. That same spell took our infants and youngest children, and those women pregnant with the next generation. You killed both our past and our future, and now you think we will grant you peace with nothing in return?"

"Our own kin died in the backlash." Minerva's hand tightened on her cane.

Ship-bane bared her teeth. "And I am supposed to feel sorry for you? That some of those who murdered our elders and infants, who sought to wipe out our entire colony, paid for their actions with their own lives?"

"Please." Basil glanced frantically back and forth from Minerva to Ship-bane. "Surely Mrs. Whyborne—that is, Speaker of Stories—told you what's at stake. If we don't take back Balefire, we might all die, your people and ours alike!"

"Silence!" Minerva snapped.

"The ketoi have fought the masters before and won," Ship-bane replied. "I choose to believe we can do so again. You stole our future, and though children have been born since, nothing can reclaim the generations we lost. So either agree to our terms, or leave our territory and never return."

For a long moment, a tense thread seemed to pull tight between Minerva and Ship-bane. I held my breath, unsure what to do if it should snap. Which side would I take, if the situation degenerated into violence? I needed the Endicotts, but Ship-bane's anger was just. Though no doubt Father would scorn her for not thinking strategically.

"The terms are these," Mother said. "The ketoi will allow you to return to Carn Moreth. In exchange, no Endicott will venture past Seven Stones Reef for the space of ten years. You will return what your ancestors stole from our people." She paused. "And the Seeker of Truth will present herself to us after Carn Moreth is retaken, for judgment of Endicott crimes."

"No!" Basil said. Rupert motioned him to silence.

Minerva's jaw tightened. "What do you believe we stole from you?" she asked, but something in her voice suggested she knew exactly to what Mother referred.

"The great treasure of the Endicotts, hidden away since Sir Richard built Balefire upon the bones of our ancestors." Mother's smile widened, showing more teeth. "The Sword, the Spear, the Shield, and the Source."

CHAPTER 17

Whyborne

"THE WHAT?" I asked blankly. Rupert and Basil also seemed confused. But Minerva's sharp eyes narrowed.

"Absolutely not," she said. "You ask far too much."

The ketoi hissed. Ship-bane displayed her teeth in a snarl. "Then you will never set foot on Carn Moreth again, land dweller."

"No!" I stepped forward reflexively. "Seeker, remember what you told me last night. What good will these items do you if the masters return?"

"That is quite beside the point," Rupert said. "Even if they are real, the Seeker cannot simply hand herself over to the ketoi to be murdered."

"For judgment," Mother corrected.

Rupert's eyes narrowed. "Pretty it up however you wish. We all know the outcome of whatever sham trial you would orchestrate."

"I am the one conducting these negotiations, Rupert," Minerva cut in. "As for your question, Dr. Whyborne, these artifacts are hinted at in what you know as the Wisborg Codex.

They are said to be able to kill anything from the Outside." She arched a brow at my expression of surprise. "We have the key to the codex. Did you imagine we don't possess a fragment of it ourselves? Not the whole," she added quickly. "Only you have that."

The late Reverend Scarrow had said as much, before his fellow sorcerers had murdered him for wishing to share his knowledge with me.

I should have realized they would seek such things out. A thought began to congeal. "The Codex, at least the copy owned by the Ladysmith, dates from the fifteenth century. Sir Richard took Carn Moreth in 1498. Was he acting on some information from the fragment?"

Minerva gave me a short, sharp nod. "Yes."

"He had a fragment of a book the Fideles are using to help the masters return," I said. "And used a spell created by the masters to prevent the ketoi from setting foot on the island. Is anyone else concerned by this?"

Rupert's expression grew even more troubled. "It isn't auspicious, I grant you. But that was five-hundred years ago. Surely it has no relevance now."

The wind off the sea threatened to snatch away my hat. I removed it, and the breeze ruffled my hair. "If it's one thing I've learned over the last few years, it's that the past doesn't remain buried forever, Mr. Endicott."

Ship-bane tossed her head. "None of this means anything to me. You will return what is rightfully ours."

"The weapons will do you no good," Minerva replied. "They are inert. Whatever magic once lived in them is long gone."

"Then what does it cost you to give them back?" Mother asked.

Minerva didn't respond. "She's afraid the ketoi might be able to wield them," I said. "Or she hopes that the full codex will contain some information on how the Endicotts might restore them."

Rupert shot me a glare. "You have no say in these negotiations."

"Then you shouldn't have brought me along." I fixed my gaze on Minerva. "I've come here, at your invitation, to help prevent a disaster that might consume Widdershins and end the world. Nothing else matters in the face of that. If this is the price the ketoi ask, give the objects to them."

Cold fury lit Minerva's eyes, though she kept her face schooled. "They have been locked in our vault for five-hundred years, known only to the Keeper and the Seeker. They are our *heritage*. Our legacy."

Mother stared fixedly at Minerva. "They are not *your* heritage or legacy, Endicott. They are the ketoi's birthright, which you stole. You can uncurl your grasping fingers from them—or you can lose them and everything else. The choice is yours."

Basil's face was drawn with worry. "If we give them to you, will you forget about judging the Seeker?"

"No," Ship-bane said, giving him a sinister grin that showed too many teeth.

God. The weapons and the Source, whatever the devil it was, might be of use to the ketoi in the fight against the masters. But the life of the Seeker was pure revenge. As I tried to think of some way of swaying Mother and Ship-Bane, Minerva spoke.

"Very well," she said at last. "Loath though I am to see our family's legacy given over to the hands of monsters, it would seem I have no choice. If you allow us safe passage to Carn Moreth, we will have ten years peace and we will give you the Sword, the Spear, the Source, and the Shield." Her mouth twisted in anger. "And I will submit to your savage judgment."

"Excellent." Ship-bane's teeth shone in the night as she drew a knife from where it was secured to her net skirt. "Let us seal the compact in blood."

CHAPTER 18

Griffin

THE ENDICOTTS WASTED no time. As soon as Whyborne and the rest of the party who had met with the ketoi returned to Old Grimsby, preparations began. We went back to the yacht with Rupert and Basil, and the whole of the little harbor was soon abuzz with activity as the flotilla prepared for launch.

Whyborne recounted the meeting to the rest of us over a hasty dinner. Christine worked her way through most of a roast chicken while we spoke, then stole the boiled potato from Whyborne's plate when he was momentarily distracted by the deck hands shouting to one another above our heads.

I hoped the Endicotts meant to pack several meals for the assault on Balefire.

"I wish the ketoi had been a bit less unbending," Whyborne said at last. "I expect the Endicotts to betray us, of course, but if the Seeker feels her life is in danger, she may act rashly."

"She doesn't strike me as a woman who fears death," I said. "But resentment will certainly sway her against us."

"Bah," Christine said through a mouthful of potato. "The woman can't wait to stab us in the back. We've all seen how she looks at Whyborne as though he's a dog who can't be trusted not to bite his handler as eagerly as his foe."

"Thank you so much for that description, Christine," Whyborne said, turning back to his plate. He frowned perplexedly at the space where his potato had been. "Of course, it's possible the ketoi *don't* mean to summarily execute the Seeker. Perhaps Mother wishes to teach her humility, and the judgment will be rather different than what Minerva assumes."

"I suppose we'll find out sooner or later," I said. "Whyborne, you've never come across any mention of these ketoi items in your researches? The Sword, the Spear, the Shield, and the Source?"

"No." He turned his attention to me. Christine snuck the roll from his plate. "I've asked myself if I might have heard reference to them under another name, but there's nothing I recall. They must be some deep secret of the ketoi—and of whoever created the codex in the first place."

"Another thing we don't know," Iskander said. He retrieved our dessert—slices of chocolate cake—from the sideboard, while I took up our dirty dishes. Whyborne watched me remove his empty plate with an air of befuddlement.

Basil clattered down the stairs. "We're getting ready to put out to sea," he said. "Rupert wants to speak with everyone before we get too far from shore."

Whyborne looked mournfully down at his cake and pushed it away. "I suppose we should attend him."

"I'll catch up in a minute," Christine said, snagging his slice and adding it to her own.

"Er, yes," he said in slight alarm. "We'll fill you in on anything important."

We followed Basil up the stairs. As we reached the deck, Whyborne shook his head. "How did I eat an entire meal and still end up hungry?"

"It's a mystery," I said, patting his arm. "We'll find something from the galley after we're done with Rupert."

The dark sea spread all around us, with only the westering moon and the light of the other ships to offer any illumination outside of the circle of our lanterns. The vast emptiness stretching all around gave me pause. This had once been land. Even now, the keel of our ship passed high over drowned meadows and villages, streams and forests. The bones of the people and animals who had once called it home.

What had the inundation been like? According to the legends, sudden enough to kill almost everyone. Though the tale of Lyonesse was clearly a fanciful retelling, tailored to fit the much later Arthurian myths, the souls who had died here had been real people with real lives.

Up until this moment, the threat posed by Morgen's Needle had felt dire, but also somewhat abstract. Now, though, sailing above the lands it had drowned and seeing only empty sea, I fully appreciated the power of the artifact and the danger it posed.

We found Rupert standing at the bow of the ship. With him was Hattie, dressed in her trousers and with her witch hunter's daggers at her waist.

My lips tightened. Every time I looked at her, the only thing I could remember was her blade at Whyborne's throat, while she tried to convince Rupert that killing him was the only way to keep the Endicotts safe.

"Where's Iskander?" she asked when we approached.

"Dining with his wife," I said, not bothering to hide my dislike. "What are you doing here?"

"Coming with you, ain't I?" she asked, clearly unperturbed.

Whyborne folded his arms over his chest. "To keep an eye on me?"

"To fight the Fideles." Rupert interposed himself between them. "Not one another. Now, would you care to hear our plan of attack?"

Whyborne's lips pressed together, but he nodded. Rupert went to stand at the rail, staring out at the night-shrouded water.

"The sea around Carn Moreth is too treacherous for larger vessels," he said. "We will draw as close as is safe, then take the lifeboat the rest of the way. Basil will remain aboard the *Melusine* and return to Old Grimsby for safety."

"I could fight with you," Basil objected.

"The Seeker has ordered everyone below the age of twenty to stay in safety." Rupert turned to Basil. "No one is questioning your courage. But if things go badly, there must be some of us left to carry on the Endicott legacy."

"Ah, yes, the legacy of making enemies wherever you go," Whyborne said. "A proud tradition indeed."

I tried to turn my chuckle into a cough. From the look on Rupert's face, I didn't succeed.

Basil's shoulders slumped, but he nodded. "I understand, Rupert."

"Good lad." Rupert returned his attention to us. "The western and southern sides of Carn Moreth are nothing but wave-scoured rock, far too treacherous to land on. The northern and eastern flanks, however, are accessible by boat. The causeway connecting the island to Penmoreth lies in the northeast, dividing the shore into two wide beaches. This is where we'll put in, once the Seeker has unlocked the barrier."

I frowned. "Surely the Fideles will have set watch there. They'd be fools not to expect some sort of attack, or to assume sorcerers such as yourselves could find no way through the barrier."

"You're correct, Mr. Flaherty," Rupert said. "We'll use what magics we can to conceal the ships, but I won't pretend we aren't going into extreme danger. Our ultimate goal is to escort the Seeker into Balefire, where she will hopefully be able to turn the estate's magics against the intruders. But the fight to get there will be a hard one, of that I have no doubt. My hope is Dr. Whyborne will be able to draw upon the arcane lines that flow around Morgen's Needle, as he did in the Draakenwood."

Whyborne frowned slightly. "If it becomes necessary."

I hoped it didn't, for his sake. I thought him magnificent when under the influence of the power surging through the lines, but he'd confessed to me that he was uncomfortable with the effect it had upon him. Not to mention channeling too much arcane energy became physically painful even to him. He was never one to yield to pain, but I hated that he had to endure it at all. Perhaps we would be lucky for once, and the small force of Endicott sorcerers would bring a quicker end to things than Rupert feared.

A pair of clawed hands wrapped around the rail. Rupert leapt back, and the rest of us started as Heliabel heaved herself onto the deck. She'd shed her ceremonial regalia, and seawater streamed from her sleek form.

"Mother!" Whyborne exclaimed. "What on earth are you doing here?"

"Joining you, of course." Her tentacle hair lay nearly quiescent over her shoulders, save for the ends, which twitched like the tail of a cat trying to decide whether or not it was annoyed with something. "The rest of the ketoi will merely watch from afar, but I'm not sitting by while you go into danger."

Rupert looked pained. But after a moment, he forced himself to nod. "Of course. We'd be grateful for your assistance."

CHAPTER 19

Griffin

THANKS TO THE short nights, dawn was breaking when Carn Moreth came into sight.

The Endicott ships reacted to some signal I couldn't perceive, heaving to and weighing anchor almost as one. The boats had been readied, and we scrambled into our places. None of us trusted Whyborne with the oars, so Iskander, Hattie, Rupert, and I took them up, while he and Christine perched in the bow and stern, respectively. We'd already stowed our supplies: a small waterproof box for Rupert containing his alchemical supplies, canteens for each of us, a packet of food for Christine, and our weapons.

"I'm bringing my bow," Christine said. "Oh, and Whyborne, I thought to pack rags and oil."

He stared at her blankly. "What on earth for?"

"Flaming arrows, of course!" Her eyes all but shone with excitement. "I'll soak the rags, tie them around the arrows, and then you light them on fire once they're in flight."

"Er," Whyborne said, clearly less convinced of the merits of her plan than she was. Then he brightened. "Actually, that is an excellent idea. You stay near the back of the fighting—or perhaps find a good vantage point—and we'll press on, while you shoot over our heads. I'm afraid your bow won't be of much use inside, so you should probably remain in whatever place you take up to begin with."

"Really, Whyborne, do you think I didn't bring a cudgel with me as well? Use some sense, man."

I glanced at Iskander, who looked pained but knew better than to argue. Whyborne, however, had apparently forgotten his instincts of self-preservation. "But surely you shouldn't be lifting anything heavy, let alone swinging it about."

"Heavy? It weighs three pounds, if that." Her dark brows dove into a scowl. "Wait a moment. Are you attempting to trick me into staying behind?"

Thankfully, the sailors swung us over the side at that moment, preventing an argument. As soon as we hit the water, we began to pull for the island. Heliabel dove in beside us, her sleek form keeping pace alongside, just beneath the surface.

Carn Moreth reared up above the sea, a windswept mount which had stood against centuries of assault from the waves. Gulls took off from the crags, screaming to one another as they departed for the morning hunt.

Above the steep cliffs overlooking the sea sprouted an incongruous sight. The ordinary walls and windows of a manor house seemed to grow from the rock itself, but rather than form a flat sprawl, they crawled up the steep hill to the very pinnacle of the island.

"Daft, ain't it?" Hattie asked with a nod. "Forms a spiral, or as close to one as they could build. You can't see it from here, but Morgen's Needle is at the center. Right at the very tip-top of the island."

Early sunlight shimmered off the waves, obscuring the details. I squinted—wait. That wasn't sunlight. "I can see the defenses from here. A great wall, or veil, of magic."

The closer we drew, the more obvious it became to me. Beautiful, in a strange way: a curtain of arcane light, woven into a complicated tapestry meant to repel the Endicotts' many enemies. Whyborne had mentioned Minerva said the barrier had been added to over the years. Probably that explained what appeared to be seams, as it were, where the new layers were attached to the original. I wondered what Basil would have made of it all, had he been able to view it as I did.

The Seeker sat in the lead boat, her black dress ruffling in the wind. The flotilla split in two, some boats circling around to the northern beach, while others, including ours and the Seeker's, made straight for the eastern one. The barrier met the sea perhaps a hundred feet out from the sand.

"Take the glass and see what the Fideles are doing," Hattie ordered Whyborne. He complied, lifting it to his eye and peering at the sprawling, spiraling manor.

"I don't see anything moving," he said after a long moment. "Just gulls. Perhaps they haven't spotted us yet?"

Unease ran a cold finger across the back of my neck. "One would think they'd have a watch set. Surely they can't be that secure in their ability to hold us off."

"Maybe there ain't many left?" Hattie said hopefully. "The Endicotts trapped on the island wouldn't give up without a fight. With any luck, they decimated the bastards."

Without warning, a titanic voice boomed out over the water, emanating from the island. "Turn back! Turn back, or you will die. The barrier cannot be breached."

Hattie's brows rose. "Huh. That's new. I guess they had someone watching for us after all."

"Perhaps it means they're frightened," Iskander suggested. "With any luck, you're correct, and only a handful survived the confrontation with your relatives. They hope to scare us away, because they have no hope of repelling a force of our size."

Whyborne perked up at his words. "This may be easier than we thought. With any luck, we'll be on our way back to Widdershins by tomorrow."

The boat bearing the Seeker drew near the great barrier. How she knew its precise location without being able to see it, I was unsure. Minerva rose to her feet despite the rocking of her boat and held up one hand. The rising sun glinted off something gripped in her fingers.

"That'll be the pendant Ned brought back," Hattie said.

I kept a close eye on the barrier. The Seeker's voice echoed across the water in some sort of chant, and the pendant flashed. In response, the barrier drew aside in front of her boat, as though it were a curtain she'd parted.

"It worked!" I exclaimed. "Thank goodness. We should aim for..."

The words died in my throat. Threads of arcane power began to fray out from either side of the curtain, reaching toward one another. "No. It's closing again."

Rupert's eyes widened. "We have to warn them."

"The barrier is reforming!" Christine bellowed. As she was used to shouting orders at a dig site, her voice carried easily over the water, even with the growing crash of waves against the shore. "Use the pendant again!"

Some of the Endicotts in the boats separating ours and the Seeker's took up the cry, relaying the warning to the head of the flotilla. The Seeker held up the pendant a second time, even as the barrier reknit into a whole. As her words echoed again, it shuddered—but remained firm.

"It isn't working!" I called.

"Fall back," Rupert shouted. "Fall back before we encounter the barrier!"

Heliabel surfaced beside us and grabbed the gunwale. "You need to slow the boat. You're moving too fast."

I shipped the oars, as did Hattie, but it seemed to make no difference. We were still rushing toward the barrier at an alarming rate. Sunlight dazzled my eyes, reflecting from the waves, but was there something moving beneath the water?

"Arcane energy," I warned. "We're under attack."

"Rupert," Hattie yelled. "Look!"

Even though the Seeker's crew had set themselves to rowing away from the barrier, tentacle-like shapes of arcane energy had caught them fast, dragging the small craft toward the wall of magic. I expected some sort of impact, but the boat passed harmlessly through, and for a moment my heart lifted.

Then I realized the boat was passing through, but the people on board weren't.

The Seeker was knocked overboard, while those behind her were dragged from their benches. One unfortunate man fell to the bottom of the boat and became caught between the barrier and the stern. As the boat continued to be pulled forward, he was crushed in a froth of blood and bone. Rupert's cry of anguish rang out over the waves.

Screams and shouts of panic rang throughout the flotilla. Those farthest away managed to break free by dint of hard rowing, but the magic was too strong for the rest.

Including us.

I unsheathed my sword cane. "Whyborne, ready your curse breaking spell," I said.

"Ready."

I plunged my arm into the waves, stabbing the sword cane through one of the streamers of magic clinging to us. "Now!"

Magic coursed through the blade, but nothing happened. Apparently I'd not found the proper weak spot to break the spell. "Damn it! Heliabel, move back. Hattie, try to chop at the water with your daggers. Give me one and I'll take care of this side."

I'd expected an argument, but she passed me a witch hunter's dagger instantly. Unfortunately, my shadowsight vanished under its influence. I stabbed at the places where I thought the arcane tentacles had been.

It worked. Iskander and Rupert pulled hard on the oars, and we began to move south and west, away from the beach. For a moment, I thought we'd managed to break free.

Then we slowed...and reversed. Now our little boat was heading toward both the barrier and the rocks jutting from the waves on the impassable part of the island.

I put down the dagger, and my shadowsight returned. "They've reformed," I said, trying to keep the despair from my voice. Christine let out a string of Arabic curses, and Whyborne's expression took on a grim determination.

"Hold on," he said.

He thrust one hand into the water. The waves swirled in confusion, spinning us around. I seized the gunwale so as not to be dumped out of the boat, as did Hattie. Rupert let out a surprised yelp.

The sea roared, and we seemed to drop and slow. As the boat steadied, I realized what Whyborne had done—was still doing. His water spell had always been one of his strongest. Now he used it to force the sea—or at least the area around us—away from the barrier, against its natural flow.

The result was a tumult of currents. Sweat stood out on Whyborne's brow, and his mouth was a line of grim determination...but we were still moving slowly, inexorably toward the barrier, drawn by the magic even without the help of the incoming tide.

"Now what?" Christine asked.

Whyborne shook his head, a sharp motion. "I don't know, but I can't hold back the sea forever."

I peered at the section of barrier before us. The curse breaking spell might work against it, but we'd never have time to actually cast it before being dumped in the sea or crushed. I focused my attention on the warp and weft of the barrier, trying to ignore my pounding heart and the little voice certain we were all about to end up dashed to pieces or drowned.

"There's a seam—a weak spot—in the barrier just there." I pointed to what no doubt seemed empty air to everyone else. "Hattie, if you can use your knives to cut it fast enough, perhaps we can slip through."

Hattie paled. "I can't swim, can I? And it's too far to reach."

Curse it. "Christine, aim us to port. Heliabel, if you can give us a push to help turn the boat, please do."

"And hurry," Whyborne grated.

Christine leaned on the tiller. Heliabel flung herself at the boat, kicking her feet, her toes spread to fan their webbing to the fullest. Our angle shifted gradually, fighting against the magic dragging us shoreward. We drew nearer and nearer to the barrier—and the seam.

"We're almost there," I said. "Get ready, Hattie."

She moved into a crouch, then leaned as far as she dared over the prow of the boat, knife outstretched.

"Back to starboard, Christine," I called. "That's it—now straight—"

"Hurry," Whyborne said through clenched teeth. "I'm losing—"

"Now!"

Hattie didn't hesitate, bringing the witch hunter's dagger down in a savage slash.

The torn edges of the spell peeled apart, as though under tension from either side. At the same moment, Whyborne slumped—and the water came rushing back.

CHAPTER 20

Whyborne

THE WORLD DISSOLVED into a mad confusion of water and darkness. Salt stung my eyes, and I no longer knew which way was up, my body spun head over heels by the sea. I thrashed wildly, but the spell had stolen much of my strength, and my flailing did nothing. My lungs burned, crying out for oxygen.

Leave it to the accursed Endicotts to get me drowned.

A hand seized the back of my collar, heaving me toward the surface. Rock scraped against my knee, and then against both shoes. Somehow I got my footing and staggered upright, only to be knocked down by another violent wave. I clawed at the rock, but it was too slick to grip.

Another heave, and I was dragged fully out of the water. Mother's golden net skirt glittered in my vision for an instant, before she dove back into the water. I peeled a strand of seaweed from the side of my face and tried to get my bearings.

I sprawled atop a huge rock that in some long-ago era had fallen from the cliffs above, and now canted out of the sea. Rupert, Christine, and Iskander had all made it onto the rock as well, though our boat had failed to survive the encounter.

Of Griffin and Hattie, there was no sign.

"Griffin?" I spun frantically to the ocean. "Griffin!"

Christine grabbed my arm. "Heliabel went back in."

The seconds seemed to take hours. I stared at the churning waves, heart in my throat. Had he been dashed against the rock? Drowned?

The possibility filled my lungs with ice.

Mother's head broke the water. With her ketoi strength, she hauled two figures onto the rock.

Griffin blinked as I reached him. Both he and Hattie began to cough. I caught my husband beneath the arms and half-carried him farther up the incline, away from the hungry waves. We both collapsed to our knees, and I patted him on the back while he brought up the seawater he'd swallowed.

"Thank goodness!" Iskander exclaimed. Griffin sat back, and Iskander clapped him on the shoulder. "There you go, old chap. Feeling better?"

"Right as rain," Griffin managed.

I went to put my arms around him, but the sight of his torn shirt and abraded skin stopped me. The sea must have dragged him against the rough rocks. "You're hurt."

"I'll be fine." He stood up, moving slowly, and took stock. "My revolver is soaked through, and I dropped my sword cane."

"I'll get it," Mother said. "And the Endicott's knives."

While she dove, Rupert and Iskander dragged some of the flotsam from the waves. Oars, Christine's bow—now sadly waterlogged—and Rupert's box.

"My alchemy supplies," Rupert said as he carefully set the box down. "Or what little I could bring. If you will allow it, Mr. Flaherty, I have a salve that will aid with the pain and speed healing."

Griffin nodded. "I'd be grateful."

Christine wrapped her arms around herself. "I don't suppose you have any warm blankets in there?"

Though the sea was no colder than that off the coast of Widdershins, it was cool enough to discourage prolonged immersion. The shadow of the island fell across us, and the wind bit through our sodden clothing.

"Perhaps I can help," I said. "I sense an arcane line."

Griffin nodded. "I can see it. And others. The vortex here isn't as large as the maelstrom by any stretch of the imagination, and the lines feeding into it are much thinner, but we shouldn't be very far from one anywhere on the island."

Though the line might be thinner as Griffin said, it provided more than enough energy for what I needed. I placed my hands on the rock and carefully channeled my fire spell into the stone. The surface quickly warmed beneath my fingers, and I let it spread out from me.

"Ah, that feels much better," Christine said as she lay on her back against the stone. "I don't suppose you can dry our clothes?"

"Not without the risk of setting them aflame," I replied ruefully. "I can heat smaller stones to put into our pockets or hold in our hands, as I did in Alaska."

Mother emerged from the waves, carrying Hattie's knives gingerly in one hand, Griffin's sword cane thrust through a loop on her skirt. While Rupert tended to Griffin, I took stock of our surroundings. Unfortunately, there wasn't much to see. A large rock protruding from the waves, surrounded by smaller rocks. Barnacles clung to the tide line, clicking and popping as the incoming surf splashed against them. Above us loomed a sheer wall of dark gray stone. Though the cliff face was weathered and split by countless storms, I couldn't imagine scaling it, even if we'd had the equipment to make the attempt.

"I must say, this doesn't look very promising." Iskander eyed the cliff above us as well. "Perhaps we can swim out a bit and return to land at a more favorable location?"

"No," Griffin said. Rupert had finished his ministrations, and though the abrasions still looked painful, their redness already seemed to be fading. "The barrier re-sealed itself behind us."

"Or someone caused it to," Rupert said darkly. "And it reaches all the way to the sea floor, to keep ketoi from swimming under. Sod it." He caught himself and took a deep breath. "Forgive my language."

Hattie snorted. Rupert ignored her.

"There must be something we can do." Christine sat up and glared at the cliff face and scowled, as though she meant to collapse it through will alone. "Kander, did my lunch survive? I think better when I'm not hungry."

"You ate immediately before we left the ship," I pointed out.

"Just be happy she's not invoking the custom of the sea, my dear," Griffin said. "At least, not yet."

Christine cast him a withering glare. "For that remark, you're first on the menu."

"I don't think that will be necessary," Mother said. "I think I spotted something when I was retrieving Griffin's sword cane. If you can wait a few minutes before resorting to cannibalism, I'll be right back."

With nothing to do but watch the tide encroach on our very temporary refuge, I sat beside Griffin. Hattie and Christine both inspected the cliff face, Hattie going so far as to climb a short distance before giving up.

"Never thought I'd wish the manor was a bit less well defended, eh Rupert?" she said.

I took Griffin's hand, curling our fingers together. "You frightened me," I confessed. "I thought you'd drowned."

"I won't leave you that easily," he said with a smile. "Though I am glad Heliabel was with us."

"Indeed." I shuddered to think what would have happened if she had remained behind in Widdershins, or with the ketoi at Seven Stones Reef.

Mother returned a few minutes later. I rose to my feet at the sight of her smile. "You found something?"

"Yes. Not a solution you'll care much for, Percival, but our options are limited at the moment." She gestured to the waves. "The drop-off here is fairly steep. Carn Moreth must have been defensible on this side even before the sea drowned the land around us. But when I swam down to retrieve the sword cane and knives, I noticed what looked like a cave, or at least a split in the rock. I found it again and swam up it. It comes out somewhere within the island, in a…well, not a cave. More a passageway."

Rupert frowned. "A passageway?"

"You'll see. The air is fresh, and it seemed to lead up. I'd say it's our best chance for now." She glanced from one of us to the next. "I'll swim you down one at a time."

"Oh," I said, at the same moment Hattie muttered, "Bugger." I started to exchange a commiserating glance, then recalled she'd tried to kill me in cold blood, and scowled instead.

"I don't see as we have any choice," Rupert said, taking a step back from an encroaching wave. "Heliabel—cousin—do you have the strength to take all of us?"

"Of course. I can swim for most of a day without tiring."

"I'll go first." When Christine opened her mouth to object, I said, "You don't have a weapon, Christine."

"My bow is probably ruined, but I still have my cudgel," she argued.

"Even so, Whyborne is best equipped to face any danger alone, at least in the short term." Iskander put a gentle hand to her arm. "If anything attacks, he can draw on the sea and try to drown it, at least long enough until you can arrive and finish it off."

"Oi!" Hattie exclaimed. "My knives ain't nothing, you know."

"I know," I said darkly.

"Here." Rupert opened his alchemy case and retrieved what appeared to be two sealed bottles of clear glass. I took the one he held out to me, mystified.

"Read the Aklo phrase inscribed in the metal ring around the mouth, then give it a good shake," he said.

I did as instructed, and within seconds, a greenish-white light shone steadily from the liquid in the bottle.

"Witch lights," he said, holding up his own bottle. "They should glow for a few hours, though they will eventually fade."

"Thank you."

Those of us wearing coats stripped them off in preparation for the swim. I took a secure hold on the witch light, glanced back at Griffin, then walked to the edge of the crashing waves. My mother stretched out her clawed hand. I took it, and followed her into the sea.

CHAPTER 21

Griffin

The wait for Heliabel to return seemed interminable, though in truth it couldn't have been more than a few minutes. I started forward the moment she appeared, intending to go next. But she held up a hand. "Percival asked for Christine," she said.

Iskander and I exchanged a look. Christine, however, marched forward, her skirts swirling in the incoming current. "Naturally."

Once they vanished, I leaned toward him and said, "Let's hope Christine doesn't get any hungrier than she already is. I fear there won't be much left of him."

Iskander let out a quiet laugh. "I made the mistake of reminding her the babe is quite small at this stage."

"And you're still ambulatory? I congratulate her on her restraint."

"Indeed." His eyes hadn't left the spot where Christine had vanished beneath the water.

"Perhaps you should go next," I said.

He cast me a grateful look. "I'd prefer it."

I clapped him on the shoulder. Soon enough, Heliabel returned, and he was gone.

"Me next," Hattie said. "Don't want the ketoi to get any funny ideas about leaving the two of us here to drown."

"We have a truce," Rupert reminded her.

She looked at Rupert as though he'd gone mad. "You don't trust them, do you? Been talking with Basil a bit too much."

"Basil is—"

"A coddled idiot," Hattie shot back. "The Seeker should have drilled some sense into his granite skull years ago."

I made myself still, hoping they would forget my presence. It sounded as though there was more than one split within the Endicotts. The information might not offer any immediate advantage, but it might come in useful at some later date.

Unfortunately, Heliabel's return interrupted their discussion. Hattie's face paled, but she took Heliabel's hand without complaint.

"She is an interesting woman," Rupert said unexpectedly, once they were gone.

"My mother-in-law? She embraced me from the start," I said, in case he was plotting to sow some sort of discord between us. "And, should you ever doubt her resolve, know that Theo and Fiona took her hostage. She stabbed herself to avoid being used against her children."

Rupert's brows arched in shock. "Truly? Then I take my initial assessment back. She is an extraordinary person."

Had the Seeker sent Basil to be the *Melusine's* windweaver, or had Rupert requested him? When I'd first met Rupert, he hadn't hesitated to call Whyborne an abomination. Still, perhaps his views had already been softer than those of other Endicotts, as he'd been willing to treat with Whyborne from the start.

I didn't want to push the matter at the moment, however. "She is that. There's a reason Whyborne always said he was his mother's son."

When Heliabel returned, I gestured to Rupert to go first. I didn't believe she would abandon him on the beach, but I knew for a fact she wouldn't leave me behind. "Percival wants to speak to you," she told me cryptically, before taking Rupert and his alchemy box with her.

With nothing to distract me, I became aware of the scrapes on my back, the ache in my throat from my brush with the sea. I peered out across the water; past the barrier, I could see empty, drifting boats and one or two objects that might have been bodies.

God. How many Endicotts had drowned today? We'd come so close to being among them, both in the water, then after. Had Heliabel not been with us, we'd be trapped here while the waves crawled ever higher.

Unless someone else armed with anti-magic weapons had made it through by slashing blindly at the barrier until they happened to hit a weak spot, we were probably the only ones who had set foot on Carn Moreth. It was up to us, and us alone, to take back the manor.

I drew in a deep breath, seeking to calm my nerves. We'd faced bad odds before. With any luck, Hattie was right, and the Endicotts had winnowed the Fideles's numbers to the point where we had a real chance against them.

Heliabel reappeared. "Are you ready?" she asked, holding out her hand.

"Yes," I said, but I hesitated. "Heliabel, I don't think I've ever properly thanked you. For…well. Everything. Including saving my life a few minutes ago, of course."

She smiled. Like all ketoi, the expression was borderline disturbing, showing rows on rows of shark teeth. "Of course, Griffin. You have been a gift to us all." Her hair rose from her shoulders. "Now, if I don't escort you below, Percival will probably swim back to get you himself."

I took her hand and joined her in the water.

Despite taking the deepest breath I could, my abused lungs ached by the time we reached the opening in the rock. The weight of the ocean pressed against my eardrums as Heliabel guided us into the darkness of the cave. One of her arms tightened securely around my waist as her powerful legs propelled us through the water at a speed I couldn't have hoped to achieve on my own. Her certainty kept me from panicking. It couldn't be much longer until I took a breath. A few seconds at most. Just a few more. A few more…a few more…

Light shone through the water. But not from above, as I'd expected. Rather, arcane power threaded through the stones themselves, outlining a submerged passage that seemed far too regular in shape to be natural.

Then we were moving up, fast. The pressure against my eardrums decreased—and we broke the surface.

I took a great, heaving breath. My heart felt as though it wanted to pound out of my chest. "Magic," I gasped. "All around us."

"I'm not surprised," Christine said grimly.

The passageway gradually sloped up, growing shallower and shallower until it rose above the level of the water. Whyborne held aloft the witch light, peering closely at walls that had obviously been carved out of the living rock itself.

I saw instantly why he'd asked for Christine to be brought next. Bas-reliefs covered the walls of the passage, interspersed with curious clusters of dots that might have been writing. Combined with the magic threaded through the stone itself, the connection was obvious even to my eye.

"It's like the city in Alaska," I said, as I stumbled out of the clinging water and onto dry land. "Dear God. Balefire is built atop a city of the masters."

CHAPTER 22

Whyborne

"There must be some mistake," Rupert insisted for at least the third time. I started to wish Mother had left him on the rock.

"There isn't," Christine replied. She traced the bas-reliefs with one finger. "Look, Whyborne—there were cycads like these depicted in the city of the umbrae, do you remember? Was this once a tropical climate?"

"Science has discovered the fossils of clam shells atop mountains," I said. "Certainly it is possible."

The sheer age of the place seemed to press down on me, just as it had in the city of the umbrae. These ruins were older than the pyramids. Older than Jericho. And yet they looked to have been abandoned only recently. No cracks showed in the walls, no masonry had collapsed. The reliefs were as clear as the day they'd been cut, thanks to the magic permeating the stone.

"I can't believe Balefire was built atop the ruins of some abominable city," Rupert said, staring aghast at the walls. "How could we not have known?"

"You believed Morgen's Needle to be the work of the masters," Griffin said. "Why wouldn't you expect this?"

"Because this is our home!" Rupert's shout echoed eerily up and down the passageway. He caught himself, closed his eyes, and took a series of deep breaths. "This isn't some…some mining camp in Alaska. This isn't an abandoned stretch of desert, or desolate valley no one with any sense would set foot in. I grew up here."

"And I grew up atop a monstrous arcane vortex." Of which I carried a fragment inside myself. In terms of shocking revelations, I rather thought Rupert didn't have that much to be upset about.

Hattie had remained silent throughout. Now she roused and said, "Do you think the Keeper knows?"

Rupert's lips parted. "I don't…perhaps?"

"If he does, he's kept it a secret for a reason." Hattie nodded, as if that settled the matter.

"But why?" Rupert stared at the walls, as though he expected them to alter into something more palatable. "If we'd known, we could have investigated these murals, not to mention the magic in the walls. Perhaps we might have learned something of the masters, rather than being blindsided by their return."

Hattie shrugged. "Maybe it was investigated. A lot can happen over five centuries, things that end up sealed away in the Keeper's archive and meant only for his heir. The Keeper knows more than we do—that's his job, innit? Same as with those artifacts the fish want back."

"I suppose." Still, Rupert looked as though it had been a blow. "At any rate, we have more important things to attend to at the moment. We need to focus on finding a way out of here."

I turned to Griffin. "Does your shadowsight tell you anything that might be of use?"

"Not really. But the stone is completely threaded through with magic, just as it was in the city of the umbrae." The one they'd taken from the masters, before being sealed away within. "Which hopefully means our way forward won't be blocked by any collapses. As for finding a way out, I say we walk until we find a fork, then take whichever seems to lead upwards."

Rupert removed a belt equipped with a series of pouches from his waterproof box, then tucked away his supplies in the belt for ease of transport. Once he was done, he took the lead, holding up his own witch light to guide the way. It gleamed off the damp walls, the play of light and shadow making the carvd images seem almost to move.

As we followed, Christine and I took the opportunity to compare the bas-reliefs with those we'd seen before. The groupings of dots, which seemed to form the language of the masters, were clearly the same. If only we had some version of a Rosetta Stone, that would allow us to translate it.

"Perhaps, if we survive the end of the world, we might write a paper," I suggested. "We can't bring the city of the umbrae to the attention of the wider world, but perhaps the Endicotts would allow scholars on Carn Moreth."

Mother had been listening to us closely. "I would have had Ship-bane add that clause to the agreement, had I known."

"A shame I wasn't able to take any photographs of the other city," Iskander remarked. "Not that I suppose we would have brought them with us, but at least we might have compared them at a later date."

"If you don't mind, we have other things to worry about more important than archaeological zeal," Rupert snapped. "Stop dawdling."

"Hmph," Christine muttered. "More important than archaeology, *really*."

Soon after we started walking, we came across an interruption in the murals. A band of featureless greenish-black stone had been inlaid in floor, ceiling, and both walls. Rupert slowed as we approached.

"That looks like a trap," Christine said.

But Griffin shook his head. "No. An arcane line passes through here. For some reason the masters wished to mark it."

"Could they have considered it a boundary of some kind?" I stepped across it, felt the energy spark beneath and around me.

And something else. For a flicker of a moment, so fast my mind barely even registered it, I seemed to be somewhere else. A rocky peak, marked by a great black stone spearing toward the sky.

And a feeling of shock—followed closely by one of recognition.

Then it was gone. I stumbled, catching myself on the wall. "Whyborne?" Griffin called, and hurried to my side. "Are you all right, my dear?"

"Yes." I put a hand to my temple. "For a moment, when I stepped through the line, I thought I saw something. Morgen's Needle, I suppose."

Griffin frowned. "I didn't feel or see anything."

"Nor did I," said Mother, crossing along with the others. "Mr. Endicott?"

"No." Rupert shook his head. "Dr. Whyborne, has this ever happened to you before, when encountering a line?"

Unease soured my gut. "No. It hasn't." I paused, concentrating on the memory of that brief flash. "I was right. It was a boundary. And something noticed me crossing it."

Worry darkened Griffin's green eyes. "I can't say I care for that."

"Nor me." Hattie rested her hands on the hilts of her blades. "Everyone be on your guards."

There was nothing to do but push forward. Very soon after we crossed the line, we came to rooms and corridors leading deeper into the heart of the island mount. As with the city of the umbrae, the rooms all maintained a hexagonal shape, their walls covered with reliefs of animals that seemed like distant relations of our modern fauna. Unlike the maze of the massive city, however, the passageway we were in was clearly a main thoroughfare of some sort. It was much larger than any of the others which burrowed off into the rock, and continued upward in a gentle, curving slope.

A curving slope.

"It's a spiral," I said, coming to a stop.

Christine nearly walked into me. "Good gad, man, watch yourself. What are you talking about?"

"The passageway we're in." I stepped aside to let her pass. "Mr. Endicott, didn't you say Balefire is built in a spiral up the peak?"

"Bloody hell." Hattie halted beside me. "I've been wondering why this place felt familiar. The layout's same as the house."

"Not the same," Rupert said. "But similar…you're quite right, Hattie."

"Old Sir Richard must've known about this place." Hattie's white skin took on a sickly pallor. "But why would he base Balefire on *this*? There are damned ketoi on the walls, in the murals!"

"He used a spell created by the masters to build the barrier, possessed a fragment of the Wisborg Codex along with its key, *and* constructed his house according to the plan of a city of the masters?" I liked Richard Endicott less and less, which was saying a great deal considering.

Rupert's expression said he shared my unease. "It's said he planned Balefire based on visions that came to him in dreams. If his mind was influenced in some fashion...well, I'm not sure what that means for us, to be quite honest."

I was surprised to hear him even entertain the notion, rather than dismiss it out of hand. I'd yet to meet an Endicott who liked the implication any of them could possibly be influenced by malign sorcery, or anything else. Theo and Fiona had reacted in violent disgust when they'd found out my Endicott ancestor had married a ketoi woman; certainly they'd instantly ceased to regard me as part of the family. The suggestion the Endicotts' entire history might have been affected by the masters and their creations surely wouldn't go down easily.

Hattie's response was more typical. "But we hunt these things." She didn't bother to hide her distress. "We ain't like those other sorcerers, Rupert. We don't have any truck with the Outside."

A horrifying thought struck me, one I had no intention of sharing with either Rupert or Hattie. I'd always assumed the maelstrom had collected Mother to Widdershins because she had the incredibly rare mingling of both ketoi and sorcerous lineages. But what if it had begun its work long before then?

The maelstrom, like the ketoi and umbrae, was a creation of the masters. Did it have some special affinity with places of power such as this, where they had once lived? Was it a mere coincidence that I was descended from the man who had taken this island, who had perhaps been influenced by the works of the masters? A simple twist of fate that my great-great-great grandfather had fled to the colonies, though of course he had died without ever setting foot in Widdershins?

The maelstrom was connected with the arcane line in Fallow. Could it somehow be linked to this vortex as well?

God. Surely not. The maelstrom didn't have infinite control over those it touched. It merely weighted the dice of chance toward the outcome it wanted.

But over centuries, no matter how many throws it lost, those it won would gradually begin to accumulate. To aggregate into a pattern I suddenly wasn't sure I liked at all.

Mother gestured at the passageway ahead of us. "Does this mean we're going in the right direction?"

"Yes." Rupert's voice gained confidence as he spoke. "This should take us to the end of these...diggings. I know the way out."

"Let's just hope it isn't blocked," Christine said. "Come along, Whyborne."

Hattie and I had fallen to the rear of the group. She strode ahead of me, and I found myself playing the part of rearguard. Not that there seemed to be anything to guard against. Probably no one had been in this passageway for centuries.

I tried to escape my dark speculations about the maelstrom by turning my attention to my immediate surroundings. The air in the corridor was surprisingly fresh, and, once we left the sea behind, smelled only of cool stone. There were no traces of animal intruders, not even insects.

And it was silent. I hadn't noticed it at first, as Christine and I had been talking, but there were no sounds besides those our group made. No rustle of animals, not even the fall of a loose pebble thanks to the magic sustaining the walls and ceiling. How long had it been since so much as a sigh had disturbed the profound quiet? Even our footsteps faded quickly, without echo, as though the silence resented us for breaking it.

We passed a bas-relief depicting one of the dwellers in the deep, surrounded by a host of comparatively tiny ketoi. The detail really was quite extraordinary. If only we'd been able to take photos or rubbings in the umbrae city to compare the styles. Were they as identical as our memories suggested, or would some variation show in a direct comparison? Had Carn Moreth and the city in Alaska been inhabited at the same time, or had they been separated by millennia?

One of the ketoi in the bas-relief turned its head and looked directly at me.

I came to a sharp halt, staring in shock. I hadn't actually seen it move, had I? A trick of shadow and light must have confused my eye.

The others drew ahead of me, but I hesitated, unsettled. I leaned in closer to inspect the carving. Just my imagination…but I couldn't get over the feeling it was watching me.

I shook my head and took a step back. My shoulder bumped into someone. "I'm so sorry," I said, turning to see which of my companions had come up soundlessly behind me.

A man stood there, dressed in once respectable clothes now stiff with grime. His hands and bare feet were encrusted with filth. Blond hair hung limply around his ears, clearly untouched by either scissors or comb in quite some time.

Where his face should have been, there sprouted a blood-red tentacle, dripping with slime.

CHAPTER 23

Griffin

WHYBORNE'S SHOUT OF horror echoed up the passageway.

I'd thought him right behind us, but when I spun to help him I glimpsed only the reflection of his witch light from around the curve. Damn it.

"Percival!" Heliabel exclaimed, even as she rushed back down the passageway. My heart in my mouth, I ran after, my heart pounding with fear, and left her quickly behind.

Wind screamed down the passageway, tearing at my hair and damp clothing, and nearly knocking me off my feet. I rounded the curve and spotted Whyborne cringing away from something, hands in the air as he summoned a gale.

"Ival!" I shouted.

His attacker struck the wall with stunning force, propelled by the blast of wind. A man, I thought, at least judging by the clothing. One of the Fideles?

"Griffin!" Whyborne let the wind die away and backed toward me, his eyes locked on the slumped figure. "Don't get too close to it."

It?

His assailant pushed itself to its hands and knees, then

surged onto all fours. Though it seemed human at first glance, it moved more like an animal. Then it turned toward us, and my gorge rose at the sight of the enormous tentacle protruding from its head where its face should have been.

"Dear God in heaven," I whispered through a dry throat.

Reddish slime dripped like blood from the writhing appendage. A slit of a mouth gaped open beneath the tentacle, allowing it to draw breath and presumably feed, but it had no nose, no eyes. How it navigated, I hadn't the slightest idea, but the lack of sight didn't hinder it from charging directly at us.

"The fire spell," I barked, even as I thrust my sword cane at it.

Whyborne channeled power down the blade. But before I could close with the creature, the ruddy tentacle snapped out at me, like the tongue of a frog striking at a fly. I tried to skip back, but it seized my wrist and yanked me toward it.

My wrist felt as though encircled with acid. I let out a cry of surprise and pain, and dug in my heels to keep the creature from wrenching me to the ground.

Then Heliabel was there. She sprang onto its back, her tentacles stinging its exposed flesh in a furious assault. It let go of me, a pained shriek sounding from its slit-like mouth. The creature bucked, and Heliabel was flung to the floor. Still squealing, it reared up onto its feet, standing like a man again. The great tentacle lifted, no doubt preparing to lash out at her.

One of Hattie's knives sliced through the horrid protuberance. It fell to the ground with a disgusting plop, even as she buried her other blade in the thing's throat. A gurgle escaped it, before it crumpled to the floor, dead.

"Griffin!" Whyborne seized my injured arm, pulling it to him to inspect my wrist. "Are you all right?"

The strange slime clung to my sleeve. Where it had touched my skin, it had left behind an angry red mark, as though I'd been scalded. "The tentacle seems to secrete some sort of acid," I said through gritted teeth.

"Here." Iskander and Christine had arrived; Iskander removed the cap from his canteen. "Hold out your arm, and I'll rinse it off."

Heliabel stepped cautiously over the severed tentacle and

joined us. "Percival? Are you hurt?"

"Thankfully, no." He shivered. "I was able to use the wind spell to repel it, before it could attack me. Griffin is the only one injured."

"The water helped," I said, lowering my arm. My skin still stung, but not as badly, and the rest of the slime was gone from my clothes. "Thank you, Iskander."

"What the devil is that thing?" Christine asked, nudging its leg with the toe of her boot. "One of the Fideles, being punished for disobeying Nyarlathotep? They didn't drip acid slime before, but perhaps he's refined his technique."

Hattie took one step back, then another. "It ain't one of the Fideles," she said, her voice shaking. "Rupert, look. The ring on his hand."

Rupert crouched beside the body. Now that I had the chance to actually examine the thing, I was struck by its poor condition. Its clothes were filthy and crusted with old blood. They hung loose on a boney frame that looked as though it were slowly starving. A silver ring encircled one stick-like finger, close to slipping off. Rupert tugged it the rest of the way, then held it up.

It seemed a simple enough ornament, just a plain band set with three tiny emeralds. But Rupert stared at it as though it held horror.

"Earnest," he whispered. "No. It can't be."

"It is." Hattie continued to back away, shaking her head. "It's bloody Earnest!"

Dread leached the warmth from my extremities. "One of the Endicotts who was trapped here?"

Rupert nodded wordlessly. He slipped the ring into his pocket and turned away.

"I'm sorry." It seemed a hopelessly inadequate thing to say, but what sentiment could soften such horror?

"The Fideles did this to him." Hattie turned away, staring at the wall, her hands shaking in fury. "How long was he like this? What about everyone else? To hell with that, what about the *kids?*"

My stomach rolled over. Iskander's skin took on a grayish hue, and Rupert closed his eyes.

"We'll make them pay," Christine said firmly. "We'll kill

every last one of the bastards and send them screaming to hell."

Hattie nodded once, sharply. "Yeah." Her shoulders straightened. "I'll gut them all myself if I have to. Come on."

She strode ahead, and everyone moved to follow. I put a hand to Whyborne's elbow. "Best stay close, my dear."

"I almost forgot." He turned to the mural behind us. "Look, Griffin. The..."

He trailed off, head cocked to the side in bafflement. "This ketoi." He hesitantly touched one of the carved figures. "It's back to normal now, but it moved earlier. Looked at me. Or at least I thought it did."

Even through the lacework of ancient spells that kept the walls from crumbling, I could make out the fading luminosity of enchantment. "There was sorcery done here recently. You say it looked at you?"

He nodded. Unease crept through me, growing by the minute. "And you said earlier, when you crossed the first arcane line, that you felt something had noticed you doing so?"

The witch light already lent his pale skin a greenish cast, but I fancied the unnatural hue deepened. "Oh dear."

Blast. Something had taken note of his presence, and I didn't imagine for a moment it had anything good in mind for him. Or the rest of us, for that matter. "Exactly." I forced my fear down and tried to speak lightly. "We'd best stay with the others. Whatever noticed you has already caught you alone once." He'd been fortunate, but what if things had gone differently? What if I'd raced down the curving corridor to find him strangled by the horrid tentacle?

"You think it sent the...creature?" he asked unhappily.

"I think we should assume the worst." I hurried him up the gentle curve. "Something in Carn Moreth is hunting you."

CHAPTER 24

Whyborne

THE SKIN BETWEEN my shoulder blades itched, and I found myself jumping at every unexpected scrape of boot on stone or glint of light on metal. I wasn't the only one; Mother kept casting looks back, and even Hattie slowed each time we approached a side corridor or doorway. Christine kept her cudgel ready in her hand, and Griffin held his sword cane unsheathed.

I couldn't imagine what Hattie and Rupert must be feeling, to have seen someone they knew so hideously transformed. The Endicotts might have tried to kill us all in the past, and likely would do so again, but no one deserved such a fate. Certainly not any innocents who'd been trapped in Balefire alongside the adults when the Fideles took control.

God. Surely even mad cultists weren't so evil as to twist the bodies of children.

My clothing clung to me, unpleasantly damp, and salt and sand caused it to chafe against my skin with every step. I longed for a hot bath, preferably with my husband in the same tub, followed by a soft bed and his arms. It seemed like the eye of every carved animal watched me as we passed by, even though I knew Griffin's shadowsight would betray the presence of such a spell.

Hattie, who had taken the lead, slowed. "The walls look different ahead."

We crowded behind her. The passageway didn't come to an end, but there was a doorway set into it, as if marking the extent of the masters' ruins. Any door that had been there was long gone now, making it easy to see what lay beyond.

Rather than the masters' smooth sculpting from solid rock, decorated with bas-reliefs and writing, the passage from here on out was formed by large, upright stones. They stretched from floor to ceiling, packed tightly shoulder to shoulder, like misshapen sentinels. The ceiling seemed composed of smaller stones carefully layered to create a slightly arched roof. For the most part, they appeared undecorated, though here and there a spiral or other symbol had been carved into one.

Iskander pushed to the front, his eyes bright with curiosity. "This construction appears neolithic. Very much like a passage grave, wouldn't you say, Christine?"

"You're the expert on this area of the world," she replied. "I'll rely on your judgement."

"Fascinating," he murmured, running his hands over the stones. "It looks no different than other neolithic construction made by human hands. The ancients must have discovered the ruins left behind by the masters and added on to them. Do you think the ketoi directed them here? Perhaps the builders were even hybrids."

"Possibly." Mother's hair slithered restlessly over her shoulders. "It seems the island was used as a meeting place long after the ketoi forgot anything but the most distant legends of the masters, though. The discovery could have been accidental."

"Or something else directed them to build here, the same way something seems to have directed Sir Richard," I said. Rupert winced but remained silent.

Griffin touched one of the ponderous stones. "The only magic here seems to be that of the vortex."

After the wide corridors of the masters, the neolithic passage felt claustrophobic. The walls were closer to one another, and the ceiling lower. The weight of the earth seemed to press down more heavily. At least it lacked the maze of side corridors, with only the occasional niche meant to mimic the rooms below.

The rocks of the wall were roughly shaped, which meant their width and depth was rather uneven. One in particular seemed to bulge out from the wall as we approached. Hattie came to an abrupt halt, holding up her hand.

The rest of us stopped as well. In the silence that fell around us, there came wet smacking sounds. They were followed by heavy breathing, then more tearing, smacking noises.

Something ahead of us was eating.

The fine hairs stood up on the back of my neck. Hattie had gone the color of milk, but she gripped her knives and started to step forward.

Rupert grabbed her by the shoulder. He shook his head at her startled look. Clearing his throat, he said, "This is Rupert Endicott. Is anyone there?"

There came a groaning shuffle, and three people mutated in the same fashion as Earnest emerged from behind the rock. One of them still clutched a half-eaten rat in her dirty hands.

"We're here to help you," Rupert said. "We're going to fix—"

The hideous red tentacle of the nearest one snapped in his direction, uncoiling with tremendous force and speed. Iskander yanked Rupert back by his collar, barely preventing the thing from grabbing him. Droplets of acid slime must have struck Rupert in the face, though, since he cried out and wiped his sleeve across his cheek.

Christine stepped in and bashed it across the head with her cudgel. The other two lunged in her direction, and I lay frost across their skin. They cringed back, and I grabbed Christine's arm and hauled her out of their reach.

"Blast and damnation! If only I had my rifle," she exclaimed. "Or at least my flaming arrows."

Mother and Griffin both rushed to help. Should I channel fire through Griffin's sword cane again? Or perhaps—

"Whyborne, look out," Christine cried, pointing behind us. "More of them!"

Another three loped up the passage on all fours, their limbs moving in such an unnatural manner it brought bile to my throat. One of them howled wordlessly, and the pack began to race toward us much faster than I'd imagined such twisted creatures could move. They must have been in one of the side corridors in the ruins of the masters below, and come up behind us after we'd passed.

Christine gripped her cudgel. "Don't just stand there, Whyborne, do something. Cast a spell!"

"I would if you'd give me a second to concentrate," I snapped.

Centering myself, I drew in a deep breath. Arcane lines flowed beneath my feet, and though this vortex was but an eddy in a pond compared to the maelstrom, its power was more than adequate.

"Hold on," I advised her.

For a second time in an hour, I seized the air itself, pushing it to obey my will. The blast roared before me, wind funneled from a thousand tiny cracks in the rock, building on itself until it exploded in the faces of the monsters closing in on us.

The gale tore at my clothing and Christine's hair, but I braced myself. The full brunt was reserved for the mutated Endicotts before me, but startled shouts betrayed the fact some of it had caught my companions as well. Griffin's tie blew past me, accompanied by centuries of dust and grit.

The mutated forms closing on us staggered back, one striking the wall with stunning force. Before the other two could regroup, I reached out with my will again, focused on the roof above them—and pulled.

Stones shattered and toppled. The ground shook beneath my feet, and for a horrible instant I thought I'd gone too far, and caused a collapse that would bury us all. I shoved Christine down, seeking to shield her with my own body.

A few errant pebbles struck my shoulders and a cloud of dust enveloped us. But the roof didn't crush us, and the sounds of the collapse died away.

Christine pushed me off of her. Before she could speak, Rupert Endicott appeared out of the dust, fists clenched.

"You may lack anything resembling subtlety," he said, "but I didn't expect you to try to kill us as well!"

Iskander rushed to help Christine up. I hung my head. "I'm sorry. I didn't think it would be quite so...large...a collapse. Is everyone all right?"

Griffin wiped dust and blood from his sword cane. "We're fine, my dear. But please, do try to exercise some caution in the future."

Christine fixed me with a glare of cold fury. "This is a unique archaeological site, Whyborne. How could you vandalize it in such a fashion?"

Horror swamped me. "Oh God." I put a hand to my mouth. This was what I'd come to—destroying a neolithic monument like some sort of ignorant treasure hunter dynamiting a tomb. "I didn't think."

"Obviously." She turned her back on me with a disdainful sniff.

Rupert splashed some water from his canteen onto a handkerchief and used it to clean his spectacles. While everyone else took the opportunity to catch their breath, I cautiously approached the Endicott I had blown against the wall. It had been—still was, I supposed—a woman. Her hair was matted, body starvation-thin, and clothing disheveled and stiff with dirt. I drew just close enough to be certain she was dead, her neck at an unnatural angle.

Except, even as I started to turn away, she stirred. The tentacle protruding from her face seemed to dissolve, revealing features that shimmered oddly, as though viewed through water. Her head turned with the grate of broken bone, but the gaze that met mine was utterly lifeless.

"I know what you are," she said.

CHAPTER 25

Griffin

"**Dear God!**" **Whyborne** shouted, taking a step back from the corpse.

The fading glow of an abandoned spell clung to its head. I swore and rushed to his side. "What happened?"

His dark eyes had gone round, and all the color drained from his skin. "Didn't you hear it? See it?"

Christine frowned. "What are you going on about?"

Whyborne swallowed and pointed at the dead woman. "Her face...the tentacle disappeared. She looked at me and said she knew who I was. No, that's not right—she said she knew *what* I was."

My heart sank. This was what I'd feared, when I argued for him to remain behind in Widdershins. Someone—something—in this wicked pile knew his true nature. Whether the Fideles or some evil of the masters that lingered in this lightless place, it would surely turn its efforts toward his destruction.

But it was too late to resurrect our argument now, and "I told you so's" useless, so I only said, "I can see the remains of the spell. It's similar to the enchantment on the bas-relief."

"None of the rest of us saw or heard anything." Rupert's

expression was grim. "This must be some trick of the Fideles. Perhaps one of their sorcerers has something of yours, allowing him to focus his magics on you? Blood or hair would do it, as would seed."

"Dear lord!" Whyborne exclaimed, face going red.

"I was merely listing the most common substances used in such magic," Rupert replied mildly.

"I don't see any traces of a spell on Whyborne," I said over Whyborne's wordless sputtering. "Whatever is at work here, it isn't traditional sorcery." Which wasn't at all comforting. If it had been so simple, we could have used the curse breaker spell. As it was, I had no idea how to protect him from it.

"And what does that imply?" Rupert asked.

I shook my head. "I don't know. I doubt I would have seen the influence of the dweller, if I'd had my shadowsight at the time, because it was something that came from within. Something intrinsic to Whyborne's nature thanks to his ketoi blood, not a spell per se. But Heliabel is unaffected, so it can't be that." I hated not knowing; I hated feeling helpless to shield my husband.

Rupert sighed heavily. "I wish I had learned more about the creation of warding amulets, but it's a bit too late for that now. As it seems there's nothing further to be done, let's continue on."

"One moment, Rupert." Hattie stepped into his path. "First, tell me what the bloody hell were you thinking?"

Impatience thinned his lips. "About what?"

"Giving us away." Hattie pointed at the corpses. "We might've snuck up on them. Gotten the drop. Instead, you go shouting and give them the chance to attack first. Why?"

"Because they're our family." His hands clenched at his sides. "We can't just go murdering them. We have to give them a chance. We have to try to save them. *Supra alia familia.*"

The anger drained from Hattie's face, replaced by grief. "Look at them, Rupert," she said softly. "Would you want to live like that?"

He didn't reply. An unexpected ache arose in my chest. "My partner, Glenn...an enslaved umbra dissolved his face. I found him still screaming, and I...ended his suffering." Whyborne put a comforting hand on my shoulder, and I touched the backs of his fingers in thanks. "It was the only mercy I could offer him. These poor wretches...their minds are gone."

Rupert's hands relaxed. "I know."

"I'm sorry," Iskander said to him. "Truly. But Griffin and Hattie are right. They seem to have no notion of who they are or what's happening to them. God only knows how long they've been like this. Months, probably. You've given them relief from their pain."

Rupert didn't say anything for a long moment, and I suspected he fought back tears. Then he nodded. "You're right. Let's just...let's just keep going."

We all fell in behind him. "I never thought I'd feel sorry for the Endicotts," Whyborne murmured in my ear.

"Agreed." I kept my sword cane unsheathed in my right hand, but with my left I hooked my fingers loosely around his for comfort. But as we followed the slow climb of the passageway, I realized the mutated Endicotts were the least of my fears.

Whatever had done this to them, whatever was using the very walls and dead to stalk Whyborne...it was powerful. And if we were to take back Carn Moreth and Balefire Manor, we'd have to face it sooner or later. I could only pray we were prepared.

CHAPTER 26

Whyborne

THE PASSAGEWAY CONTINUED to spiral upward. I clung to the hope we might soon emerge from this underground hell, but after a few minutes of walking we came not to the upper air, but instead to another set of ruins.

By the time we reached the end of the neolithic passage, the witch lights had grown noticeably dimmer. I didn't bother to remark on it, but I hoped we'd soon be back in the daylight. Ordinarily I might at least be able to set fire to a torn piece of cloth to supply a temporary substitute, but our clothing was still far too damp from our immersion in the ocean.

The passage ended in a sort of crude doorway, just as the initial corridor had done. And once again, the spiral continued on, this time in what was unmistakably Roman construction.

"How very interesting," Christine remarked. She paused and examined the masonry walls, the arched ceiling. "Was there a Roman outpost here at one time, I wonder? Mr. Endicott?"

Rupert seemed glad to have something to think about other than the horrors visited on his relatives. "I believe so, yes. A small garrison—more of a lookout than anything else. The records are fragmentary, but there is mention of Roman era ruins being cleared away when Balefire was constructed."

"Appalling!" Christine's nostrils flared in indignation. "Your ancestors destroyed an archaeological site to build their accursed house? I knew your family was evil at the root, but I didn't realize just how far it went. No wonder Whyborne has turned into a wrecking ball."

Iskander put a hand to his forehead. "Christine, please. This isn't the time."

"I didn't mean to," I protested, though of course she was right. "But there is some good news. If Balefire was built atop Roman ruins, then we should be getting close to the surface."

"I'll be glad to see the sun again," Griffin said. "I'm much better with underground spaces that I once was, but I'll admit the situation is beginning to wear on me."

"On us all," Iskander agreed.

I glanced at Mother. "You've been out of the water for a while now. How are you feeling?"

"My feet are sore," she confessed. "These stones aren't kind, but I fear they don't make shoes in my size."

Christine let out a bark of laughter. "True enough."

Mother nodded at Christine's feet. "How are yours?"

"Swollen and hurting like the devil." Christine tapped her cudgel in her palm. "I do hope I get to take my frustrations out on a few Fideles before this is over."

"Perhaps you should sit down and rest for a bit?" I asked uncertainly, though there wasn't really anywhere convenient save the hard floor.

She let out an exasperated huff. "Oh yes, we'll just ask the Fideles to hold off for a bit while I take a brief nap."

We'd only gone a short distance further when a breath of fresher air touched my face.

"Does anyone else feel that?" Rupert asked. "I think we're getting close to the surface."

Hattie held up a restraining hand. "We need to go slow. Not get excited and rush right into a trap."

I swallowed back my impatience, knowing she was correct. For a time, nothing other than the breeze indicated we were drawing closer to the surface. But eventually the silence, which had been broken only by our footsteps, changed in character. A sort of hum I felt in my teeth, more than heard with my ears.

As we curved steadily upward, the sounds of distant howls and cries joined it.

"Does anyone else hear that?" I asked cautiously.

Griffin nodded. "Yes. It's real, not a spell."

"What the devil is it?" Christine wondered. "More of those mutated people?"

"Probably." Rupert looked haggard, but his mouth was set in a determined line. "Hattie, scout ahead. The rest of us will wait for you here."

She nodded. How she would see without a witch light, I couldn't guess, but she vanished quickly into the shadows ahead.

It seemed we stood there forever in the encroaching dark. The glowing liquid in the glass bottles had faded now to offer no more radiance than a candle. My skin crawled, and my imagination populated the shadows behind us with loping figures.

Hattie reappeared at the edge of our light, so suddenly I jumped. My heart sank at the ashen cast to her skin.

"The passage lets out into a big room. Huge. And it's...it's crawling with them."

Rupert closed his eyes. "How many?"

"Nine or ten, probably. We might be able to sneak around them, though. They're all clustered near...well, you'll see for yourself. But we have to go through the room. There doesn't seem to be any other way out."

"Did you see an exit?" Griffin asked.

She nodded. "There's a door. A regular looking door, like anywhere else in the house. It was shut, but I bet it leads out into Balefire. If we can just get through the room, we'll finally reach the manor itself."

CHAPTER 27

Griffin

WE MOVED FORWARD as stealthily as possible. Hattie took the lead, and I followed her. My shadowsight would reveal any magical traps or active spells, which could prove essential if her plan was to work. Behind me came Whyborne, followed by Christine, Iskander, Heliabel, and Rupert.

The room ahead would have to be truly vast if we were to slip past the mutated Endicotts undetected. At least there was no need to douse what remained of the witch lights. The creatures had no eyes to see us with.

As we moved closer, I became aware of a purple light, which seemed to hover right on the edge of vision. "Do you see a glow?" Whyborne whispered behind me.

"Yes," I murmured. "We shouldn't speak unless we must, lest they hear us. Just stay with me, my dear."

The violet glow grew stronger. The white cloth of my shirt reflected it strangely, and a glance back showed Whyborne's did as well. It made him look like the disembodied ghost of a man hacked to pieces, arms and collar floating independently in the air. Heliabel's markings went from dark blue to an eerie purple, and all of our teeth looked shockingly bright, though tinged with violet.

"What the devil?" Christine whispered. "Is this some sort of strange spell?"

"No," I replied. "I see no trace of the arcane. It seems to be some property of the light."

The endless spiral of the passageway finally came to an end. Beyond was a truly colossal room, just as Hattie had said.

It looked as though someone had hollowed out the hill itself. The room was riven from solid rock, massive columns left in place to support the titanic weight of the earth and manor house above. Magic, similar to that in the ruins built by the masters, striated the stone, no doubt doing its part to prevent a collapse.

Someone—or something—had carved patterns into the floor, though the scale was too large to make out what was being represented from ground level. The patterns glowed in the bizarre light, purple here, orange there, shocking green elsewhere.

Was this where the ketoi and their hybrid kin once carried out their rituals? Or was this great hall older still?

The source of the unsettling violet glow pierced the center of the cavern. A great hexagonal pillar of purple-black stone rose from the floor and vanished into the ceiling. Strange carvings, similar to those far below, spiraled up the stone; the whole thing glowed with arcane energy in my shadowsight.

Streams of arcane fire poured through the walls, floor, and ceiling, twining around the black stone like yarn around a needle. The stone stood at the very heart of the vortex, rooted unimaginably far below us, and towering up through the layers of earth and rock until it reached the free air somewhere on the other side of the chamber ceiling.

"Morgen's Needle." Hattie's whisper was scarcely louder than a breath. Her lips parted with shock and her skin appeared dark in the unearthly light.

Mutated Endicotts clustered all around the Needle where it pierced the floor, and it was from them the piteous howls came. Their filthy clothes barely reflected any of the violet light, but the slime and red skin of their tentacle faces glowed horribly bright. Some stood on two legs, others on four, but all were uniformly filthy. The gnawed bones of rats lay scattered about on the floor, but they were accompanied by other bones which had clearly once been human.

God. Had the Fideles transformed them, only to lock them away down here to starve in the dark?

The only mercy was that none of the bones appeared to belong to children. My hands shook with suppressed fury, and I felt sick that we'd joked so lightly about Christine's hunger earlier. As soon as we were face-to-face with the Fideles, I wouldn't hesitate to destroy them. They deserve to be wiped from the earth for this horror.

Hattie stepped cautiously into the chamber, clinging close to the wall. What she must be going through at the moment was beyond my power to imagine, and yet she bore it stoically, as did Rupert. I couldn't help but feel a touch of admiration for her. Whatever else could be said about them both, neither lacked courage.

We crept along the outside wall, clinging as tightly to it as possible. Carvings covered the lower half, though they seemed far more crude than those at the bottommost reaches of the island to my untrained eye. Many glowed in the light with the same gaudy colors as marked the patterns on the floor.

The door we made for was difficult to spot in the murky light from the black stone. It was set back in a slight recess, but as Hattie had said, it was an ordinary door of wood, banded in corroded iron and set with a latch. Its presence seemed jarringly out of place in this ancient hall. Unfortunately, it was set on the opposite side of the cavern from where we'd entered.

I made sure I had a good grip on my sword cane. Even if we successfully evaded the creatures, there was no telling what might await us on the other side of that door. Something, or someone, knew Whyborne was here. It would be the perfect place to set an ambush, in case the wretches on this side didn't kill him first.

We kept our movements slow and careful, and had crossed half the distance when Rupert's foot slipped on a finger bone.

The sound wasn't loud—but it was loud enough. The mutated Endicotts instantly fell silent, and their hideous heads turned in our direction.

We all froze, and I held my breath. My pulse drummed in

my ears and a metallic taste filled my mouth. I was painfully conscious of every tiny rustle of cloth, every sigh of breath from my companions.

The tentacles squirmed in the air, as if longing to lash out at some prey. Heads cocked, and I prayed the horrible alterations hadn't included enhanced hearing. My legs cramped from being held in the same uncomfortable position, but I didn't dare move a muscle.

One by one, the Endicotts turned back to the Needle.

I kept my sigh of relief silent. Disaster averted, at least for the moment.

Until beside Whyborne, one of the crude carvings on the wall opened glowing eyes.

CHAPTER 28

Whyborne

THE PAINTED EYES opened practically at my elbow, their pigments reflecting the mad light to make their appearance that much more startling. I jerked away instinctively, and my foot caught on a gnawed femur. Griffin lunged to grab my arm and keep me from falling, but he was too slow, and I tumbled to the ground with a loud clatter.

The mutated Endicotts erupted into howls and shrieks.

Hattie cursed. "Run!" Rupert shouted. "Run for the door!"

"Come on, my dear!" Griffin grabbed my hand and hauled me to my feet. The corrupted Endicotts charged at us, most of them on four legs, one still on two. His clothing seemed in slightly less disrepair than the others, and thus glowed more brightly in the Needle's light.

Iskander and Christine fell in to provide a rear guard. A scarlet tentacle lashed at Iskander, and he nearly severed it with a knife. Christine swung her cudgel, bashing the same creature in the shoulder. But the rest were almost upon them.

This was my fault. My friends were about to die right here in front of me, and it was my fault.

No. I couldn't let that happen. "Run," I ordered. Christine flashed me an uncertain look. I dropped to my knees, pressing my hands to the stone floor. "I said run, blast it!"

"Come on, Kander," she said, and they both broke off, racing past me. I dimly sensed Griffin at my back, but I had no concentration to spare.

The earth spell had always been the most difficult for me. But thanks to the vortex this place was drowning in power.

All I had to do was drink it down.

I opened myself to the arcane energy burning against my skin. The scars on my right arm ached. The scent of scorching cloth filled my nose. I closed my eyes and forced my will onto the patch of floor in front of me, even as the Endicotts closed the distance between us.

Their feet and hands struck stone suddenly gone soft as mud. Yelps of surprise and fear rang out. I sensed Griffin lunge over me with his sword cane, driving one off. "Ival!"

I hardened the stone again and fell back with a gasp. Six of the Endicotts thrashed in front of me, some only inches away, their hands and feet trapped in the floor.

"Good work," Griffin said, helping me up. "Come on."

Two of the remaining creatures had circled around us and made for the rest of our companions. As Griffin and I sprinted toward them, a third collided with me. I fell heavily, certain I was about to feel the stinging acid on my skin, or teeth tearing into my throat.

Griffin stabbed his sword cane into it. The blow wasn't deadly, but was enough to make the creature leap off me and at him.

I seized it by the ankle, clinging to it with all my strength. "Stand back," I warned, and drew on the power of the arcane lines once again.

This time, I poured the raw energy directly into the warped form. My bones ached as arcane fire funneled through my body, and I gritted my teeth against the pain. The Endicott screamed and thrashed. The odor of scorched flesh rose from its clothing. I continued to draw on the power in this place, making myself into a conduit, holding nothing back, until the monster ceased to move.

I scrambled to my feet and we ran again. Hattie had slain another of the Endicotts, and Mother spread sorcerous frost over a second. Griffin stabbed it through the back as we ran past. Christine reached the door first and shoved on it. "Locked!"

"Out of the way," I said. "I'll smash it open if need be."

"If you do that, we won't be able to close it again behind us." Rupert reached Christine's side. "And we've no idea how many others might be stumbling about below us."

He had an unfortunate point. "Then what?"

"Magic, of course." Rupert laid his hand on the latch. "Not all of us smash our way through the world, Dr. Whyborne. Some of us are capable of subtlety when it suits."

I bit back a retort, mainly because I wasn't certain I could contradict him. Iskander and Hattie stood guard, and I listened intently for approaching footsteps. According to Hattie's original count, there might still be a lone Endicott missing. They moved with a hellish silence, so I strained my eyes, even though the violet light from Morgen's Needle seemed more to enhance shadows than shed illumination.

"We need to be wary of ambush on the other side of the door," Griffin said in a low voice. "The Fideles might have set a guard, in case the wretches in here didn't take care of us for them."

The locked clicked. "It's open," Rupert said. "We shouldn't—"

In that instant of distraction, a figure rushed Hattie. Its tentacle whipped out, striking her across the face and sending her to the ground with a scream of agony. Iskander whirled on it, but it was already past him and bearing down on Rupert.

Christine swung her cudgel into its knee. It tumbled forward, and Iskander stabbed it. It collapsed to the ground, breath wheezing as blood filled its lungs.

"Hattie!" Rupert ran to her. "Someone give me a canteen."

I passed him mine. He poured it over her face, murmuring reassurances.

"Bloody hell, that stings," she moaned. "I can't see out of my right eye."

The mark of the tentacle stood out on her face like a brand.

The acidic slime had caught her directly across the eye. Rupert peeled the swollen lids apart while he emptied the canteen onto the reddened orb. I cringed at the sight; she'd be lucky to retain any vision in it whatsoever. At least it had only hit one eye and not both.

There came a gurgling sound from the dying creature. "Rrrruperrt."

Hattie shoved Rupert's hand away. "Charlie? Is that Charlie?"

"Dear God." Rupert stared at the figure for a long moment, as though loath to approach. Then with a shake of his head he went to kneel by it. "Charlie? Can you hear me?"

"Rupert." Charlie's breath wheezed in and out of the slit of his mouth. Horror rooted me to the spot. At least before we'd been able to tell ourselves the mutated victims didn't keep their minds. To be in such a state, and still retain awareness…

This was the one who had gone on two feet, and his clothing seemed in better condition. Had he been transformed later than the others?

Rupert gripped Charlie's hand. "What happened here? Can you tell me?"

"B-betrayed us." The words were growing more slurred as Charlie's life drained away. "Something in the Needle woke up. Whispered to him in dreams. I believed at first. Wrong." His body spasmed.

Tears shone in Rupert's eyes, but his voice remained steady. "Who betrayed us, Charles? Tell me, so I can make sure he dies screaming."

Charlie swallowed convulsively. "Justinian," he whispered. "The Keeper of Secrets."

Then he went limp, and breathed no more.

CHAPTER 29

Griffin

"It ain't true," Hattie said. "It can't be."

"We should...should go through the door," Rupert said heavily. "Assuming there's no ambush, as Mr. Flaherty suggested, we can bind your wound. Keeping the eye shut will hopefully help."

No one else spoke.

I positioned myself in front of the door, and Whyborne stepped to my side. I scrutinized it with my shadowsight, but saw nothing. Still, there was no telling what might lurk on the other side: Fideles, more Endicotts, whatever sorcerer or servant of the masters who had been watching Whyborne through the very stones. My heart beat quickly, and I readied myself to act. A glance at Whyborne told me he was prepared to use magic should anything attack us.

I flung the door open, as hard as I could, in case anything lurked behind it. It crashed back with a loud boom that made me wince. Nothing but darkness and silence lay beyond.

I'd hoped to glimpse sunlight, but the dying witch lights illuminated only windowless stone walls. Still, I was relieved when a quick inspection of the room revealed nothing more than dust and cobwebs. Square sarcophagi lined the floor in rows, and urns sat in niches on the walls. When the door shut behind us, it proved to have been disguised on this side as a memorial plaque, inscribed with the Endicott motto: *Supra alia familia.*

"I suspected we'd come out somewhere in the family crypt," Rupert said. Hattie leaned on his arm as he guided her to one of the sarcophagi. "Judging by the layout of the spiral."

Thick silence seemed to press in on us from every side. Christine went to an unlit torch set into a sconce and took it out. "Whyborne, will you do the honors?"

It burst into flame, spreading a pool of flickering orange light over the scene. Christine looked tired in its light, her mouth pinched and dark shadows under her eyes. The rest of us were no better, our clothing stiff with salt and spattered with blood. Only Heliabel appeared much as she usually did. She padded around the room, stopping occasionally to trace her clawed hands over a sculpted bust of some long ago progenitor, or examine the names carved into the funerary plaques on the walls.

Hattie perched on the edge of a sarcophagus decorated with the lifelike effigy of a man in armor. Rupert took out his handkerchief and began to bind it around her head. "It won't be much of a bandage, I'm afraid. Hopefully we can find something better once we reach the rest of the house."

"The Keeper can't have betrayed us, right?" she asked, an uncharacteristically plaintive note in her voice.

"I'm not sure what other possibility makes as much sense." Whyborne's hair, stiffened by salt, stood up in even wilder spikes than usual. He no longer glowed as brightly as he had when drawing on the arcane lines during the fight, but he was still a flame in my shadowsight. "If he knew some secret concerning Sir Richard and the works of the masters, he might have possessed the knowledge to reweave the barrier spell after Minerva breached it. It would also explain the voice that boomed out as the flotilla approached—he wanted to warn as many of the family back as possible. And—"

"Shut it, abomination!" Hattie shoved Rupert aside and drew one of her daggers, waving it menacingly in Whyborne's direction. "We would've made it through the room if something wasn't after you. We wouldn't have had to kill Charlie. Maybe *you're* a traitor!"

I moved to put myself between them, as did Heliabel. Christine thumped the cudgel menacingly into her hand.

"Please, Hattie." Rupert's features were drawn, his eyes heavy with exhaustion and grief. "I know you want to lash out, but Dr. Whyborne is right." He gestured to the hidden entrance. "This door dates from the Tudor period. It's possible the Keeper of Secrets didn't know it was here, but how likely? I believe he knew about the room beyond. And if he's the one responsible for...for..."

"He wouldn't." Hattie stabbed a finger in the direction of the inscription on the door. "*Supra alia familia,* Rupert. The Keeper wouldn't do this to his own blood. Wouldn't turn them into abominations. Wouldn't torture them in the dark."

"Families will do all sorts of terrible things to one another," Christine said. She rubbed at her arms, as if she'd taken a chill. "My own sister tried to kill me. Whyborne's brother murdered their sister and tried to do him in as well."

"Yes, but your sister was possessed by a monster, and they're a bunch of abominations." Hattie shook her head. "It ain't the same."

I could have given Hattie examples from my time with the Pinkertons of purely human families being cruel to one another beyond words. But I suspected she already knew as much, and merely clung to anything that would let her deny the plain truth. So I only said, "What possible motive did Charlie have to lie to you?"

She had no answer to that. Whyborne shifted his weight uncomfortably. "Charlie also said there is something in Morgen's Needle, which spoke to Justinian in dreams. Mr. Endicott, didn't you say family lore holds Sir Richard dreamed the spiral architecture for Balefire?"

Hattie brightened. "You're right. Maybe it ain't Justinian at all. Maybe he's being mind-controlled by whatever is inside the Needle."

"The Fideles are fond of mind domination," Whyborne agreed hesitantly.

I caught Rupert's grim look. Though he didn't disagree, he

surely must be asking himself if the explanation was truly adequate. Balefire, the barrier, the fragment of the Wisborg Codex, even the very office of the Keeper of Secrets, all pointed to a pattern too large and too old to be easily dismissed.

But he only said, "Whatever the truth, we must press on. Perhaps there is some other explanation, but for now, we must be ready should Justinian have turned against us, no matter the cause. I propose we attempt to reach the alchemy laboratory. There are things there we can use against the Fideles, and against whatever they might summon, including Hounds of Tindalos."

Hattie rested a hand on one of her knives. "What about the crèche? We should check there, find out if..."

If the children still lived, she meant. But she didn't say it aloud, and neither did any of the rest of us.

"Quite." Rupert pushed his spectacles higher onto his nose. "Balefire is essentially divided into two parts. The lower, outer part of the spiral consists primarily of living areas. The main library, bedrooms, dining hall, kitchens, and such, including the crèche. Then there is the Great Hall. Beyond that is the upper house, which is devoted to our family's calling. Training rooms for both fighters like Hattie, and sorcerers and alchemists like myself. Libraries containing more specialized books on magic. Laboratories. And of course the armory and the vault, where the most dangerous magical items are locked away."

"The crèche first, then, as it's closest," Heliabel said. "And we try not to be caught by the Fideles."

"There are many secret passageways within the walls of Balefire," Rupert said. "I'm familiar with a few, though only the Keeper knows them all. If he has betrayed us, willingly or not, perhaps he at least hasn't told the Fideles everything about the estate."

"Something isn't right here," I said uneasily. "Charlie only mentioned Justinian. We've seen no signs whatsoever of the Fideles since we've arrived. I know this is a place of the masters, and it does make sense for them to be here, implementing the next phase of the Restoration, but...are we certain they are the ones behind everything?"

"They should have been here in the crypt, waiting for us,"

Christine agreed. "They have to know we're here—they've been tracking us since we passed the first arcane line."

"They've been tracking me," Whyborne said unhappily.

"*Something* has been tracking you," I corrected him. "What, I don't know, but it can't be the Fideles or Justinian. Otherwise they would surely have prepared an ambush for us."

"They might still have," Iskander pointed out.

Rupert frowned at us. "If not the Fideles, then who could it be? Even the Keeper couldn't overcome the rest of the family here and transform them all into monsters on his own."

I didn't have an answer for him. When no one spoke, Hattie said, "Only one way to find out, and it ain't standing around here. Come on, Rupert. Let's get moving."

CHAPTER 30

Whyborne

THE CRYPT LET out onto a flight of stone steps. After a long moment of listening at the door at the top for any sounds beyond, Rupert let us out and back into the sunlight at last. Which was a good thing, since the witch lights had faded almost to nothing, forcing us to rely on the torch I'd lit. Christine started to leave it in a sconce, but Rupert shook his head. "The island has no gas lines. I fear we still rely on oil lanterns and candles in this remote locale. Hopefully we will find a lantern soon, but keep the torch just in case."

"Did you hear that, Griffin? They don't even have electricity," I said smugly. "I, for one, have always been in favor of modern progress. Our house has been wired for several years now, due to my insistence."

"That reminds me, Whyborne," Christine said. "With the baby coming, we've decided to install a telephone in our house. I'll be able to contact you any hour of the day or night."

"Oh dear lord—"

Griffin elbowed me hard. "Please, keep your voices down."

We found ourselves in a wide hall, which ran level, though

with a definite curve. Diluted sunlight filtered through an oriel window, but it was nearly blotted out by the thick storm clouds which had gathered. The floor was paved with dark gray flagstones, covered by a long carpet down the very center. The walls and ceiling were also of somber stone, lined with ancient iron sconces and candelabra. Beyond the window, the sea heaved restlessly, gray waves reflecting the low clouds.

Rupert led the way cautiously down the hall. Portraits of Endicotts lined the right side, which must have been pressed against the rock of the island, as it had no windows. I was no expert in the art of portraiture, but the first appeared to be from the Tudor era and showed a rather martial looking man posing with a halberd, the point of which was thrust into a dead octopus. I supposed the octopus was meant to symbolize the ketoi who had been killed and driven off Carn Moreth.

Christine leaned close to me. "A shame Mr. Durfree and Mr. Farr aren't here to see the paintings. They'd expire from joy."

"Or kill one another over some trivial disagreement," I whispered back. Or, given that Griffin was convinced they were lovers, do something else to settle their dispute. I tried very hard not to consider what form such a settlement might take.

From there, the portraits lessened in age, depicting increasingly recent relatives. A pair of identical twin men stood in one with their arms around each other. "Zachariah and Jeremiah," Rupert said in a low voice as we passed it.

Zachariah. My great-great-great grandfather, who had murdered his brother, fled to the colonies, and taken a ketoi woman for a wife. So much for *Supra alia familia*.

Had Zachariah hesitated before ending his brother's life? Had there been an instant when fate might have fallen in either direction? When he might have chosen not to strike, returned to Balefire and his ordinary life, rather than slay his brother, flee to the colonies, and marry a ketoi?

And if so, was this one of the moments when the maelstrom, sharing the same arcane energy that even now swirled around us, weighted the outcome?

Last February, I'd confessed my fears about the maelstrom to Griffin. That it wasn't moral in the way we were. That it collected terrible people like Blackbyrne, or Fear-God

Whyborne, to it. Encouraging one brother to murder another surely wasn't beyond its capability, considering what some of the old families had done.

I could drive myself mad, wondering what was chance and what was part of some design.

The island topography must have widened enough to allow side rooms to be built, because doors began to appear to both the left and right of the main passageway. Some of them stood open, and I glimpsed bedrooms and parlors, drawing rooms and dining rooms. A layer of dust covered everything, and cobwebs hung in the corners. An air of desertion seemed to cling to the place, as though no one had walked here in some time.

"Where is everyone?" Hattie asked. She kept turning her head to the right, and I guessed having a blind spot had put her even more on edge.

Rupert only shook his head. I couldn't help but wonder what this place must ordinarily look like, brightly lit and with people moving around, talking and arguing and living their lives. Or did it always have a layer of gloom about it?

We hadn't gone far before Rupert opened one of a pair of large doors. We followed him into an enormous library. Light streamed in through the windows, illuminating floating motes of dust and warming the leather bindings of what must have been thousands of books. Like the rest of the house, the furniture was dark and brooding: tables that looked to have been used by generations of scholars, a worn rug over the gray flagstones, and heavy exposed beams crossing the high ceiling.

We shut the door behind us; unfortunately it had no lock. "We've been lucky so far," Rupert said. "Why whatever has sensed Dr. Whyborne's presence hasn't raised the alarm, I cannot guess. We shouldn't assume the situation will remain the same for long, which is why I want to use the secret passageways to reach the crèche."

He went to one set of shelves and began to run his hands over the titles, though what he was looking for I had no idea. There came a strange rustling and chittering from behind one of the desks. A rat?

Horror swept over me—what sort of damage might the thing have already inflicted on the books here? "You're always going on about subtle magics," I said to Rupert. "Don't you at least have something to keep vermin out of the library?"

"We don't have time for this, my dear," Griffin said.

"But the books—"

"I'm afraid he's right, old fellow," Iskander said.

I scowled but turned toward the shelves Rupert was busy inspecting. He reached out and pulled on a book, and there came a muffled click.

More rustling. And a chitter that sounded more like laughter.

I spun, just in time to see a brown form streak from behind a chair, heading in the direction of the door. Though covered in brown hair and possessed of a naked tail, its forepaws looked more like hands, and the face that leered back over its shoulder at me was disturbingly human.

Rat thing.

I let out a cry of alarm, even as I spread a layer of frost over the floor. The rat thing's hand-like paws slipped, and though it didn't fall, it was forced to slow to stay upright. One of Iskander's knives whistled through the air with deadly accuracy. The point slammed into the rat thing. It let out a squeal of agony and went into convulsions.

"Good show!" Hattie exclaimed.

Iskander drew his other knife and went to finish off the thing. "We've encountered one of these creatures before. It helped the Fideles back in Widdershins, when Bradley Osborne was trying to take over Whyborne's body."

"Nasty bits of work, they are." Hattie joined him, nostrils flared in disgust at the sight of the thing. "Seen one a few years back, when we killed a sorcerer who was causing trouble in Dartmoor."

"They serve Nyarlathotep," I said uneasily. "He brings them from the Outside to tutor human sorcerers in magic. That was why Bradley had one." Surely this must be evidence that the Fideles were indeed the ones who had taken Balefire.

There came a soft click, and the section of shelves Rupert had been working on swung open. "Hurry. Someone is bound to have heard all that commotion. Hattie, hand me that lantern if you would. Dr. Putnam-Barnett, I think it's time to put out the torch so as not to set fire to anything in the walls." Hattie passed him a lantern from one of the desks, and he held it up. "Dr. Whyborne, if you'd be so kind?"

I lit the wick with a thought. "Watch your head," Rupert advised me, then ducked into the secret passage.

As he'd warned, the passage was both low and narrow, forcing me to walk hunched over. Once the doorway closed behind us, we had only the light of the single lantern to guide us. "Hold onto one another," Rupert called back softly. "I wouldn't want anyone to get separated from the group. And do be cautious—there are steps where the passage climbs the hill."

Mother entered behind me; her claws snagged in my clothing when she set her hands at my waist. We made our way as quietly as possible, but the passage was narrow, and it was hard not to bump into the sides with an elbow. Cobwebs brushed across my face, and the scent of dust in my nose made me want to sneeze. I squeezed watering eyes shut and tried to resist the urge.

The passage narrowed and widened, climbed up and down. Every so often, we passed a concealed door or peephole. Rupert took the opportunity offered by the peepholes to sneak a glimpse into the rooms, no doubt searching either for invaders or members of his family. Each time, he closed them again with a disappointed shake of his head.

Where was everyone? Had all the surviving Endicotts been transformed? And what of the Fideles, assuming the rat thing meant they were in fact here? Had their numbers been so vastly reduced during the struggle to take Balefire that there weren't enough remaining even to patrol the halls?

The longer we went without encountering signs of life, the greater my unease grew. The emptiness seemed to take on an air of malice, as though some vast thing crouched over Carn Moreth, patient as a spider as we worked our way toward the center of its web.

Rupert came to a halt at one of the doors. It had a peephole set into it, so he looked through before reaching for the latch. "We've arrived at the crèche. I don't see anyone," he said in a low voice. "But we have to check."

God. If we found nothing—or worse, some sign that the children had been among those consigned to the subterranean passages beside the adults...

The door swung open and Rupert stepped out. I followed, and Mother emerged after me.

A woman lunged from where she had stood concealed just to one side of the hidden door, and swung an iron poker at Mother's head.

CHAPTER 31

Griffin

"Back, abomination!" the woman shouted as she brought the iron poker down.

Whyborne barked the true name of fire, and the poker went red-hot in the woman's hand. She let out a shriek of pain and dropped it onto the carpet beneath us; the scent of scorched wool joined that of burned skin.

"Katherine, no!" Rupert grabbed her arms. "As impossible as it sounds, the ketoi is with us."

"Rupert?" She blinked at him, eyes going wide. She looked to be middle-aged, her graying hair swept into a bun, clad in a somber black dress that hung loosely enough about her frame to suggest she'd lost weight recently. "You came for us. Oh God, you're really here." She flung her arms around him. "It's over. This nightmare is over."

I lowered my sword cane. Clearly, Katherine hadn't thrown in her lot with the Fideles.

Rupert hugged her back. "Katherine. Thank heavens you're alive. After what happened to the others, I was beginning to fear everyone had been..."

She drew back. "The others? What do you mean?"

Hattie emerged last from the secret passage, shutting the door behind us. "You don't know what happened to them? Earnest and Charlie and the rest?"

"I'm not allowed to roam," she said. Her eyes widened at the sight of Hattie's face. "What happened to your eye? And who are these…people…with you?"

Rupert gestured to Heliabel. "Katherine, this is our cousin, Heliabel Whyborne. She and our other cousin, Percival Endicott Whyborne, have come to help, along with their companions."

Katherine glanced warily from their faces to Rupert's, obviously struggling whether or not to believe him. "Since when do abominations help us?"

"Since the world is in danger," Heliabel said coolly.

"Never mind all that," Hattie said impatiently. "What happened to the little ones? Are they…alive?"

Katherine turned away from us. "Children, you can come out."

One by one, wary faces appeared: from behind furniture and doors, within cupboards, and under chairs. Hattie clutched at Rupert's arm, as though to keep from collapsing. I felt a wave of relief wash over me also, as one fear slowly let loose its stranglehold. I'd tried not to think about the possibilities: that we'd find the crèche empty…or worse, filled with smaller versions of the horrors we'd faced below ground.

But they were all right. Frightened, obviously, but none of the children seemed sick or too thin.

"You remember Rupert and Hattie," Katherine said to them. "And these people are apparently here to help."

A boy with brown skin had the courage to step out in front of the others. He looked from one of us to the next, clearly uncertain as to whether we were trustworthy.

The fear in all their eyes wrung my heart, so I went down to one knee, to be more on their level. "Hello," I said with a smile. "My name is Griffin. Are you Sadik?"

He nodded mutely.

"I have a message for you from your mother." I kept my voice as light as possible, as though they'd been separated by a routine business trip rather than six months of terror. "We met her in Old Grimsby. She misses you very much, and she can't wait to see you again."

God, I hoped she hadn't died at the barrier, or drowned in the sea after. I'd been unable to note what happened to the boat she was in, too concerned with our own survival at the moment to worry overmuch about anyone else's.

"Th-thank you, sir," the boy said in a shaky voice.

More children closed around me now, clamoring to know about their parents. I wished I had answers for them. Some might have lost one or both during the assault on the barrier, and though I hated to offer words that might prove untrue, at the moment I rather suspected they needed reassurance of some kind.

One young girl toddled up to Heliabel, finger in her mouth, eyes wide as she stared up. Katherine made a move to intercept her, but Rupert put out a restraining arm.

Heliabel crouched as I did. She looked fierce and wild in this place, with its ancient tapestries and soft carpets. Her jewelry glittered in the light of the lantern, and the tendrils of her hair rippled around her shoulders.

"Hello, little one," she said softly.

The girl took her finger from her mouth. "You're pretty," she lisped.

Heliabel smiled, careful not to show her teeth. "Thank you. So are you." She paused, tilting her head. "I have a grandson about your age."

"Is he pretty, too?"

Her eyes darkened. "I've never seen him. But his mother was very beautiful, so I imagine he is too."

Whyborne cleared his throat. "Miss Endicott—Katherine—we need to ask you some, er, difficult questions."

"Come with me." She beckoned us to one end of the room. "Children, entertain yourselves for a few minutes."

We congregated near the window with her. The waves heaved far below the oriel window, gray as iron beneath the cloudy sky. Lightning danced on the horizon, accompanied a few seconds later by a growl of thunder.

"What happened?" Rupert asked without preamble. "How did Balefire fall?"

Katherine shook her head. "I don't know the details. I was

here, as usual. It seemed to be an ordinary day, much like any other. Then I heard the distant sound of fighting. I told the children to stay put, locked them in here, and ran to see what I could learn. I met Earnest in the corridor. He...he told me the Keeper had gone mad. Earnest and some others were going to stop him."

Rupert's skin took on an ashen hue. "What had he done?"

"I don't know. Earnest didn't have time to say, just told me to lock myself in the crèche and protect the children." Katherine closed her eyes. "I never saw him again."

"He's dead." Hattie's voice was flat with suppressed emotion. "So is the Seeker. And Charlie. And a lot of others."

"Charlie. No. I thought...but let me continue." Katherine straightened her shoulders, as though gathering her courage. "I did as Earnest told me. At first I believed we were under attack from the ketoi. That Justinian had done something to the barrier to allow them to pass inside, perhaps. I wish to God that had been the case. But it wasn't."

"He'd let in the Fideles?" Rupert suggested gently.

"Fideles? No." Katherine gave him a puzzled look. "There aren't any outsiders here, not that I know of. No, this was Endicott against Endicott. Those loyal to Justinian, fighting against those who refused to join him."

God. No wonder we'd seen nothing of the cult. They'd never been here to begin with.

Rupert sagged, as though he'd received a blow. "But that means...what we saw below...if the Fideles didn't do that to them..."

I couldn't imagine his shock, to discover people he'd known all his life, his own family, had turned on one another in such a horrifying fashion. "I'm sorry," I said.

Katherine looked uneasily from Rupert to Hattie. "This is the second time you've hinted at something terrible."

"Unspeakable," Rupert said hoarsely. "At least for now. I don't want to say anything within possible hearing of the children. What happened when the fighting ended?"

"Justinian came here." Katherine rubbed her arms as if for warmth. "He said things were changing, and there would be a period of adjustment. That if I took care of the children and did as I was told, everything would be fine. But if I roamed too far, or asked too many questions, or tried to leave the manor, I'd come to the same end as everyone who defied the family."

"Defied the family?" I exclaimed, incredulous. "Was that his excuse for all of this?"

"I was afraid, but I went along with things for the sake of the children." The lines on her face seemed to grow deeper as she recalled the months since. "Each day, I'm allowed to go to the kitchen, prepare food for the children, and bring it back. Once a week, I go to the laundry. At first, Charlie went with me, as a guard. When I dared to ask him what was happening, he only said Justinian was doing what was necessary to keep us safe."

"Funny idea he had of safety," Hattie muttered. "Stupid sod."

Katherine stared blindly out the window. "Later, Charlie let other things slip. That we were cut off from the mainland, and no one outside knew what had happened here. That Justinian had a plan, but our enemies would do anything to stop us, including foment treachery among our own ranks."

Rupert slid his fingers beneath his spectacles, pressing against his closed eyes. "We thought we were coming to rescue everyone—we thought the Fideles were behind this. So many died trying to breach the barrier. Justinian's own sister. His own twin. How could he?"

Whyborne shifted uncomfortably. "It's possible something is controlling his mind. He might not be acting rationally."

"And he did try to warn us," Hattie put in uncertainly. "Told the flotilla to get back. Maybe the Fideles are involved. Maybe they got him mind-controlled and he was able to fight through just long enough to warn us."

No one bothered to answer her obvious grasping at straws. I couldn't blame her for her desperation, though. She and Rupert must surely be heartbroken at the horrors their family had inflicted on one another.

Katherine crossed her arms. "I don't know. I tried not to ask too much, or learn too much. I didn't trust anyone else to properly care for the children." She sighed. "In time, Charlie seemed to become...less sure, shall we say. He never spoke much to me, but I think his initial certainty, that Justinian had acted for the good of the family, began to fade." She shook her head. "Then he stopped coming. I hadn't caused any trouble, and I didn't dare ask what had happened to him, so I was allowed to keep on my routine unsupervised."

"You did the right thing." Rupert let his hands fall. "Thank you, Katherine."

She put a hand to his shoulder. One of the toddlers tripped over a carpet and began to cry. Katherine excused herself, picked her charge up, and bounced the girl in her arms.

I beckoned the others to form a tighter circle. "What do we do now?" I asked in a low voice. "I know we meant to go to the alchemy lab, but we were expecting to fight the Fideles, not your own family."

"Justinian might be under outside control, but all of them?" Rupert stared into nothing. "It seems unlikely, to say the least. Which means some of them chose this."

"Then they ain't family," Hattie said. Her expression of helplessness began to give way to one of anger. "If they willingly went along with turning people like Earnest into monsters, they're lower than any abomination I've ever put down. We have to stop this, no matter what."

"We're talking about potentially killing cousins, uncles, aunts," Rupert protested. "I know you say they aren't family, but when you're face-to-face, will you really be able to strike a blow?"

"I did below, didn't I?"

"These will have human faces still," I said. "Faces you know and perhaps love."

"It don't matter."

"It will," Whyborne said. He folded his arms over his chest. "Speaking as someone who killed his own brother. You think it will be easy, and maybe it will in the moment, when everyone you love is about to die if you don't act. Or perhaps it won't be nearly as simple as you think."

"And what other choice do we have?" She spread her hands apart. "If we don't act—"

There came a loud rustling from the wainscoting.

She fell silent, and we all froze, listening. More muffled sounds, followed by a soft chitter.

Then more rustling, and more, tiny feet and claws moving through the walls. It grew louder and louder, the children falling silent in fear and horror, until it sounded as though a veritable army of rats closed in on the crèche.

"Run!" Katherine hastened to the door leading to the hall and flung it open. "Get out. Draw them away while you still can!"

CHAPTER 32

Whyborne

"**We're going to** remove the barrier!" Rupert shouted over his shoulder to Katherine as we bolted out the door. "Be ready to get the children across the causeway the moment the way is open. With any luck, some of those in the flotilla were able to swim to the headland and will meet you there."

The patter of rat feet grew louder and louder as we raced out the door and into the hall. There was no point in secrecy anymore; we had to draw the rat things away from the children if Katherine was to have any hope of getting them out of this prison. We dashed up the wide hall, past suits of armor on pedestals, up stairs, farther and farther along Balefire's mad spiral.

A lookout tower opened to our left, and as we passed it, the mass of rodents found their exit from the walls. A rat thing burst forth, followed by a tidal wave of normal rats beneath its thrall.

"Good gad, where did they all come from?" Christine panted.

"It doesn't matter—run!" I exclaimed.

We fled as quickly as we could. Unfortunately, Mother's

legs, while well-adapted for the water, were less so for sprinting. Her batrachian feet smacked against the gray stones, then back onto a runner, and her breath came in harsh gasps.

I took one of her arms and Griffin the other, but there was only so much we could do. The hideous squealing behind us dinned in my ears, and I knew we'd soon feel the first teeth sinking into our heels. I had to do something, or else we'd surely be stripped to the bone.

"Rupert, the oil lamp!" I shouted. "Throw it!"

Thankfully, he didn't question, but hurled it behind him in an arc. It hit the stone and burst.

"Keep running," I gasped, and stopped.

Griffin cried out, but I didn't have time to see if he and Mother had obeyed me. The oncoming horde had already reached the oil streaming across the floor.

It exploded into flame at my command, so hot and close I singed my own hair. The rat thing was caught in the conflagration; it shrieked and twisted, along with a few unfortunate thralls.

Released from the rat thing's magic, the natural beasts immediately panicked. Squealing in terror, they scattered, fleeing both the flames and our presence as swiftly as possible.

"Well done, Whyborne." Christine ran back to clap me on the arm, then leaned in to peer at my face. "Oh dear."

"What?"

"Didn't you used to have eyebrows?"

"Curse it." I felt my forehead; the skin was tender and a good deal of the hair on the right brow seemed to be missing.

"Never mind that," she said. "That was some quick thinking. You kept us from…"

She trailed off as three figures emerged from one of the side rooms we'd dashed past. All of them held swords, and with a sinking feeling I recognized them as witch hunter's blades.

"Very quick indeed, abomination," said a hard voice. Four more Endicotts had bottled us in from the front, three armed with the same swords. The fourth, a woman with flaxen hair, I assumed to be a sorcerer.

"Aunt Ophelia," Hattie said. Her voice grated in her throat. "I'd hoped I wouldn't see you here."

"There is much you don't know." Ophelia tilted her head to the side. "By order of the Keeper of Secrets, surrender your weapons." When Hattie didn't move, she arched a brow. "Hattie? The Keeper orders you. Do it."

Hattie's knives hit the floor.

I looked around wildly, but there seemed no escape. The sword wielders closed in. Thanks to the witch hunter's blades, my magic was useless against them.

"Surrender," Ophelia repeated. "You can't win this. You can come quietly...or we can paint the floor with your blood."

No one moved. My heart beat in my throat as I tried to calculate odds. Neither Rupert nor I could fight the witch hunters. Hattie had already surrendered. Iskander, Christine, Griffin, and Mother might stand a chance, but it would be poor odds against six armed fighters and one sorceress.

Christine cursed and hurled her cudgel to the floor. The rest followed suit. A few moments later, a pair of the witch hunter's manacles clamped around my wrists. Rupert and Mother were restrained in similar cuffs. Everyone else they quickly bound with rope.

"Bring them," Ophelia ordered. "They have an appointment with the Keeper of Secrets."

CHAPTER 33

Griffin

I FOUGHT TO maintain my composure as Ophelia and her guards hustled us down the passage. We should never have come here; we should have stayed in Widdershins and left the blasted Endicotts to tear each other apart like rabid animals. If we died here in this God-forsaken mansion...

I glanced at Whyborne. His face was fixed in the haughty expression he adopted whenever he was angry or afraid. God knew I was both at the moment.

The corridor ended in what must have been the Great Hall Rupert had spoken of. The room was enormous, roughly the same size as the cavernous dining hall in Whyborne House back home. Centuries of soot darkened the thick rafters, and iron chandeliers filled with hundreds of candles spread flickering light over the scene. The cold fireplace was large enough for a man to stand upright in. A pair of heavy oaken doors had been left open to catch the summer breeze. Beyond them a long, crooked stair descended to the causeway far below.

At one end was a dais, set with two chairs. One chair was empty, but in the other sat an older man with a thick white beard, who must have been Justinian. A few dark strands remained amidst the snow of his hair and beard, and he seemed Minerva's elder by years, even though they were twins. Perhaps his actions over the last few months had aged him prematurely.

My heart pounded, and my mouth had gone dry with fear. I cast a quick look around the room, desperate to find some means of escape. But none presented itself. The Endicott who'd taken my sword cane dropped it along with the rest of our weapons onto a long table near one wall. Witch hunter's manacles encircled Whyborne's wrists, preventing him from using any arcane power. Rupert was in similar straits, and two different Endicotts trained their weapons on Heliabel, whose power was also bound by the manacles. Christine glared daggers at Justinian while Iskander stood stiffly beside her.

We were in very bad trouble.

"Well, well." Justinian rose to his feet and stepped closer to Whyborne, peering at him like a man inspecting some hapless animal at a county fair. "I thought that the abomination who murdered my children would be more impressive."

Christine and I both moved to step between Whyborne and Justinian. The guards leveled their weapons at us, and Ophelia said, "Hold still if you value your lives."

Whyborne put his shoulders back and met Justinian's gaze. "If you refer to Theo and Fiona, they left me no choice. I didn't seek their deaths. I wanted to be an ally to the Endicotts, until they—"

"Silence!" Justinian barked. I tensed, certain he would strike Ival, but though his fist clenched he didn't raise it. "My children did their duty proudly. The last communication I received from them was a farewell. They realized that foul town of yours needed to be wiped off the face of the earth if any of us were ever to be safe, and to that end they meant to give their lives." Tears filled his eyes, and he swallowed hard. "If they had never met your sister, never met *you*, they might have returned to me safe. Instead, you destroyed my legacy and left me without even ashes to bury."

"Keeper, I must speak with you," Rupert said urgently. "Something is very wrong. I—"

Justinian rounded on Rupert. "How dare you presume to speak to me, when you return in the company of *this*. You and

Fiona worked together in the alchemy laboratory, and yet you ally yourself with the man whose hands are stained with her blood."

Rupert hesitated, no doubt asking himself what approach might reach Justinian. Whether to address him as a grieving father, or a victim under control of other powers, or simply a madman. At last he said, "The Seeker of Truth sought the alliance. When Balefire was cut off, we feared the worst. Surely you didn't imagine your own sister would abandon you?"

Emotions chased one another across the Keeper's countenance, almost too fast to categorize: grief, resignation, anger. He turned away, clasping his hands behind him, and stared at the cold fireplace. "I tried to warn you all. I told you to turn back. I didn't want..." His shoulders trembled, then steadied. "But that was before I knew Minerva had betrayed me by allying not only with ketoi, but with the murderer of her own niece and nephew."

My patience was rapidly reaching an end. "You dare speak of betrayal? Of murder? Do you think we haven't seen what's been done to your kinfolk who opposed you?"

"Does Ophelia know?" Rupert asked on the heels of my questions. "Does she realize how you twisted Earnest and Charlie and the others?"

"I know the duty I owe this family," Ophelia snapped, at the same moment as Justinian said, "The oath-breakers had to be dealt with somehow, and of course I didn't wish to kill them. I was offered this compromise, so I took it."

"Compromise?" Christine spat. "Torturing your own people? Breaking their minds and leaving them with the choice to either starve or kill and eat one another?"

Out of the corner of my eyes, I saw Ophelia jerk slightly. But then she firmed her stance once again, as if to make up for her lapse. "I did not break my oaths."

"What oath?" I asked.

Ophelia's gaze went to Rupert, then to Hattie. "The oath we all take upon reaching twelve years of age. To obey the Seeker of Truth and the Keeper of Secrets. To place the good of the family above our own lives, our own happiness, our own desires. *Supra alia familia.*"

"And those who died at the barrier?" Hattie asked. Her voice was low, and her remaining eye fixed on the floor rather than any of us. "What oath did they break?"

"Never mind any of that," Whyborne said. "What do you mean you were offered a compromise? Have you been seeing things in dreams? Are you allied with the masters? What the devil have you been in contact with?"

Justinian's eyes hardened. "You might be a spark of something greater, but you know nothing, abomination."

My breath caught. There should be no way Justinian could have learned of Whyborne's true nature. Balefire had been cut off long before Rupert and Hattie found out Whyborne was part of the maelstrom. "How did you know that?" I asked, though perhaps the better question would have been what he intended to do with that knowledge.

"Keeper, please." Rupert bowed his head. "I beg you, listen to me. Far beneath our feet, there are ruins constructed by the masters themselves. Sir Richard built Balefire according to dreams, but the manor echoes those ruins. The barrier that has kept us safe for so long is a spell of the masters. If something has been influencing you, speaking to you through dreams, it may not have any of our best interests in mind. Please, just take a moment to really think about your actions. I don't—I can't—believe they originate with you."

To my surprise, a look almost of sorrow touched Justinian's face. "Oh Rupert. You have always chafed at the idea there are secrets you aren't entitled to know. Minerva you trusted without question, obeyed without hesitation, but me?" He shook his head. "I knew of the ancient passageways beneath our feet. I knew about the voice within the Needle that spoke to Sir Richard in dreams. The Keepers who followed after him all knew of it—and knew better than to trust something the ketoi and their wretched hybrid offspring had once worshipped."

He walked a few paces to stand before Whyborne, studying him once again. "The Needle is a source of great power, but only when handled cautiously. Responsibly. The alchemists of old summoned creatures from the Outside they named demons, but so long as they were careful in their dealings, they could come away with valuable knowledge."

"So you're some sort of imitation Dr. Faustus?" Whyborne demanded archly.

Justinian frowned. "Hardly. The intelligence within the Needle slept for five hundred years, its dreams touched only a handful of times by prior Keepers, and then only within very controlled circumstances. Our law was to learn only how to strengthen the barrier, nothing more."

Rupert's expression had grown even more wretched than before. "So what caused you to break that law?"

Justinian began to pace, hands still clasped behind him. "When the Fideles arose, I began to learn everything I could about the masters. Our duty to defeat them seemed clear. I read our fragment of the Wisborg Codex. I combed every inch of the Pnakotic Manuscripts. And I came to a terrible realization." He paused. "We cannot hope to fight them and win."

My blood ran cold, and a part of me wondered what he'd seen, and if what he feared was in fact the truth. "If you know anything that might help us—"

"Nothing will help us," Justinian cut me off. "All who resist are doomed. Every time I shut my eyes, I saw the fate awaiting us. All dead, from the youngest babe to the oldest grandmother."

"So you were influenced through your dreams," Whyborne interrupted.

Justinian waved an angry hand. "Don't be absurd. I hadn't awakened the Needle yet."

Whyborne's eyes narrowed slightly. "Perhaps *you* didn't. But the Restoration proceeds, despite all our attempts to stop it. If all the arcane lines are in fact connected, if it serves as a sort of, of control switch for them, then—"

"Don't presume to lecture me on my own family's legacy!" Justinian shouted. A wild look had come into his eyes, one that instantly put me on edge.

Whyborne's mouth shut with a snap. Into the ensuing silence, Rupert quietly said, "Justinian, what you have done?"

Justinian ran a hand across his face. "What I had to do. We Endicotts have fought monsters for a thousand years...but that is not the oath we take. That is not our motto. I had to put our family first and find a way for at least some of us to survive, no matter what." He bowed his head. "I awoke Morgen's Needle and it showed me how to create a barrier that would keep us safe. But it is merely the tool of something larger. There was only so much I could learn from it. I had no choice but to reach for greater assistance. Not if I was to keep the children safe."

This was bad. This was very, very bad. It sounded as though Justinian had dealt with something from the Outside. Whether the dreams from the Needle had warped his mind, or whatever being he'd called forth had driven him mad, I didn't know.

As for what he had planned for us, I didn't want to contemplate.

"Rupert, Hattie, now you understand," Justinian said. "Everything I did was for our family. For our future. To preserve our legacy."

Rupert's head bowed, too broken in spirit perhaps to say anything. Hattie continued to stare at the floor, as if lost in thought.

"You cowardly, sanctimonious prick." Christine's words rang across the Great Hall. She drew herself up, glaring at Justinian with an expression of utter loathing. "You claim to be doing this for the Endicott children, but you're doing nothing but indulging your own fears."

"How dare you—" Justinian began.

"Your duty is to make a better world for them." Christine's dark eyes flashed fire. "Instead, you mean to help ruin the one they will inherit."

"You know nothing," Ophelia snapped.

"I know a great deal," she shot back. "I know that my mother wasn't the best, for either myself or Daphne. I know I've been terrified I won't be any better than her, that I'll drive away or fail my child. But having seen you lot as an example, I'm feeling a great deal more confident in my abilities, because I at least won't sell its future to monsters!"

"Time is growing short, and I am done entertaining you." Justinian glanced at Ophelia. "You know what to do. I trust your judgement in this matter."

She nodded curtly.

Justinian turned back to Whyborne. "I hope you're ready to meet your maker."

Ival returned his stare coolly. "I'm an atheist."

An odd grin twisted Justinian's mouth. "That isn't what I meant. You have no soul. Just a fragment of arcane power where it ought to be. But this is where the architect of the maelstrom did his work, using Morgen's Needle to weave and twist the very veins of the world."

Fear threatened to freeze my limbs, my lungs, my heart. "You cannot mean to summon Nyarlathotep."

"I would do anything to save this family," Justinian replied, his smile still fixed in place. "And to finally have revenge against the creature who slaughtered my children." He gestured to two of the guards closest to Whyborne. "Take him, and follow me."

"No!" I tried to put myself in between the two Endicotts who came for him, but a third struck me a heavy blow across the back of the head. I crumpled to the ground, the room spinning around me.

"Griffin!" Whyborne shouted. He tried to run to me, but the guards grabbed him around the elbows and hauled him back. A confusion of yells rang out as Heliabel, Christine, and Iskander attempted to intervene. "Griffin!" he called again. I blinked; they dragged him backward by the arms, his heels scraping the stones as he fought to stay with me. "Hold on! I'll come back for you!"

"Ival," I whispered.

Then a door slammed shut, and he was gone.

CHAPTER 34

Whyborne

I fought like a mad thing, twisting and bucking against the grip of the Endicott guards. Again and again, I instinctively reached for the arcane fire beneath my feet, but the manacles around my wrists left my hands numb and my senses dead. I was cut off, nothing but a little spark in human flesh, bound and trammeled.

And on the way to meet with my maker. Literally.

Nyarlathotep had twisted the arcane lines to create the maelstrom. He had set Morgen's Needle in place, or forced the umbrae or ketoi do so for him. Last February, he'd meant to emerge into the Draakenwood at Stanford's call, pluck my essence from my body, and give it to my brother. And do the same with Persephone's. It would have given Nyarlathotep a means of controlling and corrupting the maelstrom, through the fragments within Stanford.

What he meant to do to me now, I couldn't guess as to the details, but I doubted it included killing me outright. Perhaps after Stanford's failure, he'd concocted some secondary plan, should either Persephone or I be foolish enough to fall into his hands.

My captors dragged me bodily through the upper half of Balefire, but the rooms and doors barely registered. I struggled and kicked, but they ignored me.

I had to get free. God, what did the Endicotts mean to do to my family? To Griffin and Mother, Iskander and Christine? I'd been so proud of Christine when she'd told Justinian precisely what she thought of him. She'd be a wonderful mother.

I just had to ensure she lived long enough to get the chance.

The Keeper strode well in front of us, so I turned my attention on the guards. "Don't do this," I said, even though I doubted they would listen to me, if they hadn't listened to other Endicotts. "The Keeper has been led astray by despair. Even if we can't win, there must be a third path, one that doesn't end in either complete extinction or wholesale slavery."

They didn't answer.

"Was this even discussed?" I asked frantically. "Did the Keeper even ask your opinion? Or did Justinian just make this decision on his own?"

"That's his job," one of them said.

I was so shocked to have gotten a reply, I almost lost my train of thought. "But...but surely strategy, warfare, that's usually considered by more than one person. He's the Keeper of Secrets, not the Dictator."

"It doesn't matter," the other said. "It's too late. And we aren't listening to the words of an abomination."

"Oh no, but you'll deal with an entity that gives people tentacle-faces!" I exclaimed. "What is wrong with this family? Can't I be related to a single ordinary person?"

Neither had a good answer to that. We caught up with the Keeper at the end of the passage. The doorway blocking our path was a dozen feet tall and sealed by a pair of large iron doors. Though the design matched the rest of Balefire, it reminded me instantly of the doorways we'd passed through below. If any future civilization added to Balefire's spiral, it would begin here.

Assuming the masters allowed a new civilization to rise. They'd abandoned our world once before, after the umbrae and ketoi rebelled. If they regained a foothold, I doubted they would vacate so easily a second time.

Justinian placed his hand on the doors and murmured a spell. They swung open in response, and he strode through, followed by the guards.

The doors let out onto the very pinnacle of Carn Moreth. It was a landscape of tumbled gray stone, worn smooth by centuries of storms. From the very center of island, Morgen's Needle thrust toward the sky. So close, I could see the purple-black stone it was hewn from seemed semi-opaque; if sheered off in a thin enough sliver it might border on transparent. The menhir jutted perhaps fifteen feet above the ground, the spiral of arcane symbols we'd seen below continuing up its surface.

Iron gray clouds seemed to scrape the top of the Needle. Far off to the west, the setting sunlight escaped beneath a break in the mass just above the horizon, turning the cloud's bellies blood red. Rain spattered down around us fitfully, thunder rumbling low and threatening somewhere to the east.

Even with the manacles on my wrists, I dimly sensed the lesser vortex around me. It wasn't the maelstrom, but I could still draw from its energy—if only I could reach it.

The guards flung me roughly against the black stone, then stepped away. Surprised to have been released, I scrambled to my feet.

"Remove the manacles," Justinian ordered. He stood a few feet away, his white hair blowing in the wind, an eager glint in his eyes. He wanted me to suffer, I realized. And perhaps whatever lurked in the Needle had influenced his mind, used his grief for Theo and Fiona as a crack to be widened, but his desire to see me die screaming came solely from within himself.

"Are you sure?" one of the guards asked uncertainly.

Justinian's words cracked like a whip. "Obey me!"

I readied myself, the shape of the lightning spell in my mind. As soon as they released me, I'd call down the lightning directly on Justinian's head. With any luck, I'd hit at least one of the guards as well. The moment the manacles left my skin, I reached for the arcane power surging beneath me.

And something reached back.

CHAPTER 35

Griffin

I took one deep breath, followed by another. My head ached and my heart slammed against my ribs. Warm blood flowed down the side of my face, but I didn't think I'd been concussed.

Heliabel snarled. "Let me go to him!"

"You aren't going anywhere," Ophelia said, her voice so cold I expected frost to spread out from her feet and over the stones. "Save to your deaths. As Nyarlathotep has no interest in you, I am allowed to decide your ultimate fate."

No. We had to escape, had to get to Ival. What Nyarlathotep planned for him, I couldn't guess, but clearly it wasn't a swift execution. I struggled to sit up, and then climbed swaying to my feet.

"You'll regret this," Rupert told Ophelia. "Justinian is a fool if he thinks the masters will spare any of us. Earnest and Charlie—"

"Were traitors," Hattie cut in.

Rupert gaped at her. "You don't mean that."

"'Course I do." She finally looked up, turning to him. Her remaining eye was red-rimmed, as though she'd been weeping silently. "We felt bad for them, because we didn't know the whole story. We thought the Fideles had done it to them. But they betrayed the family. Broke their oaths."

"Nothing could possibly justify—"

"Shut it!" She took a step toward him; had her hands been free, she doubtless would have punctuated her words with a blow. "You think you know everything, but you're just spoiled. You didn't have to grow up outside the family like I did. The Seeker saved me from the gutter, and Aunt Ophelia finished raising me, and the only thing anyone asked in return was a bit of loyalty. I just wish I'd been here to help earlier."

Rupert looked stunned. But he should have seen it coming. Hattie had always acted solely for the good of the family. It was why she'd spared Whyborne. Why she'd initially saved Whyborne from Stanford instead of Iskander, even though the choice had pained her. Why she'd come with Rupert to America in the first place, swallowing her revulsion at working with what she considered abominations. Of course she would continue to choose the side she'd always chosen before. Why would any of us have ever expected otherwise?

"I'm sorry, Rupert," she said. "I'm sorry Earnest and Charlie and the others couldn't make the hard choices. I'm sorry they decided to turn traitor instead. But I ain't sorry for keeping my oaths." She looked at Ophelia. "Just tell me what you want me to do."

Ophelia smiled. "That's my girl. But you know I'll require a bit of proof before I untie you."

I held my breath. Hattie's mouth tightened. "Katherine ain't on our side. I don't mean she's actively plotting against us yet—she's too worried about the kids. But you're going to want to do something about her soon, before she gets the courage to try anything. I definitely wouldn't let her roam around unguarded anymore."

Christine unleashed a blistering string of curses. Fury and raw despair mingled in my veins. Hattie had betrayed Katherine's confidence, even knowing what the end result would be. The thought of the woman transformed into one of the faceless monsters turned my stomach.

"Thank you," Ophelia said. She cut Hattie's bonds, then took her knives from the table. "Now, with your help, we'll draw this to a close. Rupert is of our blood, so we will of course spare his life."

"The way you did Earnest and Charlie?" I demanded.

She shrugged. "Eventually. Once Justinian is finished with the spark. Until then, Rupert comes with us. I fear there aren't enough of us left to spare a separate guard on him."

Another pulse of fear for Ival went through me, but I struggled to ignore it. I couldn't think about him right now. I had to concentrate on surviving the next few minutes, whatever it took.

There had to be a way out of here. Somehow.

"As for the rest," Ophelia went on, "They are not our kin, and the one is a ketoi. I say we take them to the cliff's edge, slit their throats, and cast their bodies into the sea below."

The guards marched us out of the Great Hall, not to the stair but through the same door Whyborne had been taken earlier. It let into the upper portion of Balefire's spiral. We passed a library and what looked to be an infirmary. A tower opened to the right, and the guards shoved us in its direction.

A tight stone stair rose to one side, and directly across from us stood a small door. My shadowsight revealed magic sealing it, but a word of command from Ophelia dismissed the spell. She unbarred the door and led the way outside.

We found ourselves on a small outcropping of rock, covered in thin grass. The tower wall bounded it on one side, and a long drop into the ocean on the other. The sea wind blew stiffly, flattening our hair and rippling Christine's and Ophelia's skirts. We faced east, but the setting sun reflected strangely from the heavy bellies of the storm clouds, briefly making the overcast sky seem lighter than the land and sea below.

I cast about frantically for some avenue of escape. There were six of them, counting Hattie, and five of us. Hattie and the other guards were all armed, and Ophelia was a sorceress. Our only exit was the door back into the tower.

There had to be some way out. It couldn't end like this.

Ophelia stepped to the cliff's edge and looked down. "Hattie?"

Hattie had escorted Iskander from the Great Hall, one hand on his shoulder as she steered him along. Now she stepped out from behind him and went to Ophelia's side. "Yes, Aunt Ophelia?"

Iskander had ended up closest to me. He took a small step in my direction and bumped against my hip.

"You have done well so far." Ophelia swept her gaze over us. "Your task now is to strike the killing blow when the prisoners are brought to you."

Iskander bumped me again. The devil?

Hattie nodded. "Whatever you say. I've got a request, though."

"What is it?"

Hattie locked her single-eyed gaze on Heliabel. "I want the ketoi to go first."

Fingers brushed against mine, picking at the knot of my bindings. Iskander's fingers.

Heliabel fought, and it took two of the guards to drag her to the edge where Hattie stood. One got too close, and she stung his hands with her hair. He cursed and let go. Even from a distance, I could see the red spot on the back of his hand, the skin swelling rapidly around it.

"That's why you always wear gloves when dealing with ketoi," Ophelia snapped. "You know better than that. Just because we're currently sealed away from the outside world doesn't mean we can let discipline relax."

The remaining guard seized Heliabel by her hair and yanked her head back, exposing her throat to Hattie's knife.

The ropes around my wrists began to loosen. Had Iskander somehow managed to free himself, even though Hattie had been right behind him? Or...

"Go on, Hattie," Ophelia urged. "Kill the abomination. If there's one good thing about the coming days, it's that the ketoi will finally be wiped from the earth. A fitting end for monsters like them."

Hattie raised her knife. "And what about monsters like us?" she asked.

And buried her blade in the guard's throat.

CHAPTER 36

Whyborne

I RECOILED IN horror, but whatever lived within the Needle already had a grip on me. An invisible force curled around my body, holding me tight to the column of black stone. Simultaneously, a mental assault slipped past barriers I'd not had time to strengthen.

"*I know what you are.*" Curiosity and wonder flowed from it, tempered by uncertainty. "*How is this possible?*"

What was it? A consciousness similar to the one that had developed within the maelstrom? Or something else?

"*I've watched you. I didn't tell them you were here. I wanted you to come to me in the chamber below, but I had no way to speak to you.*"

I struggled to shut it out, but I couldn't summon the concentration. It rifled through my thoughts, burrowing deeper into my memories, until it suddenly stopped on the moment during the battle on the Front Street Bridge, when my consciousness had briefly been joined with that of the maelstrom.

Shock and hope flowed out from the being in the Needle, so

strong it took my breath.

"Come to me."

For an instant, I felt half outside of my body, as though the Needle wanted to drag me into it as well. I glimpsed the cavern below our feet, where mutated Endicotts fed on the remains of their kin we had slain or trapped. I saw the empty corridors built by the masters, and the library with the secret passage, and half a dozen other places within Balefire.

And at the very edge of awareness, I perceived the arcane lines spiraling away from me, spreading over the face of the world.

"I've brought the abomination," Justinian said. My consciousness snapped back into place at his words, though I could still feel the thing in the Needle tugging at my thoughts.

"Thank you, Justinian," said a young woman. "You've been so helpful."

She stepped from somewhere behind me, though I couldn't have said where. Her pale skin all but glowed in the sun's last light, her blonde hair arranged in the fanciful crimps and waves popular forty years ago. Her dress appeared to date from the same era. For a moment, I thought she must be an Endicott, because of the strong resemblance she bore to Fiona.

But she wasn't. I didn't have Griffin's shadowsight, but my every sense screamed the thing before me was only a mask, worn over something utterly inhuman. Beneath her girlish tones there rang the howling of the void, and I shuddered.

No one else might have perceived it—clearly Justinian didn't —but the very arcane lines whispered her monstrousness to me. I couldn't imagine how she would appear to Griffin, but I knew the sight would be horrible.

"Anything to bring this abomination to justice at last," Justinian said. "Tell me what I can do to assist you."

This being had no need of his assistance, that much I knew. Whatever it was, Justinian was deluding himself to think otherwise.

Which no doubt it intended. Its face, so reminiscent of his dead daughter, combined with a small stature and the styles popular in his youth, were nothing more than a trap meant to lull him into complacency.

I tried to pull free from the stone, but I was still held fast. I reached again for the arcane fire, but that only allowed the thing in the Needle to more thoroughly invade my thoughts, which I couldn't afford.

The girl turned to me. She carried a cloth-wrapped bundle in her arms. Something moved and twitched beneath its coverings.

She paced toward me, accompanied by Justinian. When they were a few feet away, she smiled guilelessly. "Would you like to see my pet?"

"No," I said with absolute certainty.

"Are you sure?" She grinned and reached for the edge of the covering. "I think he wants to see you."

She pulled aside the tattered cloth. At first glance she held nothing but a repulsive mass of squirming tentacles. Their pallid hue appeared sickly, and many of them dangled limp and unmoving, though far too many still stirred. Mouths gaped at the end of some, needle-like protrusions emerging from their tips.

Then the writhing mass shifted, some of the tentacles drawing apart to reveal the lumpish tumor forming its body. Staring out at me, embedded in the oozing flesh, were the familiar features of my brother Stanford.

CHAPTER 37

Griffin

Several things happened at once.

My bindings gave way. The guard Hattie had stabbed let out a strangled gurgle and collapsed. Heliabel flung herself at Ophelia, teeth exposed and hair ready, even though her hands were still bound at her back.

Hesitation could prove deadly, so I turned and punched the guard behind me with all of my strength. His nose gave way beneath my fist with a gush of blood, but he didn't go down.

"Iskander!" Hattie shouted, and tossed him one of her knives.

He caught it easily and stabbed another guard with it. Ophelia called out something in a language I didn't speak, and Heliabel went flying back, as though blasted by a shotgun.

Then I had no more attention to spare. The guard I faced had stumbled slightly, but now raised his sword. I grabbed his wrist, trying to force the blade down and to the side, away from me. But that left one of his hands free, and he struck me hard on the side of the head—directly atop the wound already there.

Fresh blood sluiced down my face, and what had faded to a dull ache turned into a white spike of pain. My hold loosened, and he wrenched free.

Christine, her hands still bound, head-butted him in the side. His arms windmilled, trying to catch his balance. I kicked his knee, and he fell to the ground with a most satisfying thump. Christine tried to boot him in the head, but he rolled out of the way, and she missed.

I attempted to grapple with him, but he swiped his sword at me, forcing me to jump back. The blade of the guard Iskander had killed lay in the grass nearby, and I snatched it up, blocking the guard's blow just in time.

Metal rang off metal. The witch hunter's sword was heavier than my cane, making my moves slower and clumsier than they would ordinarily have been. Things might have gone badly for me, but Christine hurled herself into his back, sending him off balance—and directly onto the point of my blade.

His weight nearly tore the sword from my hand, but I managed to pull it free as he slumped to the ground. "Good work," I called to Christine, before turning to the fray.

Ophelia had backed up to the edge of the cliff, a wand in her hand. The last guard lay dead, Iskander standing over him. Heliabel struggled to sit up; one half of her face was badly blistered, and the tentacles on that side were blackened and shriveled. Hattie stood before Ophelia, her knife held out before her.

"Traitor," Ophelia snarled. "We lifted you from the gutter my accursed brother left you in. I took you under my wing, reared you alongside your cousins. I made sure you learned the knives from the best, even if it meant going outside the family. Where before you had only known want, I—*we*—gave you everything you could possibly need. The only thing I ever asked in return was your loyalty." Rage and pain darkened her eyes. "And this is how you repay me?"

"Earnest was a good man." The wind ruffled Hattie's hair, but otherwise she was still as a stone. "He didn't deserve what happened. The Keeper should've called a council. Should've brought us all home so we could decide together what to do. But Justinian was too afraid we'd choose different, so he tried to force us. He says he never turned his back on our family, but he's lying to himself. And so are you."

"Surrender," Rupert said. He held up his manacled hands. "We'll bind you with these and leave you safe and unharmed, somewhere you can't cause trouble."

Ophelia's eyes narrowed. "And then what, Rupert?"

"I don't know," he replied honestly. "We'll decide that after we prevent Justinian from summoning Nyarlathotep."

Ophelia's brows arched, and an ugly laugh escaped her. "Summon him? Don't you understand? He's already here."

Shock and horror froze me, so that when she took a step back, out into the air, I couldn't even react. Hattie lunged to grab her, but it was too late. Ophelia toppled out of sight, a brief scream quickly cut off as her body struck the rocks below.

I stared at the empty air where she had vanished. "She was lying," I said, past lips that had gone numb with anxiety. Not because I didn't believe her, but because I didn't wish it to be true.

My fingers went cold, and my heart seemed to seize, like an engine without oil. Whyborne was in Nyarlathotep's grasp, which meant everything I'd dreaded for months had likely come true. The masters' greatest servant wouldn't simply let him survive, not after the defeat in the Draakenwood.

My husband—my love—was either injured, dead, or enslaved. And I was already too late to save him.

CHAPTER 38

Whyborne

I screamed.

Bile rose in my throat, it was all I could do not to vomit. I shut my eyes, but then opened them again to horror.

This monstrosity couldn't be Stanford. This was some terrible joke, some trick meant to break me.

The face made a burbling sound, unable to speak either because he no longer possessed lungs and a larynx, or had no mind left to form words. Watery eyes fixed on me, and there might have been a spark of recognition somewhere within their tormented depths.

"Your brother failed me," the girl said. "But as you see, I am not unmerciful."

Dear God, no wonder I'd sensed a vast presence hiding behind the mask of the young girl. Hadn't I read of the different forms taken by the thing before me? To the mad pharaoh Nephren-ka, it had been Nyarlathotep, a god of chaos. To medieval sorcerers it had taken on the shape of the Man in the Woods. Across eons and continents, it had put on whatever form would most easily help it accomplish its dark designs. This was simply the one best to present to Justinian, nothing more.

"There was still too much of this world in his body," she went on, "and not enough of the Outside for him to survive after you pushed him through the rip in the veil. I might have let him die, but instead I removed what was needed so he might live. You should thank me for being so good to your brother."

My head ached, and a wave of faintness swept over me. Stanford had been a terrible man and a worse brother. If there had been anything left of the boy Mother remembered, it had been unable to withstand the hate and greed infecting him.

Perhaps Stanford deserved everything that had befallen him. Surely he had brought it upon himself by agreeing to graft a thing from the Outside onto his own flesh.

And yet the repellent monstrosity he'd become revolted me on a soul-deep level. As though a rock had overturned and revealed a squirming mass of maggots underneath. He'd been this way for months, assuming time even worked in a similar fashion in the Outside. Did anything remain of his mind? Was he mercifully mad, or agonizingly aware of his condition?

There had been no mercy in this, any more than there had been when Justinian transformed his family, or had Nyarlathotep do so for him. There was only mockery and torment, a blasphemous horror from the Outside laughing at mortal pain, delighting in suffering.

The thing that had created the maelstrom—created the essence that was me—was a howling void of madness and cruelty.

"Well?" Nyarlathotep cocked her head at me. "Aren't you going to say 'thank you,' little spark? Or perhaps you aren't grateful for your brother's wretched life. You *did* mean to kill him, didn't you?"

The being in the Needle recoiled. I fell to my knees, freed from its curious grasp. Heart pounding, I scrambled up. If I couldn't get away, I had to fight, somehow. Though what I would do against a god of sorcery, I couldn't begin to imagine.

"Kneel." Nyarlathotep's voice thrummed in my brain, my blood. "Kneel before your creator." She raised one of her slender, girlish hands and gestured to Morgen's Needle. "Long ago, at the behest of my masters, I stood in this very place. I used the black stone and through it commanded the arcane lines, the very blood of the world. I turned some of them from their original course, twisted them together, and wove an arcane vortex larger and stronger than any in existence. So powerful it could open a gateway to the Outside massive enough to admit armies."

She dropped her hand to her side. The wind howled over the island and flung handfuls of rain from the darkening sky. "But mistakes were made. We were cast out through that selfsame gateway. The masters were cut off from this world, the world they had once ruled as gods. I returned as their emissary, sowing chaos among humans, gifting them with magic. Setting events in motion, until the masters could return and reclaim their rightful place once again."

Her cupid's bow lips turned into a petulant frown. "But in all that time, I never imagined my masterpiece would turn against me. That my absence would allow the maelstrom to grow arrogant. To forget it is nothing but a tool shaped to do the masters' bidding."

Justinian stared at me as though I were some kind of strange insect. "What could it have hoped to gain by that?" he wondered aloud. "To give itself flesh and blood." His jaw tightened. "To murder my children?"

My mind raced. Why was Nyarlathotep going to the trouble of talking to me?

She had to want something from me. Persephone and I, or at least the fragments of the maelstrom within us, could be of use to her somehow. Otherwise, why go to the trouble of organizing Stanford and the Fideles to capture us last February?

At least she couldn't simply strip the spark from me and use it herself. Killing me would seem the simplest alternative, but presumably my essence would return to the maelstrom if that happened. So either Nyarlathotep didn't want that to occur, or she still hoped in some way to make me her tool.

"If you mean to kill me, why haven't you?" I challenged, though my voice shook with fear.

"Kill you?" She shook her head slowly. "No, no. You have it all wrong. I've come to save you."

CHAPTER 39

Griffin

"I BELIEVE OPHELIA told the truth." Rupert's brown skin had taken on a sickly pallor. "Justinian himself said he'd called for 'greater assistance' than the Needle could offer. I'd hoped it meant he'd summoned some lesser creature from the Outside—a rat thing, as we'd seen them earlier, or something similar. But he's been working with Nyarlathotep all along."

Hattie shook her head slowly. She stared at the last place Ophelia had stood, despair written on her features. "Then what hope do we have?"

"None that I can see. Balefire is lost," Rupert said heavily. "Our best—perhaps our only—chance is to make for the causeway. If we can find a seam in the enchantment close to land, we can cut our way through as we did before. With luck, Katherine and the children will meet us, and the seas won't be so rough that even the smallest can't navigate them."

There seemed little chance of it, given the toddlers in Katherine's charge. For a long moment, no one spoke. My entire body felt numb with dread. Nyarlathotep was a being beyond my ability to comprehend. An entity from the Outside, with the power and knowledge to bend the very arcane lines. To instruct generations of sorcerers. He'd been worshipped as a god in Egypt and called upon by medieval cults in Europe. His shadow lay across all of history.

Now he had my Ival. Might have already done something terrible to him, or even simply killed him outright. Fear constricted my lungs—we had to save Ival, if there was any chance whatsoever. Somehow.

But how? We were five mortals, and only one of us versed in any of the arcane arts. I had my shadowsight, but as useful a tool as it was, I didn't deceive myself into thinking it would allow me to stand up to such a being.

Perhaps if we'd had Whyborne with us, or Persephone, or both, we might have had a chance. If we'd been in Widdershins, at the heart of their power, we could certainly have fought back.

But Nyarlathotep had taken Whyborne, and Persephone was far away, and we had nothing but ourselves.

Likely he would wipe us off the face of the world with barely a second thought.

But it didn't matter. Until now, I had managed to put my secret fear to the back of my mind, because there were so many immediate tasks, immediate terrors. The maelstrom had created the twins to aid its fight against the masters. Whatever came, they would be at the forefront of our defense. Even if we won, the chances of their survival couldn't be good.

Even if we won. As though there could be any victory if I lost my Ival.

I couldn't conceive of it. Couldn't imagine our home empty of his living presence. I didn't want to even consider never again sitting across from him at breakfast, or arguing amicably over whether he should add more color to his wardrobe, or shopping together at the grocer's, or any of the thousand other little moments that formed the mosaic of our life together.

I had to try to save him. Both today and in the future. No matter what it took.

"I will never see any of my grandchildren again." Heliabel said unexpectedly.

Iskander had found the key to the manacles on the body of one of the guards, and set Heliabel and Rupert free. Now she walked to the edge of the cliff and stared out over it. The blackened tentacles on the right side of her head stirred only feebly, but the others whipped around her shoulders in a frenzy of grief and rage.

"Heliabel?" Christine asked uncertainly. Iskander had cut her bonds, and she rubbed her wrists as she stared at Heliabel's sinewy form.

Heliabel didn't move. "I never even laid eyes on Guinevere's son, and Stanford's children know nothing of their heritage." And neither Persephone nor Whyborne would give her more, even if we all survived and the world didn't end. She must have had the same thought, because she said, "I wouldn't change a single thing about either of the twins. They're perfect as they are. But they're all I have left."

I swallowed. It was hard to speak the words aloud, but I had to. "And the odds of them both surviving what is to come aren't good."

"I know," she said. Our gazes met in a moment of complete understanding. "But I will not give them up a moment earlier than I must. Not even if I must face down a god."

Christine stepped to Heliabel's side. "I'm with you. My baby isn't going to grow up without its godfather, if I have anything to say about it."

Heliabel looked at her searchingly, then smiled. "Thank you, daughter."

"Christine..." Iskander hesitated, then said, "I didn't realize...you're so fearless. I never thought you would worry about...well. Becoming your mother, as it were."

She bit her lip. "It seemed easier to pretend I wasn't worried. You know me, Kander, I don't care for anything I can't fight."

He laughed and swept her into his arms. "That I do."

Rupert glanced at me. "Mr. Flaherty? I assume you are also in favor of fighting rather than fleeing?"

"I have to try," I said. "Nyarlathotep has my husband. I swore I would be with him in sickness and in health. There was no exception for kidnapping by monstrous entities from beyond the bounds of the world."

Iskander chuckled. "Drat, I knew there was something we left out of our vows, Christine."

"Hattie?" Rupert asked.

Hattie finally turned away from the precipice. She tossed one of her knives into the air then caught it. "I've got two knives and I've already picked out the holes they're going into."

"Thank you, Hattie, that was far more colorful an answer than I wished." Rupert turned to the door leading back into Balefire. "We have something of an advantage at the moment, in that no one remains to interfere with us." He didn't mention the fact that advantage came from the wholesale slaughter of his family, but Hattie flinched slightly at his words. "We should make for the armory as quickly as we can. If we're to have any chance at stopping Nyarlathotep, we'll need the weapons within."

"The ketoi artifacts," Heliabel said. "The Sword, the Spear, the Shield, and the Source. Are they there?"

Rupert looked taken aback. "I suppose they'd be in the vault, which is within the armory, yes."

Heliabel nodded. "According to legend, together they're capable of killing anything from the Outside." She smiled grimly, revealing her rows of shark teeth. "I say we find Nyarlathotep and put them to the test."

CHAPTER 40

Whyborne

"**What?**" **Justinian exclaimed.** "*Save* him?" He thrust a furious finger in my direction, even as he rounded on Nyarlathotep. "I brought you here to destroy him! To twist him into something as terrible as his brother. To get my revenge!"

Nyarlathotep smiled. The smile spread over her lips...and then continued, farther than any human mouth should stretch, curling all the way to her ears.

Justinian flinched back with a gasp of shock. Nyarlathotep's form swelled, and she let the pitiful mass that was all that remained of Stanford fall from her arms with a wet plop.

I craned my head back as Nyarlathotep finally took on her—its—true form. Or, if not that, at least a form closer to the truth than the wholesome mask it had used with Justinian. The creature before me towered at least twelve feet in height. Something that might have been a leathery cloak, or perhaps flaps of its own skin, hung loosely over most of its form. A half dozen arms of varying sizes reached from beneath the cloak. Its fingers ended in sharp points, and black chitin covered both hands and arms, as though it were as much insect as vertebrate.

It had no legs, only a writhing tentacular mass.

There was no face beneath its tattered, leathery hood. Instead a nauseating void drew the eye further and further into emptiness.

I wrenched my gaze away with effort, panting. Black mist streamed from Nyarlathotep, and it stank of frigid air and slime. Its long fingers stroked the empty air, and I could *feel* their touch through the arcane lines, as though it were a spider plucking the threads of its web, and I the hapless fly caught in them. My stomach churned, and I wanted to flee screaming, or at least curl up into a ball and hide.

Justinian called out in Aklo, attempting a variation of the earth spell. Nyarlathotep's fingers twitched on the lines, and the spell died away. Not destroyed as with the witch hunter's blades, but rather simply reabsorbed into the warp and weft of the universe.

"You were but a means to an end," Nyarlathotep told Justinian. Its voice reverberated in my skull, and it was all I could do not to clutch at my head. "The Endicotts were a force to be reckoned with. Something had to be done about them, and that was where you came in."

Justinian backed up rapidly, his mouth gaping open. Nyarlathotep loomed over him, seeming to delight in his horror. "Thanks to you, the Endicotts are now all but destroyed. Which means your usefulness is at an end."

Justinian tripped and fell to the ground, scrambling wildly back. "No," he said. "No! I did this for the family! I...I..."

"You were used," I said. "So much for the Endicott legacy."

Justinian tried another spell, and again it failed. The squirming mass that had once been Stanford struggled to drag itself out of the way. Nyarlathotep plucked one of the arcane lines, and a Hound appeared, its reptilian skin reflecting the bloody light of the setting sun. Jaws gaping to reveal teeth like a row of knives, it began to stalk Justinian.

All of Nyarlathotep's concentration was temporarily on the Keeper. I wasn't going to get a better chance than this.

Hoping to strike a powerful blow before Nyarlathotep could undo any magic focused on it, I slapped my hand against the Needle.

The thing inside of it had recoiled from Nyarlathotep's presence. Perhaps that meant it had no more affection for things of the Outside than the maelstrom did.

"Help me," I said frantically. "Let me use the vortex, please!" I started to reach within—

Before I could draw the arcane fire into me, a hand with impossibly long, insectile fingers seized me by the collar and hauled me back. "Have you been talking to someone you shouldn't? We'll have to put an end to that. I wouldn't want you giving her any ideas."

I flew through the air, crashing to the ground a few feet away from the Needle. Justinian slumped near the doors into Balefire, clutching a bleeding arm. Why the Hound hadn't killed him, I didn't know—perhaps Nyarlathotep wished to torment him further, the way it had tormented Stanford. Another Hound materialized, blinking from place to place around the Needle, as though guarding it.

Whatever was inside the Needle, Nyarlathotep clearly hadn't realized it—she?—had spoken to me. For some reason, Nyarlathotep didn't want us to communicate.

Nyarlathotep loomed over me, its stinking shadow blocking out what little light remained. One of its supporting tentacles slithered across my shoe. The thing was impossibly cold, frost biting through leather and cotton into my toes, and I had to grit my teeth to keep from crying out.

"The Endicott asked why you exist," Nyarlathotep said to me. "I know the answer. Do you?"

"To fight you on both the land and the sea." My heart pounded with terror, and my entire body ached from the battering it had taken, but I forced myself to stare defiantly at the monster towering above me.

"Foolish spark." It leaned down, its empty hood radiating the cold between the stars. "You were created to be sacrificed. If the maelstrom succeeds, you and your sister will both die."

CHAPTER 41

Griffin

RUPERT LED US rapidly up the spiral, pausing only long enough to grab a lantern, until we reached a huge pair of doors reinforced in iron. "Let's hope they didn't change the locks," he said, and laid his hand on the doors. He spoke a few words, and there came a click.

The doors swung open, revealing an enormous space filled with weapon racks, cabinets, chests, and armor stands. Kegs of oil were stacked in one corner, no doubt to be launched at enemies, then set aflame by sorcerers.

"The witch hunter's swords and daggers are useful against ordinary sorcerers," Rupert said as we stepped inside. "But I doubt they will be adequate against a being such as the Man in the Woods. I've been wracking my brain all the way here for any sort of magical weapon that might prove effective against him."

Hattie moved around the room with a determined air, picking up equipment. Caltrops that glowed in my shadowsight, a witch hunter's sword to go along with her daggers, a short flail she tucked into her belt. She opened a cabinet and took out a pair of bracers, which she held out to Heliabel. "You're the only sorceress we've got right now, so take these. They'll help amplify simple spells—fire, water, frost, that sort of thing."

As Heliabel strapped them on, she said, "And the ketoi artifacts?"

"In the vault along with…well, some rather disturbing items, or so I hear." Rupert led the way to the back of the armory, where a second, smaller door stood. Cast from solid iron, it had neither lock nor latch, and fit so closely into the frame I couldn't have slipped a knife between.

"There is one complication," Rupert said, studying the door. "It can only be opened with the blood of either the Keeper or the Seeker."

Curse the man—every moment we wasted, Ival was in danger. "You might have told us that to begin with and spared us the trip."

Hattie cocked her head at Rupert. "I get what you're thinking. Need to borrow a knife?"

"What are you about?" Christine asked.

"I believe I mentioned once before that neither Seeker nor Keeper are an inherited title." Rupert rolled up his cuff and extended his hand. "The current Seeker or Keeper usually designates who they wish to follow them, in case they are killed or incapacitated during a crisis. Once order is restored, of course, the rest of the family will vote to either make the appointment permanent, or to replace the temporary Seeker or Keeper with someone else."

Hattie pricked his finger with the tip of one of her knives. A bead of blood welled out. "Rupert here is the emergency Seeker," she said. "Minerva appointed him, what, a couple of years back? If Justinian hadn't seen fit to drown her, we'd be well and truly buggered, but he did. Which makes Rupert the Seeker of Truth."

Rupert pressed his finger to a small depression in the center of the door as she spoke. There came a series of loud clicks, and it swung open soundlessly. His shoulders relaxed slightly, and I realized he'd feared it wouldn't work.

Heliabel lit the lantern with a word. Rupert held it aloft, the golden glow of its light spreading across the interior of the room only reluctantly. Shadows clustered thick in the corners. A strange oppressive feeling to the room pressed down upon me.

The vault also glowed with magic in my shadowsight. Nearly

every object was imbued with arcane energy. And what objects they were. A severed human hand, dried into a claw, lay chained to a plinth as though it might crawl away under its own power. A crude wooden doll, its body studded with dozens of bronze nails, sat on a shelf beside what was unmistakably an Occultum Lapidem of the umbrae. There were carved bones, sullenly glowing stones, and intricately laced objects of wirework whose purpose I couldn't begin to guess at.

And above all else there were books. Some appeared to be nearly pristine, while others were mere tattered fragments. Scrolls spilled off shelves, and clay tablets such as the ones Whyborne studied were stacked high.

God, if only he could see this. He could be lost here happily for days.

"Here." Rupert went to one of the shelves and selected one of the more damaged books. He opened the cover and nodded. "Good—the cipher is sewn in."

My heart quickened. "Is that your copy of the Wisborg Codex?"

"It is." He tucked it into his vest for safekeeping. "As for the ketoi artifacts…"

"I found them," Heliabel called from the very back of the vault.

Though the artifacts were clearly of ketoi make, they were like no other weapons of theirs I had ever seen. Each one seemed to have been forged from a single piece of metal, without join or seam. As for what the strange alloy was, I had no idea. It was black, with a greenish-gold cast to it. Each was also heavily carved with what appeared to be shallow channels, which seemed more than decorative, though I couldn't guess at their purpose.

Besides the obvious Sword, Spear, and Shield, there was an odd, pagoda-shaped object made from the same metal, perhaps a foot tall and as broad across. A sphere of deep blue stone was set into its peak.

Heliabel touched it with one clawed hand. "This must be the Source."

"The Source of what?" Hattie asked.

"The ketoi have no sorcerers of their own," Heliabel said. "If they needed to use magic weapons, they would have to have some way outside of themselves to channel that power. I think the Source is meant to store magic, in essence, that can then be fed to the weapons. See how each has a stone set into it, matching the one atop the Source?"

She was right—the pommel of the Sword, the butt of the Spear, and the center of the kite-shaped Shield all had the same stone. The blue spheres sat in the middle of the maze of channel-like carvings, which must have something to do with the magic.

"There's only one problem," I said. "None of them are showing any arcane energy in my shadowsight at all. They're inert."

"The Source works only in the right hands. Ketoi or hybrid hands." Heliabel picked up the Source. "Arm yourselves, and leave this part up to me."

CHAPTER 42

Whyborne

Rain sluiced down around me as the storm arrived in earnest. Nyarlathotep's words made no sense. The maelstrom didn't create Persephone and me just so we could die.

"Liar," I said. "Or do you imagine I'm as easily swayed as Justinian? As my brother?"

The ragged leather of Nyarlathotep's cloak blew in the storm wind. "If you continue on the path the maelstrom has set, you will die at its behest. Or did you imagine it shared your pathetic human morality? Your tiny, insignificant desires? You are nothing but a vessel meant to hold water, to be abandoned, empty, when that water is cast back into the sea from which it came."

I shook my head. Though I feared he was right about the maelstrom's lack of what I would consider morality, the rest made no sense. "Why should I listen to you? You would have murdered Persephone and me on Stanford's behalf!"

"Your brother seemed more amenable. Naturally I was disappointed by his failure," Nyarlathotep said. The thing that had been Stanford flinched and drew into as tight a ball as it could, as if trying unsuccessfully to hide. "But imagine my delight when you came to me."

Curse the Endicotts. If I survived this, I was never leaving Widdershins again.

Unfortunately, my chances seemed perilously low. I could only pray Griffin and the others would somehow escape this island of horror, though how I couldn't imagine.

"One fragment will not be as good as two. But it will be better than none. Bow to me. Submit and allow me to use your power." Nyarlathotep's insectile fingers plucked the arcane lines like strings again. I felt one vibrate deep within, and a vision unfolded in my mind.

I stood in the streets of Widdershins, but not as I had left them. Some cataclysm seemed to have befallen my home. The houses were dark, windows shattered and doors torn from their hinges. Great rifts opened in the streets, and an electric trolley lay on its side as though it had been thrown with terrible force. Some of the buildings were nothing more than burned husks.

The vision shifted, and I glimpsed the shoreline. Ships and boats littered the coast, as though hurled onto land by some immense storm. I couldn't tell what might have become of their crews, if there had even been any aboard at the time.

Then I stood upon the bridge over the Cranch River, at the very heart of the maelstrom. Persephone and I lay there—or rather, our bodies did. Our hands were linked tightly together, and very distantly I could hear Griffin scream my name.

I blinked and found myself on my hands and knees on Carn Moreth. Rain poured from the sky, and I tipped my head back, letting it wash away my tears. I felt raw, as though something had scoured my very soul.

This must have been very like what Justinian had seen. Visions of despair. Of war and chaos.

Of death.

"Everything I showed you is the result of the maelstrom's planning." Nyarlathotep's dark form seemed to blot out the sky. "You will die—you are meant to die. Unless you accept my offer. Bind yourself to me, let me touch the maelstrom through you, and I will save you. Once the masters return, you will survive the conflict."

A terrible weight of certainty pressed down on me. Nyarlathotep trying to influence me, no doubt—but knowing that didn't make it feel any less real. "And my friends?" I managed to say.

"They will listen to you. They follow you already, and if you do not tell them of our deal, they shall continue to do so. On the day of the masters' return, you have but to lead them in the manner I instruct. Widdershins will be spared. You will live." It paused. "Defy me, and the maelstrom will take you back into itself, as it has always intended. The vessel of your flesh cast aside, and all your memories and desires and hopes absorbed into something incomprehensibly larger than yourself. You will have no more consciousness, no more life, than you did before it split you off and put you into this form."

My fingers tightened in a tuft of grass protruding between the stones. It clung to life, fought to survive on this inhospitable crag. Baked by the summer sun, torn by the wind, but still it struggled to continue its existence.

Perhaps Nyarlathotep lied to me, as it had lied to Justinian. But what if it hadn't? What if everything it told me was simply the unvarnished truth?

I didn't want to die.

Griffin's words about strategy and emotion came back to me. He'd chided me for insisting on coming here, for not making the sensible decision and remaining in Widdershins while my love and my friends went into danger.

The maelstrom was nothing but strategy. Centuries of planning and gathering, and it didn't care if its creation had turned out to be a horrible murder town, so long as that murder town fulfilled its purpose.

But it had made me not to strategize, but to be its heart. To feel and love and have a human life.

That love—those emotions—left me with only one possible choice now, in the face of a creature far greater than myself. My creator, in a very real way, who now offered to become my savior as well.

"My entire life, I've fought to keep what I have," I said. "First against my father, who would have remade me in his image. Then against Blackbyrne, who would have killed the man I loved. Time and again, I've struggled to hold onto what was important to me in the face of those who would have destroyed it."

I sat back on my heels. Stanford had stilled his thrashing in the grass, and his familiar eyes were fixed on my face. I tried to concentrate on them and not the surrounding horror. "But I've realized something over the last few days. That isn't enough. I have to think about the future. Justinian spoke of his legacy, about its loss, but it's more than that. The choices we make every day shape the world future generations will live in. The ketoi children, the Endicott children, Stanford's sons, and Christine's baby...they all deserve the best world we can create."

I rose slowly to my feet and lifted my gaze to the yawning void of Nyarlathotep's face. "And if giving it to them costs my life, then so be it. I'll be damned if I let you and your kind ruin this world without a fight."

CHAPTER 43

Whyborne

"Insolent spark," Nyarlathotep roared. "You dare defy me? You are my creation. You must obey me."

My hair stuck to my face, and the rain leached warmth from my body as it soaked through clothing that had never properly dried to begin with. "I spent a good part of my life refusing to obey my human father. Why the devil would I submit to a monster like you?"

The figure before me seemed to grow in size, leathery cloak flaring out around it. "If you refuse to be of use, you will suffice for my amusement. You will *beg* for death long before I'm finished with you."

The Hound that had been guarding the Needle let out a startled yelp of pain.

Nyarlathotep's attention—and mine, to be fair—jerked to it. I had the confused impression of a mass of writhing tentacles wrapping around its scaly body, feeding tubes stabbing into its flesh again and again.

Stanford.

The Hound tried to blink out of Stanford's grasp, but—

perhaps because my brother was also now a thing of the Outside—only succeeded in dragging him with it. Further from the Needle.

I had an idea. Not a good idea, perhaps, but the only one I was likely to come up with in the next few seconds. If Nyarlathotep didn't want me talking to the intelligence in the Needle, then it seemed that should be my highest priority.

The second Hound abandoned its guard of Justinian and charged at Stanford. And for an instant, all eyes were fixed on their struggle, rather than on me.

I ran for the Needle.

"Stop," Nyarlathotep commanded in the voices of the damned. Magic swirled around me, the earth gripping my feet, the air buffeting me, frost burning on my skin. I fell full-length to the ground. The rock beneath me softened and began to close over my legs, my hips.

"You are nothing but a tool." The rain turned to ice, freezing to my exposed skin. "And when a tool cannot be mended, it must be thrown away."

I bared my teeth. "We use hammers because our own fists can't drive nails. We use knives because our own teeth can't cut through hide." I stretched out my arm to the Needle. "So what does that say about you and the maelstrom?"

My fingertips brushed the Needle, and I felt the intelligence within it once again. When it had touched me earlier, I had seen its thoughts as it had seen mine. Its recognition of the maelstrom.

God, I hoped I knew what I was doing.

Rather than try to drag power from the Needle, I sharpened my will to a point and pushed into it instead.

Light exploded into being around me, the arcane vortex unfolding much as it must appear to Griffin's shadowsight. The howl of magic through my bones was nothing as compared to standing at the eye of the maelstrom. No hurricane of energy battered my all-too mortal body. Rather, the power seemed to stretch away, from horizon to horizon, taking my senses with it.

For a moment, I could see it all. Rivers of light flowed across the world, like blood through veins, silently nourishing the body of the earth around them. Slender rills fed into streams and thence into rivers. Here and there the rivers came together, currents swirling, channeling into vortexes.

I could feel them all. And, distant but unmistakable, the maelstrom beneath Widdershins turned, its vast bulk rotating eternally counter-clockwise.

It was all connected, from the tiniest arcane rivulet to the great rivers of the lines, to the maelstrom. The blood of the world, ancient as the rock, shaped and reshaped through incredible eons as continents rose and fell.

Somewhere out there, not far from where my body even now lay in the rain at the base of the Needle, was Griffin. My mother, and Christine, and Iskander, and even Rupert and Hattie. I had to find them, had to help them, before Ophelia or Nyarlathotep or anyone else could hurt them. But before I could do that, I had to save myself.

I reached out for the limitless arcane power spread before me. Nyarlathotep might be able to dissipate small spells, but I hoped he'd fare less well if I aimed a torrent of pure magical energy at him.

A shadowy form rose up before me, within the confines of the Needle. The intelligence I'd sensed before. It ruled here, blocking my reach for the power I could sense all around us.

We hung facing one another in an abyss of light. "What are you?" I asked. "You seemed to recognize me. How?"

Its shapeless form shimmered and contracted, and began to take on definition. At first it was hard to make out, like ripples distorting a reflection. Then it solidified into the form of a ketoi woman. Her blue-black markings drew spirals across her pearlescent skin, and spread to cover the tendrils of her hair. Unlike every other ketoi I'd ever met, she wore no jewelry, carried no weapon or tool.

"I recognized you," she said, though in this place she spoke directly into my mind, "because I am the one who created the maelstrom."

CHAPTER 44

Griffin

"**Through there,**" Hattie said, pointing to the iron doors at the end of the passageway. "They're normally locked by a spell, so no one can go to the Needle without the Keeper or Seeker's permission."

Only fading traces of arcane energy clung to the surface of the doors. "I think Justinian left them unlocked," I said.

We'd run all the way from the armory, terrified of arriving too late. The ketoi Sword was heavy in my hand, and I hoped it would be of use even if we couldn't activate whatever magic it was primed to contain. The Shield hung on Iskander's arm, and Christine carried the Spear. Heliabel had the Source and the magic-enhancing bracers. Rupert's hand hovered near his alchemy pouch, waiting to fling a powder or potion.

Hattie aimed a kick at the great doors. They both swung open with surprising ease, revealing a sort of courtyard encompassing the very pinnacle of Carn Moreth. The wind howled, and rain pounded the tumble of boulders and rocks forming the carn. The very last finger of sunlight shot beneath the low clouds far to the west, touching for a moment the black standing stone piercing the very heart of the island. Then it vanished, and night descended on us all.

Rupert pulled a handful of shining powder from his pouch. Shouting a string of unfamiliar words, he hurled it with all his strength into the air. Rather than disperse as powder should, the particles clung together, arcing higher and higher above the courtyard, before exploding into a brilliant white light illuminating everything below.

My shadowsight hadn't required the extra light; the courtyard blazed, arcane streams pouring in to wrap around the length of the Needle, just as they had in the cavern below. Two Hounds swung their dragonish heads in our direction as we charged inside.

Whyborne lay sprawled at the base of the Needle, one hand resting against its glassy surface. The rock around him had deformed, closing over his legs, and frost sparkled on his clothing, washing away in the rain. His stillness sent a spike of terror through me, before I realized he yet glowed steadily in my shadowsight.

Then the terror returned as I beheld the creature bearing down on him. My brain scrambled to understand what my eyes showed me, and a wave of nausea threatened to bring up bile from my empty stomach.

The creature was a blot on the world, a living darkness spreading corruption to everything it touched. Where Ival burned with pure, cleansing fire, it smeared a layer of sooty foulness across the very fabric of reality. It was every shape and none, a heaving, churning distortion that gave my shadowsight nothing to rest upon. Sharp appendages emerged from it, stabbing and gathering at the strands of arcane light, plucking smaller threads from the thick streams and weaving them into some kind of pattern. Mortal sorcerers used their spells to manipulate the warp and weft of reality. But this being seemed to weave—and no doubt unravel—it directly.

Other hands drew some of the threads into itself, where they vanished amidst the corrupt darkness of its form. Was it... feeding, somehow?

"Bloody hell," Hattie said. *"That's* what we have to kill?"

"Yes," Justinian grated.

He stood not far from the doors, back against the wall, one

sleeve soaked in blood. "You!" Christine exclaimed.

"It used me." Justinian's eyes were wild, and I wasn't certain he was entirely sane at the moment, if he had been before. "Used me, to destroy the Endicotts."

"Obviously!" I exclaimed. "We don't have time for this—we have to keep that thing away from Ival."

"Magic doesn't work against it," Justinian said, but I'd already broken into a run.

I tried not to look at the monstrous thing I was charging, instead focusing on the Hounds which moved to block our path. They blinked in and out of existence, twenty feet away one second, then five the next. My shadowsight revealed their ghostly forms, and I called, "Iskander, bring up the Shield!"

He did so without question, plowing directly into one of the Hounds as it materialized and sending it flying. The other I stabbed with the Sword; it let out a yelp of pain and blinked away to reappear in front of Rupert. Rupert flung a handful of powder on it, preventing it from blinking, and a moment later Hattie descended with her knives.

My foot caught on something half-hidden in a clump of grass, and I went sprawling. I swore, scrambling to my feet—then cursed again when I saw what I'd tripped over.

At first glance, it was nothing more than a mass of limp tentacles, torn and mauled by the Hounds. But then I realized a human eye stared out between two of them, dead and filling with rain like tears.

Heliabel stopped, lips parted, eyes wide. The Source fell from her hands, and she crouched down to pick up the nauseating thing. The tentacles slipped aside, revealing Stanford's face.

She stared at the last remnants of her eldest child, and I knew she wasn't thinking of Stanford as he'd become. Not the monster who had tried to murder us all in the Draakenwood, or the assassin who had struck down Guinevere.

She was seeing the little boy she'd described to Whyborne aboard the *Melusine*. The toddler with chubby cheeks and a bright smile. The baby she'd once cradled tenderly, her face against his soft skin, her dreams filled with a bright future for him.

This was what that future had come to. Horror and death, betrayal and jealousy, all leading here. To this scrap of inanimate flesh.

Even as she tried to hold him, his body began to dissolve. Things of the Outside never remained long after their death, and the torn flesh went to greenish slime, then to nothing at all.

For a long moment, the world seemed to hold its breath. Rain slicked her face, hiding whatever tears she might have shed. Then her expression transformed from one of stunned horror to utter rage.

"No," she said. Then she looked up at Nyarlathotep and screamed, so loud the words tore from her throat. "No! You will not have any more of my children!"

She dropped to her knees and slammed one hand on the blue sphere atop the Source. With one hand on the blue stone, she flung out the other, and channeled the arcane fire directly from the vortex.

CHAPTER 45

Whyborne

"I THOUGHT NYARLATHOTEP created the maelstrom," I said.

The ketoi woman—the entity I'd sensed within the Needle—tipped her head to the side. Her tendrils lay quiet over her shoulders, and a palpable sense of weary sorrow radiated from her.

Morgen's Needle, they'd called the stone. Morgen. Sea born. Had the name referred to her all along?

"It used me—commanded me—to twist the lines and form the maelstrom." She held up her hands. "But it was I who did the work. I who directed the arcane fire. I who made you." She let her hands fall and met my gaze. "I saw you when you came onto the island. But I did not warn the one whose dreams I touched."

No wonder there had been no Endicotts waiting to ambush us the moment we entered the family crypt. "You filled Justinian's head with visions of horror, but you want to help me? Whose side are you on?"

"I didn't wish to show him Nyarlathotep's visions. It forced me to. As for why I'm helping you, it's because I created you.

You are my legacy. Not theirs." Her nostrils flared, and her voice grew bitter. "Not Nyarlathotep's. *Mine.*"

I didn't know what to say to that, or even how to feel about it. "Who are you? You look like a ketoi, but you can't be."

"I don't remember." She tipped her head back, as though she could peer into the past. "It has been eons since I spoke to anyone. I was...not like this. I had a body, once. Like you, I was created to serve. This was how the masters decided I could best contribute. So Nyarlathotep changed me. Put me in here." She paused. "It's been so long. I can't...I can't remember. There was another, and I can't remember their face." Pain and despair distorted her features. "I promised I'd never forget them and I did!"

Her entire body went slack, head bowed, arms dangling, legs limp. "I forgot you."

Despite the urgency of my own situation, pity tightened my throat. "Forgot who?"

"Someone I loved. I can't remember them. How could I have forgotten?" Hopelessness coated every word. "I loved them more than anything in this world, and they're *gone,* and I can't even recall their name."

Dear God. Oblivion I could accept, but to still exist and not be able to remember Griffin's name? His face?

It felt an unspeakable cruelty, forced on her not by the uncaring hand of illness or age or accident, but to further the goals of the masters. "I'm so sorry."

"The masters left, so Nyarlathotep had to leave as well. I was finally allowed to sleep."

Wait. "What do you mean, Nyarlathotep had to leave when the masters did?"

"It is their messenger. Their servant. Their first creation. It is bound to them even more intimately than an umbra to its queen, or the rust to the avatar. Nyarlathotep cannot remain long in this world while they are still Outside. Only when they return will it once again be free to walk this earth as it will. And I fear that time is soon." She raised her head, just slightly. "I dreamed, sometimes, over the long years. I didn't want to wake, not ever again. But I didn't have a choice. Nyarlathotep prepares for the return of the masters. If that happens, I'll never be able to escape. Never be able to sleep and forget for a while all that I have lost."

The weariness of ages filled her voice. I couldn't imagine what she had suffered here. Locked away, her very essence changed, made into nothing but a tool for Nyarlathotep to use.

This was, indeed, Carn Moreth. The hill of grief.

"How can I help you?" I asked. "Tell me, and I'll do it."

She stirred, her eyes lifting to meet mine. "You defy them. Nyarlathotep. The masters."

I nodded, though it hadn't really been a question. "Yes."

"The you who is in front of me, but the maelstrom as well?"

I remembered what Nyarlathotep had said. That if I faced down the masters as the maelstrom wished, I was doomed.

It might have been lying. It probably was. But either way, there were far, far worse things than death.

"Yes," I said. "The maelstrom fragmented itself so my sister and I could help it stand against them. We will never submit."

To my surprise, she smiled. "Then I managed to do one good thing in this cursed existence. I will help you fight Nyarlathotep here. Now. But I ask one thing in return."

I nodded. "Anything."

"When this is done, help me sever the bonds between the Needle and the arcane streams. Redirect them, drain this vortex, and let me die."

A part of me wanted to question her further. To ask her to stay long enough for us to learn anything that might help us stand against the masters. But I could feel the weight of her grief and despair against my own heart, so I only nodded. "You have my word."

She reached out her hand. I reached back, and the arcane fire engulfed us both.

CHAPTER 46

Griffin

HELIABEL SCREAMED.

Her back arched as arcane fire blazed through her, and she bared her teeth to the heavens. Like her children, she had both the Endicott and ketoi blood, and could withstand the raw power in a way no one else could.

Had this been the maelstrom, her lack of a connection with the old families might have made a difference. But this was no titanic whirlpool such as lay beneath Widdershins, fed by enormous rivers of light. So she shrieked her defiance to the sky and held on.

The light poured through her, then into the Source, which began to shine ever brighter in my shadowsight.

In response, the stone on the pommel of the Sword began to glow as well. Magic poured through the channels on its surface, and the edge blazed as though white-hot. A glance at the Shield and Spear revealed similar effects.

"The weapons aren't inert anymore!" I called.

"So what the devil do we do with them?" Christine shouted back.

We didn't have time to determine. Nyarlathotep's attention

swung to us like the beam of a lighthouse, something with almost palpable weight. The monster tugged on the strands of arcane fire, and rifts began to open in the world. Ghostly Hounds appeared in my shadowsight, about to blink into existence.

"Hounds!" I yelled in warning.

The Endicotts were ready. Hattie threw down her caltrops, and one of the Hounds screamed as it manifested directly on them. Rupert flung a handful of powder on another, pinning it in place as well. Hattie slashed first one, then the other, with her knives, killing both.

A Hound burst into being near Christine. She stabbed the Spear at it—

And a second spear, made entirely of magic, flew out of its tip. With unerring accuracy, it lanced directly through the Hound, killing it instantly.

"Oh, that's what it does," Christine said. A savage grin spread across her face, and she began casting ethereal spears with abandon.

A rat thing and a Hound both appeared next to me. I swung the Sword, and its magical edge cut first through the rat thing, then the Hound, as though both were made from warm butter.

"Iskander, try the Shield!" I called.

He'd moved to protect Christine while she hurled magic in every direction. As she disintegrated a rat thing, another Hound charged at her. Iskander thrust the Shield in between—and the Hound was blasted back, striking the ground ten feet away.

Then the chaos of battle demanded all my attention. A Hound began to shimmer into being, but the sword in my hand was waiting and it formed around the blade, dying even as it emerged into our reality. A rat thing leapt squealing onto my leg; I kicked it off, then sliced it neatly in half.

But for every rat thing or Hound we destroyed, Nyarlathotep summoned two more. Its nightmare presence dominated the fray, calling forth horror after horror. We couldn't keep this up forever; even with magical weapons, we were only human flesh. Christine's maniacal laughter as she laid waste to our enemies notwithstanding, we would eventually tire.

"Enough," Nyarlathotep said. I cringed instinctively at the

loathsome sound. Every word felt like insects crawling through my ears and burrowing into my brain. "I tire of this amusement."

It raised two of its uppermost arms, and the sky split open. A pair of byakhee burst through from the Outside and into our world. Ragged wings buffeted the air, and their wet, mold-furred skins tainted the wind with their noxious stench. One wheeled down, making for Heliabel. She rolled away from the Source, lifting her hands and hurling a gust of wind at it. The other avoided her spell, however, and dropped straight down at Rupert.

The Needle suddenly flared in my shadowsight, so bright I flung my arm up against it. There came a sound like a bomb going off, fragments of rock exploding outward from where Whyborne had lain trapped. The byakhee started to wheel back, toward the Needle, but it was too late.

Ival rose to his feet. He still had his left hand on the Needle, and its power roared through him, turning his eyes to suns. His sleeve charred away from the scars on his right arm as he lifted his hand.

"Get away from my family," he said in the voice of something ancient.

Blue fire blazed from his hand. The byakhee shrieked and charred into ash, followed by the Hounds and the rat things. The second winged monstrosity attempted to flee, but instead tumbled like a burning star into the sea.

He turned the fire on Nyarlathotep. But it never made contact. Rather, Nyarlathotep's multitude of fingers flashed like the needles of some great machine, reweaving the flow of arcane energy.

Turning it back on Ival.

"Look out!" I cried, but too late. The blast slammed into Whyborne's chest, flinging him back and away from the Needle.

"Traitors," Nyarlathotep said. "I will make the two of you pay for your defiance. As for the mortals, your petty lives are at an end."

Its hands twitched, and Hounds and rat things poured forth from the Outside.

CHAPTER 47

Whyborne

I LAY GASPING, all the breath knocked from me. I'd fallen well back from the Needle, behind a boulder. My ribs ached, and I felt as though I'd been kicked in the chest by a horse.

"Percival!" Mother ran to me, grasping my arm. I managed to sit up. Beyond the slight cover of the boulder, I glimpsed the rest of my companions battling the Hounds and rat things summoned by Nyarlathotep. Griffin had put himself between us and anything attempting to come in this direction. As I watched, he dispatched a Hound with a single swing of an odd looking sword, as though the blade itself was somehow inimical to its existence.

I gaped at the carnage. "Are those the ketoi weapons?"

"Yes." She winced. "They're powerful, but they aren't enough. Nyarlathotep can simply continue to summon more enemies from the Outside, until we are worn down."

Morgen had spoken of redirecting the lines, destroying the vortex and draining the magic. She'd wished me to do so to set her free, but could we perhaps use such a plan against Nyarlathotep as well?

"I went into the Needle," I said. "Well, part of my consciousness did. There's—well, not is, but used to be—a ketoi woman in the Needle. She said Nyarlathotep must maintain a connection with the masters. It can only cross the veil in certain places such as this one, or the Draakenwood, or the fane in Egypt. Morgen seemed to think it possible to reorient the arcane lines around Balefire using the Needle. I could create an empty space around Carn Moreth without arcane lines. Isolate Nyarlathotep from the veil and the masters."

"A good plan," Justinian said from just behind me, "so long as we trap Nyarlathotep at the end."

I reached instinctively for the arcane fire, then caught myself before actually unleashing it on him. The Keeper of Secrets looked wretched, his white hair hanging in strings around his face, his eyes red from weeping.

I felt no pity for him, not after what he'd done to the Endicotts. But at the moment I'd take any help I could get. "Trap it how?"

"The Source." Justinian nodded at the object in question. "One of you can stuff it to the brim with arcane power. Cut off Carn Moreth from all arcane energy, and it will be the only source of magic for Nyarlathotep to use to maintain its connection with the Outside and the masters."

"Ival?" Griffin called in alarm. "Whatever you mean to do, please hurry."

I peered around the boulder. Griffin still held position, but Christine, Iskander, Rupert, and Hattie had been forced to give ground. "Just hold them off a little longer," I shouted back. To Justinian I said, "So we lure it somewhere with the Source?"

"The chamber beneath the crypt."

I thought I saw what he meant to do. "And then use the magic in the Source to shatter the stone columns? Bring the roof down on Nyarlathotep?"

"Exactly." Justinian bowed his head. "It's the only way I have to atone. I've destroyed my family. Destroyed the Endicotts. All that remains are rebels and abominations, and few enough of those. At least let me do this one thing."

The idea was madness. Luring a being beyond any of our comprehension into the accursed chamber where the mutated

Endicotts clustered around the Needle.

But we were out of time. Christine wielded the Spear with an abandon that made me thankful she ordinarily didn't have access to magic, but it was clear she was tiring. Iskander's Shield did an impressive job of keeping Hounds and rat things back, but he was flagging. Hattie looked close to her limits. She'd lost one of her knives in the fight, and was busy bashing a rat thing with a flail.

"All right," I said. "I'll need to get back to the Needle once I charge the Source."

I held my hands out for the artifact. "Percival," Mother said, as she passed it to me, "your brother…"

Oh no. He'd become a thing of the Outside, and if I'd had the opportunity to even ponder it, I would have hoped he'd dissolved before she could see what had become of him. If beholding him in such a shape had been difficult for me, what must it have been like for her?

"He distracted Nyarlathotep and gave me the chance to commune with Morgen." I folded my hand over hers. "I know that doesn't help. But I think…I spoke of his children and I believe, in the end, he remembered them." Thought of them for once in his blasted life, more like, though of course I didn't speak the sentiment aloud.

Probably I didn't need to. "I see. Please, please be careful. The moment you've cleared away the arcane lines, you need to abandon the Needle and flee."

I didn't know how careful it was possible to be, considering our plan was to collapse the island beneath us. "That's my intention. Someone will need to help Katherine and the children to escape. If you and Rupert can do that, perhaps the others can distract Nyarlathotep. Draw him away from the Needle while Morgen and I work."

"I'll let them know."

I kissed her brow; then she turned and made for Rupert without a backward glance.

I pulled arcane energy through me, my bones filling with fire, my scars aching as I funneled as much as I could into the Source. Magic poured into it, as much as I could draw, and I felt as though I heaved water into a deep well. But still I continued, until the fire spilled out around me.

"Don't fail," I warned Justinian as I held it out to him. "Wait for a moment of distraction, then run for the chamber and don't look back."

Nyarlathotep had moved away from the Needle, toward my cluster of faltering companions. As I watched, it lifted its hand and tugged on arcane lines I couldn't see.

"Iskander, Shield!" Griffin shouted.

Griffin flung himself to one side, rolling as far as he could get out of the path of whatever his shadowsight indicated Nyarlathotep was about to unleash. Iskander brought up the Shield, putting himself as a bulwark between the monster and everyone else.

A moment later, a bolt of lightning exploded from the sky with a titanic crack. It struck the Shield as though drawn to it, and even over the ringing in my ears I could hear Christine's cry.

The bolt seemed to gather into the Shield. For a moment, the metal glowed like a fallen star.

Then the lightning exploded back out, straight at Nyarlathotep.

Through surprise or some other element of luck, it struck before Nyarlathotep could unweave it. Nyarlathotep let out a sound like the hiss of a thousand furious cats, and the stench of burning rot tainted the wind.

There was never going to be a better moment of distraction. I ran for the Needle, and didn't dare look back to see what else might be happening. All of my concentration sharpened onto the task before me. My palms slammed against the slick, glassy stone of the Needle, and the world vanished around me.

Once again, I floated in the abyss of light. Morgen awaited me there, her expression one of desperate hope. "We need to use the Needle to redirect the arcane lines away from Balefire, in order to sever Nyarlathotep from the Outside," I said without preamble. "Which means..."

"I'll die." She closed her eyes. "Thank you."

I wished I'd had a chance to really speak with her. To discover more about the creation of the maelstrom, or question her more closely about the masters. "Is there anything you can tell me that will help us fight the masters when they return? Anything at all?"

She paused a moment, clearly wracking her thoughts. "I've forgotten so much."

Blast. "But you can show me how to redirect the arcane lines?"

"Of course. I can't do it myself, without Nyarlathotep's direct order." Anger sharpened her features. "It was one of the ways he made sure I couldn't act against him." She paused. "I don't know what will happen to this place, once the magic is gone."

Or me, though I didn't say it aloud. Presumably the arcane fragment that was myself would be the only bit of magic left on the island save for the Source. Would I still be able to cast spells? Or would I be cut off from the world, as surely as if I wore witch hunter's manacles?

Only one way to find out. "Very well," I said. "Let's begin."

CHAPTER 48

Griffin

THE SOUND OF fury Nyarlathotep unleashed almost drove me to my knees. Two of its arms hung useless, and the lightning had burned a hole through its leathery cape. I firmed my grip on the Sword, heart pounding and throat dry, and exchanged a look with Christine and Iskander.

Whyborne slumped at the base of the Needle. Heliabel ran toward us, and Justinian fled inside the manor, cradling the Source. "Percival has a plan," she said, speaking quickly. "He's going to redirect all arcane energy away from the island. You need to keep Nyarlathotep away from him and the Needle. Lure it into the mansion if you can."

"And Justinian?" I asked.

"He's taking the Source to the chamber below. When the rest of the magic is gone, hopefully Nyarlathotep will follow. The Keeper will use the arcane power of the Source to collapse the chamber—and probably the rest of the island—onto them both. That's why it's critical you disengage and get yourselves to safety the moment Nyarlathotep goes below."

It sounded an insane risk, but we had no other options. I nodded. "I understand."

"Rupert," she went on, turning to him, "you and I need to get Katherine and the children to safety on the causeway before things begin to fall apart."

"Of course." A moment later, they both hurried inside, leaving us to our task.

Christine gaped at Nyarlathotep. "Lure it? How are we to do that?"

"Leave that to me," Hattie said. "Hey you! We ain't afraid of you, you arse-faced prick! I've seen scarier things in the privy!"

It swept toward us on its column of supporting tentacles, moving much faster than I'd expected. "Run!" I said, and bolted for the doors.

Rat things and Hounds exploded into being, blocking the way. I swung the Sword and cut through them, while Hattie lay about with the flail. Iskander acted as rear guard, Shield up and ready in case Nyarlathotep tried to use lightning against us again.

As we entered the upper part of the spiral passageway, reality itself seemed to warp around us. The portraits on the walls altered, the painted figures horribly changed and mutated. The hall seemed to lengthen, and things gibbered from the shadows. My shadowsight offered a strange double-image, but even then I couldn't tell if what Nyarlathotep had done to Balefire was simply illusory, or fueled by magic and terribly real.

Beneath my feet, the floor began to grow softer, as though I ran through mud. The chittering shadows expanded, swallowing all light. Christine let out a string of curses in both Arabic and English, choked off as the very air thickened in our lungs.

"You have thought to defy the hands that helped to shape your very existence." Nyarlathotep's words crawled into our ears. I turned in its direction, saw its shape filling the passageway behind us. "Your resistance is pointless. You will die, and once you are gone, I will bring the spark here and show him your mutilated forms. Then, if he still refuses to submit, I will do whatever it takes to break him."

I couldn't let this creature hurt my Ival. We just needed to keep its focus on us a bit longer. "Keep running," I panted. "We have to keep running."

Rat things swarmed us, their horribly human faces utterly

revolting. I tried to kick one, but missed, and it sank its teeth into my ankle. Another leapt onto my back, its hand-like paws grabbing my hair for balance before it bit my ear. My companions shouted, and Christine managed to kill some of the rat things, but we were reaching the end of our fight.

I tore the rat thing from my back; warm blood ran into my ear as I hurled it into the wall. Hattie stabbed the other with her remaining knife, and it shrieked and died.

We stumbled into the Great Hall. The doors to the stairs and causeway stood wide, and I hoped Katherine and the children had successfully escaped, along with Rupert and Heliabel. Our weapons lay on the table where Ophelia had left them, including Iskander's knives and my sword cane.

The Great Hall shifted and shivered. For a moment I expected it to change, as the passageway had changed…but it didn't. Magic flared in my shadowsight, but then faded quickly.

In fact, all the magic seemed to be fading. The Sword in my hand no longer glowed, though I assumed that was because of its separation from the Source that had fueled it. But my breath came easier, and the shadows reverted to their usual dimensions.

Ival. Whatever he was doing with the Needle to remove the magic, it seemed to be working.

Christine motioned with the Spear, but nothing happened. With a frustrated snarl, she slammed the point into a rat thing. A second one leapt at her—and dissolved into slime in midair.

Apparently the lack of ambient magic was having an effect.

The other rat things began to die and dissolve, cut off from whatever gave them horrid life. Nyarlathotep emerged into the Great Hall, and it reached for the arcane lines, no doubt to summon more Hounds or other minions.

Nothing happened. Its searching fingers encountered no strings of the world to pluck.

It recoiled. Then its empty hood turned back, in the direction of the courtyard and the Needle. "How dare you," it boomed in a voice like the end of the world. "I will tear your mind out by the roots for this."

Was it my imagination, or was Nyarlathotep losing definition? The edges of its leather cloak seemed to be more frayed than they were before, and its arms were more like black smoke than shining chitin.

For a terrible instant, I thought it would destroy our plans, retreat up the passageway and kill Whyborne where he lay. But how could we possibly stop it?

Or perhaps we didn't need to. Perhaps all that was needed was a bit of misdirection.

For all its alien qualities, Nyarlathotep had taken an interest in humans over and over again through the millennia. From Nephren-ka in Egypt, to the medieval sorcerers who met it in the woods, to the members of the Cabal who exchanged loyalty for power.

In other words, it was used to humans bargaining with it.

"Let us go, and we'll tell you where Justinian took the Source," I called to it. "That's the only scrap of magic left on this accursed island. Let us leave here safely, and I'll divulge where he's hidden it. Otherwise, you'll never find it."

It turned back to us—and I felt its gaze again, like a physical weight, even though it had no eyes and no face. I staggered back, but it didn't linger on me. Instead, it turned its hooded head down, down, until it seemed to stare through the very stones of the floor.

Perhaps it did. Or perhaps some other sense found the Source, far below us. Either way, it let out a sound that had me clutching at my ears—then swept past, like a black wind, heading below.

CHAPTER 49

Whyborne

WITHOUT THE NEEDLE, our task would have been impossible.

But this was why it had been created—why Morgen, whatever her name had originally been, had been forced into this stone prison.

She took my hand, and my consciousness expanded as it had before. I could *see* every stream of arcane fire pouring into the island, *feel* it bound and held by the slender length of black stone.

She dove down, taking me with her, all along the length of the great menhir. I saw through the eyes of carvings, heard through the vibrations of stone. Over the centuries, Morgen's consciousness had seeped out along the arcane streams, expanding to fill not only the Needle, but the entirety of Carn Moreth and Balefire Manor.

When I'd touched the maelstrom a year ago, it had been very much like this—I'd seen all of the town, felt the thoughts of its inhabitants. The maelstrom might never have been human, or ketoi, or anything but itself, but Morgen had put something of her spirit into it nonetheless. Something about the way she had shaped it, the quiet, small choices she'd made in the midst of reorienting rivulets into streams, and streams into rivers, and rivers into the massive vortex on the other side of the ocean, had changed its essence and brought us—brought me—to this moment.

She showed me how to undo the arcane lines, to tie them on to other lines and unhook them from the Needle, shunt them away from Carn Moreth.

I recalled what Minerva had said back on Old Grimsby. "What about the capillaries, so to speak? All the little threads that permeate reality?"

"They depend on constant replenishment from the larger streams." Morgen gestured to our linked hands. "If you bind an artery tightly enough, the flesh below it will first go numb, then die."

I hoped she was right. But she'd had a very long time to contemplate her own death, so I had to trust she knew these things. And it wasn't as though I had any other option.

"I need to begin," I said. I hesitated, though, searching her eyes. "I'm sorry. I wish..."

She put a finger to my lips, silencing me. "I've longed for death. If I can take Nyarlathotep into the void with me, then I will consider it a better end than I ever dared hope for."

"I'm going to draw as much arcane fire into myself as I can." I hesitated, but it had to be said. "If I start to sound a bit megalomaniacal, forgive me."

Her eyes shone. "You're the greatest arcane vortex that has ever existed. I understand."

I winced. "Er, perhaps, but I'm really just a fellow who gets paid to translate what other people find. I ordinarily try to save my insane ranting for grant proposals."

Then I took a deep breath and let the arcane fire pour into me.

I distantly felt the ache in my body, the sensation of my blood turning to liquid flames, the scars on my arm blazing as though the lightning that had traced them in my flesh had returned. But the pain was swamped by the sense of power surging through me as the world unfolded to my senses. I felt the arcane lines around me as though they were my own limbs, and even though this vortex wasn't *me,* it was still mine to command.

I was fire and blood and power, and Nyarlathotep had been a fool to think I would ever submit.

The Needle came alive; if I shifted my perspective ever so slightly, I could see it from the carvings in the chamber below. The violet glow intensified until it blazed, and I hoped Griffin and the others had succeeded in drawing Nyarlathotep out of sight of the Needle's length.

The Needle had been created to control the lines, to weave and unweave over vast distances. If it had been set too close to the maelstrom, it would have been overwhelmed and shattered. Yet the distance suddenly seemed to me to be one of perception rather than miles. For a moment, I could see as far as I chose—could see *everything,* the complicated pattern of lines stretching across the globe, forming vortices both great and small where they came together.

But I wasn't here for that. I was here to stop Nyarlathotep from hurting my friends, myself, my town, my world.

So I focused my will and my power on the vortex around the Needle. I lost all sense of time as I unraveled the pattern made by the arcane lines and created a new one. I remembered Basil knitting in the sun on board the *Melusine,* glass needles flashing as he created a sock. Weaving in enchantment while he spoke to Griffin about magic. Casting a spell with a hole in the center.

I didn't know the art, but I'd spent hours watching Miss Emily and my Mother, and I had Morgen's guidance and the Needle's purpose. Not to mention the unusual advantage of being able to see everything from the perspective of the yarn being knitted.

I took up the lines and reworked them, into a great circle of magic, with Carn Moreth in the empty hole in the center.

My sense of the lifeblood of the world grew fainter and fainter as I worked. I continued to replenish the energy within myself, spending power recklessly and drawing it into my fragile form with equal recklessness. Until only one line remained anchored to the Needle.

I expanded my focus, searching for Morgen. For a moment, I thought I'd made a mistake, missed her passing. But she hung like a wisp in the abyss of light, barely more substantial than a thought.

Still, I wasn't much more than thought at the moment, either, at least not in this place. I reached for her.

She stared at me, lips parted. How she perceived me, I didn't know, but a smile touched her lips. "You're still here."

"Widdershins doesn't abandon its own," I told her. "And when the masters appear, they won't find us unprepared. We'll send them back to the Outside where they belong. No matter the cost."

"You must leave," she said. "Cast off the last line, and flee while you still can."

She was right. But I hesitated. "I need to make sure Justinian is where he needs to be with the Source. After everything he did, I don't entirely trust him."

"Then I'll stay with you, for as long as I can."

"I'll lend you some of my energy." I didn't know if it would work, but I could at least try. I made certain our hands were joined, and fed a little of the arcane energy I'd swallowed down into her.

Her outline firmed slightly. Our gazes met, and she said, "Do it."

I wove the final line into its new position.

CHAPTER 50

Whyborne

I instantly felt as though I dragged a great weight through mud.

Save for the Source, the last bit of arcane energy on Carn Moreth was within me. Morgen clung to my hand, the energy I lent her all that kept her in existence. She'd been changed and tormented, used and abandoned, but she'd set her revenge in motion millennia ago when she subverted the creation of the maelstrom.

And now it was time for her to have that revenge.

Justinian should be in the chamber by now with the Source. So I centered myself, honed my will into a point.

And then I dove, taking Morgen with me.

Down through the Needle, and Balefire spread out around me. I glimpsed the world through painted eyes, knotholes, and carved figures as I flew past.

Griffin stood in the Great Hall, the ketoi-forged Sword in one hand and the cane Father gave him in the other. Iskander, Christine, and Hattie were with him, and they were alive, thank heavens, they were *alive*.

"Leave," Griffin ordered, pointing at the open doors leading to the causeway. "The barrier is gone. Escape now, before the entire island collapses."

"I agree, but what about you?" Iskander asked.

Griffin shook his head. Dried blood masked one side of his face, and a small notch out of his right ear streamed fresher blood. Salt and blood matted his overlong hair, and exhaustion had stamped the flesh around his eyes. "I'm going to help Ival."

"I'm going with you," Christine declared.

"No. Christine, listen to me." He gripped her arm. "If we don't make it off the island in time, Widdershins is going to need you as it's never needed you before. You're going to have to fight in our stead, and it won't be easy, but it will be necessary."

No. No, damn it, he had to go with her. I couldn't risk Griffin getting hurt, not now when he was so close to safety. I tried to shout at him, but I had no voice, and frustration and fear burned through me.

Christine ground her teeth, but she nodded. "Fine. But if you and Whyborne die, I'll...I'll never forgive you, do you understand?"

He offered her a tired smile. "I'd expect nothing less."

Curse it, I'd let myself be distracted. With every passing moment, energy bled from me, not only into Morgen but into the Needle, the air, as though the very world tried to feed on me. I dragged my attention back, dove deeper, seeking...

The great chamber beneath the crypt opened around me. Justinian was there, and for a moment satisfaction filled me. This was going to work.

Then I saw the mutated Endicotts circling him.

The Keeper's face bore the marks of their acidic tentacles. He'd managed to kill two of them, no doubt using some of the power from the Source, but he couldn't afford to spend too much of it before Nyarlathotep arrived.

"Get back," he moaned. "I'm sorry. I'm sorry. Please, get back."

Another Endicott moved stealthily up behind him. I wanted to call out a warning, but had no means of doing so. I could only watch as it sprang onto his back and wrapped its tentacle around his throat.

Justinian screamed. He fell, and the Source bounced across the floor, fetching up against the Needle.

The mutated wretches swarmed the man who had once been the head of their household, and who had condemned them to their awful fate. Justinian's screams grew more anguished as they sank their teeth into him, feeding in a starved, mad frenzy. Within moments, his shrieks turned to croaks, and then fell silent.

Justinian was dead. And Nyarlathotep's shadow filled the open door to the crypt.

The mutated Endicotts scattered at Nyarlathotep's coming. The Source lay against the Needle, but no one remained to use it to cast the spell and bring down the ceiling.

"No one but us," Morgen said.

Far, far overhead, my heart began to pound faster in fear. "How?"

"Reach with me, through the very stones of Balefire. Use the Source and cast your spell."

Magic was dependent on will. In the absence of rat things and sigils and complicated rituals, will was the only thing that remained.

I'd spent years honing mine, but using it in this manner, when my consciousness was partly separated from my body, was nothing I'd ever imagined. As for what would happen to my mind, should the collapse shatter the Needle while I was in it, I didn't want to contemplate.

But I didn't have a choice. If I didn't act now, Nyarlathotep would escape to the Outside, and all of this would have been for nothing.

I reached for the Source.

The power I'd stored in it earlier flooded out, into the Needle, and thence into Morgen and me.

"No!" Nyarlathotep roared in the voice of a thousand screaming souls. "Stop this! I order you! I am your creator!"

Rage burst within me, partly mine and partly Morgen's. This malignant thing would have used Stanford to corrupt Widdershins. It threatened me and everyone I loved. It had done unspeakable things to Morgen's very essence, then abandoned her until it wished to use the Needle once again.

It traded in cruelty and avarice, and I despised it with every particle of my being.

I stretched out my will, and it was a battle as I had never fought before. My sense of the universe around me was gone; with no arcane energy in the ambient, I was blind. I felt as though I crawled inch by inch through the very stones of Balefire, until I found the massive columns holding up the roof of the chamber.

Already they were creaking and cracking beneath the stress, the magic that had kept them in place for centuries drained away. It wouldn't take a great deal of power to bring them down.

Which was a good thing, because I wasn't certain how much I had left. Arcane energy gushed from me into the spell like blood from a wound.

Nyarlathotep turned to flee, but it was too late.

"Your time is over," I told it, though without mouth or lungs I don't know if it could sense my defiance. "You should have stayed in the Outside." I could feel Morgen beside me, vibrating in fury and triumph. "You thought to use us as tools, but we are the weapon that will destroy you."

I unleashed the spell, and it found the cracks in the columns, wrenching them apart. The pillar closest to Nyarlathotep came down first, with a roar that would have deafened me if I'd been present in my physical form. Tons of stone pelted from above as the roof began to collapse, burying the hideous shape of Nyarlathotep beneath it.

"Go!" Morgen said. "Now!"

She'd been using my energy to remain in this world, but as she spoke, she pushed every scrap of arcane power back into me. I reached for her, but nothing remained to touch.

She was gone, her revenge complete.

More stones began to fall as the second column collapsed. I aimed my consciousness back up the Needle, rising rapidly. Balefire fell apart: floors cracking, portraits falling from the walls, roofs collapsing.

I could sense the courtyard and my body above me, but I was tiring. I'd spent energy recklessly and now had almost nothing left. If Morgen hadn't given me the last of her life, I likely wouldn't have climbed even this high.

I was so weary. It would be so simple to just float here in the darkness. So much easier than continuing to fight. I could forget about the masters, about the maelstrom's plans, about everything and just let whatever was going to happen…happen.

And then, distantly, I heard Griffin calling my name.

CHAPTER 51

Griffin

I ENTERED THE courtyard at a dead run, my heart pounding its way out of my chest. How much time we had left, I didn't know, but it couldn't be long. Why hadn't Whyborne returned from his sojourn in the Needle so we could flee together? I'd expected to meet him in the passageway.

To my horror, I saw his body still lay at the base of the black stone. The blazing vortex that had once filled the courtyard was gone; the only magic remaining in my shadowsight was in him and in the Needle. A thin line of arcane energy connected his body with the stone, which I assumed meant he was still inside it.

The light within him was dimmer than I'd ever seen. Sometimes he was a candle and sometimes an arc light, but never this feeble flicker. I dropped to my knees beside him, uncertain what to do. If I pulled him free, would it break his connection with the Needle—and if so, what would that do to him?

"Ival?" I asked. I touched his pale face. His skin was ice cold, and a fresh infusion of fear pumped through my veins. "Ival!"

There came a rumble like distant thunder—but it originated

far below us.

An instant later, the entire island shook. A rift opened in the lower part of Balefire's spiral, and a shower of masonry and glass collapsed into it. The shaking continued, cracks forming in the walls of the courtyard, and one of the big doors toppled from its hinges.

"Whyborne! Ival!" I grabbed his shoulder and shook him hard. "Wake up; please, wake up."

The arcane light drained from the slick black stone and back into him. Even as I watched, the glow within him strengthened, though it didn't achieve anything like its usual brightness. "Ival!"

He stirred and blinked. "G-Griffin? I don't feel well."

"We have to get out of here." I hauled his arm over my shoulders and dragged him to his feet. "Help me if you can, my dear."

We stumbled like a pair of drunks into Balefire. Bits of plaster rained down on our heads, and the dust choked our lungs and covered us in a layer of white. A marble bust fell from its plinth and shattered on the floor. Smoke crawled along the ceiling; the shaking had knocked over a lantern or candle, and set fire to the building.

At any instant, I expected the ground to collapse beneath us, or the roof to crush us. Somehow, we made it back to the Great Hall. Whyborne looked horrible, the whites of his eyes beginning to hemorrhage, blood leaking out his nose. I didn't know what was wrong with him, if it stemmed from the absence of any arcane energy around us, or if it was some side effect of using the Needle as he had. But there was nothing I could do to help, save try to get us off the island as quickly as possible.

The groan of stone against stone was the only warning I had. "Come on!" I shouted, and flung us both toward the doors leading to the stairs and causeway. Despite his condition, Whyborne managed to take some of his own weight, and we staggered out of Balefire and into the free air.

Not a moment too soon. The Great Hall collapsed behind us in a roar of stone and timber. A huge cloud of dust billowed out, stinging my eyes and causing Whyborne to double over with a racking cough.

We plunged half-blind down the stairs. Rifts opened in the earth as the successive layers of the spiral collapsed into each other, no longer supported by magic. The sea roared, nearly deafening, as it rushed into the deep ruins, then was flung back as tons of stone crashed down into it.

Whyborne's feet went out from under him, and he nearly dragged me down as well. "Leave me," he panted.

"Never." I pulled him back to his feet. "We're almost at the causeway."

He raised his head, blinking blearily. "Look at the sea. We'll never make it."

Oh no. I'd heard the roaring sea, but I'd been so focused on getting us down the long stair, I hadn't even thought to look. He was right—the sea thrashed like a living thing around Carn Moreth, slamming into the stones, racing across the causeway, then withdrawing, only to crash back again.

It wasn't crashing into the headland, though. Instead, the ocean became strangely calm not far from the island. Someone—probably multiple people—was using magic to prevent the waves from destroying the coastline.

There came a loud snap from only a few feet away, and a crack opened in one of the rocks jutting up by the stair.

"We don't have a choice," I said. "If we can just get past the boundary line, where there's arcane energy again, the sea is calmer."

Calmer, but deep enough we'd still have to swim. And Whyborne couldn't swim under the best of conditions. Chances were, we'd both drown before we reached the headland.

But we had to try.

A finned arm reached above the churning ocean. Then others, the ketoi fighting through the maddened waves to reach us.

Thank God.

They scrambled to meet us, two taking Whyborne's weight, two others gripping my arms. Before I could hesitate, they dragged us both into the water.

For a few seconds, all was chaos. Water crashed around me, currents ripped at my clothing and hair, and it took all my strength to cling to my sword cane. Had we been left to our own devices, we would surely have been swept away and drowned.

But the ketoi were far stronger than us, and they lived in these waters. We broke through the chaos into calmer waves, and I could see the net of magic spread over the sea, redirecting the fury of the ocean back on Carn Moreth. Heliabel stood in the shallows, casting the water spell, along with three Endicott sorcerers who must have made it to the headland after the disaster at the barrier.

A wide beach met the causeway, and Christine and Iskander ran down it before our feet even touched the shore. Grateful as I was to see them unharmed, I hurried to Ival, who had managed to stand unassisted. "Are you all right?"

"Better." He licked cracked lips; at least the soaking in the ocean had rinsed off most of the dust and blood. "Now that we're out of the dead area, and back in the arcane ambient."

I flung my arms around him. He hugged me back, and we clung to each other silently for a long moment.

Iskander put a hand to my shoulder. "Look," he said.

I didn't release Ival, but I did pull away far enough to see what he pointed at. Across the waves, the final section of Balefire slowly slid into the huge crater that now gaped in the center of the island. A haze of dust and smoke poured out, making it look almost volcanic in nature. The sea let out a terrific roar, and one of the sorcerers staggered under the onslaught, but the spell held firm.

We watched as the water around the island slowly spent its energy, until it was safe enough to release the spell. Morgen's Needle was gone. The ancient estate of the Endicotts was gone as well, along with all the magical items they'd hoarded. All the knowledge they'd gathered. The secrets they'd kept.

"Do you think that took care of Nyarlathotep?" I asked.

Exhaustion lined Ival's face. "I certainly hope so. Even if such a creature could survive being crushed beneath tons of rock, without access to any arcane energy it should have a difficult time escaping. Either way I don't think we need to worry about it for a while."

More ketoi had arrived, joining us on the strand, including Ship-bane. "Well," she said as she padded across the shoreline, "this alliance went far better than I'd ever hoped." She met my gaze and held out her hand. "The Sword, Shield, and Spear please."

We passed them to her, and she handed them to her attendants. "I'm sorry the Source was lost," Whyborne said. "But without it, Nyarlathotep would still be free."

Ship-bane didn't precisely look pleased over the loss, but she nodded. "I suppose that is a fair trade."

Rupert reached into his vest and pulled out the fragment of the Wisborg Codex he'd taken from the armory. "For you, Dr. Whyborne, as agreed." When Whyborne took it, he turned to Ship-bane. "Which leaves us with only one other piece of business to complete." He straightened his shoulders. "The agreement specified the Seeker of Truth would submit to your judgment. As Minerva died in the initial assault on Carn Moreth, that means I am the one to be judged."

Hattie opened her mouth to disagree, but a stern look from Rupert silenced her. I was under no such obligation, however. "We would surely have died without Rupert. Nyarlathotep would have won, and the chances of winning our fight against the masters would be far worse."

Heliabel nodded. "I can vouch for the truth of what Griffin says."

Ship-bane was silent a long moment. What thoughts passed through her mind, I couldn't imagine. She turned from Rupert and scanned the beach. A few bedraggled Endicotts had made it to shore after the barrier knocked them into the water. They huddled around Katherine and the children she'd so bravely cared for. Even as I watched, Padma caught Sadik into her arms and lifted him off his feet, her expression one of pure, uncomplicated joy.

The ketoi chieftess turned away from them and gazed out at the crater that had been Balefire. "There is nothing here for you now," she said at last. "My judgment is this: for you to take your people and go. Where, I care not."

Rupert closed his eyes briefly in relief, then bowed to her. "Thank you."

"We will keep watch and make sure Nyarlathotep does not escape, if it still lives." She took a step toward the waves, then paused. "Once you leave, I do not ever wish to see an Endicott set foot on, or touch the water between, the Isles of Scilly or Penmoreth. You will regret it if you do."

"I understand," Rupert said. "You have my word as the Seeker of Truth."

All of the ketoi, except for Heliabel, waded into the sea. Within seconds, they'd vanished, save for the occasional fin breaking the surface before they reached deeper water.

The sigh of the wind and the crash of the waves were the only sounds for a long moment. Hattie stared at the empty space where Balefire had stood with an expression close to heartbreak. "I can't believe it's gone," she said at last. "Where are we going to go? What are we going to do?"

Rupert put a hand to her shoulder. "We rebuild elsewhere, Hattie. The Endicotts existed before Balefire, and we'll continue to exist long after. The estate was just a place, and the objects inside just things. The important thing is, we still have one another."

"Yes, yes. That's all well and good," Christine said impatiently, "but does anyone have anything to eat? I'm famished."

CHAPTER 52

Whyborne

Two days later, I stood on the deck of the *Melusine* as it prepared to put out from the harbor at Old Grimsby. Basil was once again our windweaver, and Rupert occupied the space at the rail beside me, watching as the lines were cast off. The rest of the flotilla was in the process of getting underway, and would be following us across the Atlantic.

To Widdershins.

For the thousandth time, I asked myself if the offer I'd made was wise, or merely desperate. But the fate of the Endicotts had been bound to that of Widdershins since Sir Richard dreamed of spirals upon Carn Moreth. It was time for our war to end, and for them to come home.

"Is everyone coming?" I asked. I hadn't been present, but Hattie had told me there had been some rather heated discussion about relocating the remains of the clan to Widdershins. The vote afterward to confirm Rupert permanently in the position of Seeker had favored him by only the slenderest of margins.

"Some of the oldsters aren't happy about it—some of those

my age aren't, for that matter." Rupert sighed. "But I am the Seeker of Truth. And there are no secrets left to keep. They will follow me, or they will leave."

"If anyone tries to cause...well, more than the usual amount of trouble that happens in Widdershins..."

"Please, Dr. Whyborne there is no need for threats, no matter how mildly phrased." Rupert lifted his hand. "The younger generation, people like Basil, are disinterested in a centuries-long war with the ketoi. And we've all seen where the sort of thinking like Justinian embraced leads. Perhaps, once the war with the masters is over, we'll leave Widdershins and find somewhere else to live. Somewhere one can get a decent cup of tea, for example." He sighed. "I can't believe we're about to become colonials."

Once of the deckhands called out to Rupert, and I left him to deal with whatever matter required his attention. Mother stood at the prow, so I joined her there.

"Persephone isn't going to be at all happy with you, you know," she said. She'd gone below the waves to be tended by the ketoi healers, and her injured tentacles were plastered with kelp and mud. It looked terribly unsanitary to me, but I assumed they knew what worked on ketoi physiology better than I did. "She sent me to act as an envoy for the Endicotts, not bring them back with me to live in Widdershins."

"I know. But Rupert isn't interested in war." I sighed. "I'm thinking about settling them on the old Somerby Estate."

"Near the island in the lake?" Mother's eyes widened. "Dear heavens, Percival, you do enjoy courting trouble, don't you?"

"At least those standing stones aren't sentient."

"True." Her fond expression slid toward sadness. "I wish I could have spoken to Morgen."

"So do I." I gripped the rail as the yacht slipped out of the harbor. "She set all of this in motion, and we don't even know her real name. I wonder why she was chosen by Nyarlathotep. Was it a punishment for a rebellious slave? Or was she just a random victim, nameless and faceless to creatures such as the masters? Or was there something unusual about her, that made her more able to have her consciousness altered and fused with the Needle?" I paused. "Was she, perhaps, our own distant ancestress?"

"We'll never know," Mother said with a shake of her head. "I only hope she found peace. I hope the same for your brother."

I didn't know what to say to that, what words could possibly give comfort. She'd lost so much. And stood to lose even more.

Nyarlathotep claimed Persephone and I would have to die to fulfill the maelstrom's purpose. I had no reason to believe he'd been any more honest with me than with Justinian.

And yet I couldn't stop thinking about it.

Mother patted me on the arm after a long moment and said, "I'm going to bed. I'll speak with you in the morning."

I turned to watch her go. Griffin, Iskander, and Christine picked their way along the narrow deck toward us. Mother paused briefly to speak with Christine, then continued below.

Griffin's arm brushed mine as he stepped up to the rail beside me. We'd both spent a good deal of the last two days sleeping, too exhausted even to make love. I put my hand over his, grateful beyond words to have him still with me. If Ophelia hadn't been fooled by Hattie's apparent contrition, things would have gone very differently indeed.

"Have you started to decipher the fragment of the Codex yet?" Christine asked, taking up position on my other side.

"I've hardly had the time," I said, a bit crossly. "I wasn't feeling terribly well there at the end on Carn Moreth, you know. And after, I was a bit busy discussing the new arrangement with Rupert."

"I can't believe you invited them to live in Widdershins," Christine said. "They're probably already conspiring as to how they'll take over the entire town. Mark my words."

"I don't think so, dearest," Iskander said. "They aren't without honor, and with Rupert as the sole head of the house, I believe things will change for the better."

"Hmph. Maybe." She crossed her arms above her belly. "I do wish we hadn't had to give the ketoi weapons back, though. Do you think there's anything else like the Spear somewhere about? I could use it for staff meetings."

"And to convince donors to fund your next expedition, when all this is over," I added.

"Exactly." She started to say something else, then stopped.

"Whyborne, give me your hand."

"Why?" I asked suspiciously.

"Just do it."

I let her take my hand. She brought it to her belly, pressing my palm against the fabric. For a moment, I hadn't the slightest idea what she was about, until I felt...not much, really. Just a tiny flutter, so light I might have imagined it.

I gaped at her. "Was that the baby?"

"Yes." She let go of my hand. "I wasn't certain you'd be able to feel it. Iskander could, but there were fewer layers—"

"Er, yes," I said hastily, the tips of my ears going hot with embarrassment.

Griffin coughed, a sound I expected was meant to cover a laugh. I glared at him, and he shot me an impish wink.

We stood quietly for a while after that, simply enjoying a peaceful moment together. There would be problems enough tomorrow: settling the Endicotts, deciphering the Codex, stopping the masters from retaking our world. And yet, right now there was the sea breeze, and the stars above, and the warmth of our companionship.

I wanted it to never end.

The ship rounded the isles and made for open water. Basil's wind filled the sails, and the bow cut through the waves, each moment taking us ever closer to home.

The adventures of Whyborne, Griffin, and their friends will conclude in Deosil, Whyborne & Griffin Book 11.

SHARE YOUR EXPERIENCE

If you enjoyed this book, please consider leaving a review on the site where you purchased it, or on Goodreads.
Thank you for your support of independent authors!

AUTHOR'S NOTE

Special thanks to Courtney for her help with the Latin translation of the Endicott family motto. Thanks also to Lotta, whose suggestion inspired Penmoreth and Carn Moreth.

William Pryce's *Archaeologia Cornu-Britannica; Or, an Essay to Preserve the Ancient Cornish Language* is a real book, published in 1790. As the full title suggests, it was compiled in an attempt to preserve Cornish, which had already died out as a first language. You can find a PDF copy of it via archive.org should you be so inclined.

Interest in reviving the Cornish language began in the early 1900s, and the effort has undergone several iterations since. Some modern accepted spellings differ from those in Pryce's book. As *Balefire* takes place in 1902, I chose to go with the older source.

Carn Moreth was inspired by St. Michael's Mount, a tidal island off the coast of Cornwall. Both legend and archaeology indicate it was once a high promontory surrounded by marshy forest, located several miles from the coast. According to various tales, the forest was suddenly and violently flooded, drowning the land around it and turning the peak into an island. St. Michael's Mount, Seven Stones Reef, and the Isles of Scilly are all associated with this inundation. In time, the much-earlier folk memory became incorporated into the Arthurian stories as the drowned land of Lyonesse (called Lethowsow in Cornish).

ABOUT THE AUTHOR

Jordan L. Hawk is a non-binary queer author from North Carolina. Childhood tales of mountain ghosts and mysterious creatures gave them a life-long love of things that go bump in the night. When they aren't writing, they brew their own beer and try to keep the cats from destroying the house. Their best-selling Whyborne & Griffin series (beginning with *Widdershins*) can be found in print, ebook, and audiobook.

If you're interested in receiving Jordan's newsletter and being the first to know when new books are released, please sign up at their website jordanlhawk.com.

Printed in Poland
by Amazon Fulfillment
Poland Sp. z o.o., Wrocław